SNOWBOUND

By three o'clock it was dark and snowing heavily again. Maggie figured she'd be spending another night in her car. Her stomach growled at the thought.

She cleaned away what she could of the snow before slipping again into the car's cozy if temporary warmth. A minute didn't go by when she stopped praying. Surely God would hear her. She was twenty-four and couldn't remember asking him for anything before. If you didn't count the Barbie doll when she was eight, this was the first time, and she'd never needed His help more.

Send someone, oh please, God, send someone.

Hours laters she heard the sound of a car. She almost cried for joy. She flicked on the emergency lights and begged, "Please. Let them see me. Please."

A white blur was groping its way through hip-high snow and then, like a miracle, a gloved hand was knocking on her window.

Tears of relief slid down Maggie's cheeks. It was all right. Everything was going to be all right.

Only it wasn't. . . .

DARKEST HEART

Patricia Pellicane

ZEBRA BOOKS
KENSINGTON PUBLISHING CORP.

ZEBRA BOOKS are published by

Kensington Publishing Corp.
475 Park Avenue South
New York, NY 10016

First Printing: May, 1994

Printed in the United States of America

Chapter One

"Baby, I love you. Please, let me see you."

She'd forgotten to put on her machine and silently cursed her stupidity, for it took less than an instant for her to recognize the intrusive voice. Again. God, when would he stop? When would someone make him stop? She'd tried everything. Everything. Only to come at last to the conclusion that the man was obsessed. The trouble was, his obsession was just about ruining her life.

Maggie was tempted to hang up, to slam the receiver, as she'd done a dozen times and more, but at the last moment she brought the receiver back to her ear. Hanging up only intensified his sick compulsion to call again. Maybe if she tried, just one more time, just maybe, she could convince him to leave her in peace. "Henry," she began very gently, "you don't love me. You don't even know me. You . . ."

Henry cut her off. "I know you, honey. I watch you every night. Of course I know you," he insisted.

Henry never took into consideration that thousands watched her every night as she anchored the evening news and no other boasted of knowing her. Maggie shook

5

her head. They had been over this ground before. There was no way to make him understand. Nothing she could do, nothing she could say that seemed to matter. "I won't see you. I want you to leave me alone. Stop calling here!"

"Whore!" the gentle words of love turned into a whispering menace, filled with hate. "You're fuckin' dead."

Maggie clutched the phone to her ear, powerless but to shudder under the stream of vile epithets, even as she felt the scream of denial bubble to life in her throat and the familiar dread seep into the marrow of her bones.

His hatred stole her breath as he once again went about the horror of telling what he wanted to do to her. She shuddered as she imagined his promises and then tore her mind from the horrendous scenario. Would this never end?

As she stood there, frozen in place, the droning of the relentless dial tone went unnoticed. Maggie held the phone to her ear, her blank gaze upon the television, unaware that the program she'd been watching was over and a beautiful woman in gently flowing breezes now sold perfume. Nothing registered but the nearly crushing endless fear, the agony that had become her life.

Maggie's breath was hardly more than a ragged, choppy gasp. She couldn't bear the threats any longer. She couldn't stand the phone calls, the constant watching, the lurking in the shadows until he was ready to pounce. After almost a year, she'd reached her limit.

He had all the power. She had none.

The dial tone became a harsh, sharp beep, a reminder that the connection was broken. It brought Maggie from her thoughts, from the almost paralyzing fear with new resolve. As she replaced the phone upon its cradle, she shook her head. No more . . . she was tired of being afraid.

Tired of being a helpless victim. She was going to buy a gun, for though she felt a wave of nausea at the thought of killing anything, most especially a human being, she knew if she needed to, she'd somehow find the strength to use it.

A half hour later she jumped when the phone rang again. This time she refused to answer the insistent ring. After ten times, the answering machine clicked on and his gentle words denied the hatred that had spewed forth like a shower of poison venom. "I'm sorry, Maggie. I didn't mean it. You know I didn't mean it. I love you. I'll always love you."

She did not respond.

And then the next call. "Answer the phone, bitch—do you hear me?" And then, as always, the horrifying threats that soon turned into words of love. "I love you, honey. I love you." Click. And then it rang again, and another deranged message, and then again, until Maggie disconnected the line from the wall.

The next day, Maggie went to the police again. As always, there was nothing they could do.

Deputy Sheriff O'Mally looked at her with obvious sympathy. "You want me to talk to him again?" he asked, after listening to the tape.

"Talking to him does no good. I want you to lock him up."

O'Mally gave a helpless shrug. "Ma'am, he didn't violate the Order of Protection."

Maggie glanced at the paper laying open upon his desk. "If you mean he didn't come to my house, you're right, he didn't. But he's calling me—look at the journal." Maggie, upon the advice of the police, had begun a journal

7

where she listed the time and date of every phone call and every time the man drove by her home.

"The fact is, he didn't come near you."

"What difference does it make? He will. This won't end until he kills me."

O'Mally couldn't help but notice her uncontrollable shudder and swallowed a vicious curse. There were a lot of things he couldn't help but notice about this woman. The most obvious of all was the fact that she was probably one of the most beautiful he'd ever seen—tall and sleek, a redhead with creamy golden skin and almost perfect features, who showed just enough vulnerability beneath that sophisticated and poised veneer to bring out the protective instincts in any male. O'Mally hadn't a doubt that every night, Monday to Friday, a thousand men sat in front of their televisions, watching the evening news while fantasizing about the network's beautiful anchorwoman. He wished he had the power to end this for her, even as a small, disreputable part of him wondered how she might go about showing her gratitude, if he managed that feat. "You've got to understand. He hasn't committed a crime. What do I arrest him for?"

"He's calling me at all hours of the night. Isn't that against the law?"

"Can you change your number?"

Maggie felt a surge of righteous anger. "Why should I have to change my number? He's the criminal and I'm the one who has to hide." Maggie looked at her tightly clasped hands. Upon noticing her white-knuckled fingers, she forced a calmness she was far from feeling. "Besides, I've done that; it doesn't work. He finds it, he always finds it."

O'Mally breathed a sigh as he leaned back in his chair

and tapped a pencil on his blotter. "Colorado doesn't have a stalker law. All I can do is talk to him."

"Meaning, you can't do anything until after he kills me?"

"I don't think it will come to that."

"Really? And you're sure about that, are you?"

O'Mally pressed his lips together and avoided her gaze. Maggie grunted her disgust. "I thought so."

O'Mally only shook his head. The fact of the matter was, he was helpless to do anything. The man was a pest, but he hadn't broken any law. He didn't have the power to arrest someone on possible intent. The man had to actually do something.

Maggie, realizing this interview, like the last one and the one before that, was getting her nowhere, came quickly to her feet and reached for both her tape and journal, as well as the Order of Protection. She refolded the paper and slid everything into her purse. Her nerves were stretched to the limit. Her one and only refuge of hope taken from her, she couldn't stop the sarcastic words, "I want to thank you, Sheriff. You've been a lot of help."

Maggie was halfway to the door when his words brought her to a stop. "What are you going to do?"

She turned and looked directly into his sympathetic hazel eyes before she said, with considerably more calm than she felt, "I'm going to buy a gun. And if he comes near me, I'm going to blow his balls off."

O'Mally might have smiled at such a coarse comment coming from a woman who appeared in all ways very much a lady. Might have, that is, had the situation not been so dangerous. A gun in the wrong hands often proved fatal, and as a cop, O'Mally knew it wasn't always the criminal who died. "If you get one, learn to use it."

"I will."

O'Mally went to see Henry. He threatened him, but Henry, like many criminals, knew the law all too well. No one could stop him from calling. No one could stop him from following her, from watching. It was a free country.

The detective's visit didn't stop the phone calls. If anything, they grew only more frequent and decidedly more threatening and vile. Maggie was coming to the end of her rope. She rarely slept; her nerves were raw; she jumped at every noise. And in the last two weeks, there had been a distinct loss of weight.

A month went by and the frequency of Henry's phone calls increased. He left messages for her at work, filled her tape at home, sent her enough flowers to overflow her tiny office. Maggie gave them all away.

Daily she visited the shooting range, practicing until she could hit the target dead center at twenty-five feet. She was good, really good. All she had to do was keep calm. She'd never hit anything if she was afraid. The phone calls continued to come, but Maggie found them oddly sinister. He grew sweeter than usual. He stopped cursing. Maggie had a feeling he was trying to throw her off guard. He was planning something. She had a gut feeling that when she least expected it, he'd show up. Only, this time, she'd be ready.

* * *

Henry Collins sat alone in his small rented room and waited for the evening news to begin. A low, ragged breath of relief, almost a moan, slid from his throat as the introduction rolled by and the camera settled at last upon her smiling face.

He slid into the fantasy again. No one knew it, but she smiled just for him. It was a secret between them, a secret he'd never tell.

Her smooth, low voice drifted over him like warm honey. "Good evening. I'm Maggie Smith, and this is Channel Six News. Today, in Washington . . ." Henry listened without hearing. It was the voice he was interested in, not the words. The words were for her viewers, but the voice, like her smile, was for him. It did something to him. Henry couldn't say exactly what it was, but no woman had ever sounded like her before. He never thought to stop his hands from reaching for his crotch. It happened every time he heard her voice or saw her face. A pulse hammered in his throat, in his groin. There was no way to fight this reaction. There was nothing he could do but enjoy it.

He moaned with pleasure as he released himself from his pants and fondled his erection, exposing himself for her eyes alone. She had to see how much he wanted to love her. Henry raised his hips, so she might have a clear view. She saw his cock and smiled. Henry sighed with relief, knowing she liked it. She liked it big and thick. Henry was happy about that. Just knowing she liked it made it even better. He pulsed with need of her, and the pleasure they'd both soon know.

Henry smiled as his erection grew harder, thicker, straining toward the television, toward the only woman he'd ever loved. She knew she did this to him. Like all women, she was a bitch who loved to tease a man. That's why she kept hanging up on him, why she wouldn't return his calls. She wanted him, all right. He could tell by the way she smiled at his cock. She wanted it deep inside her, only it was part of the game to tease him first.

He watched her mouth, those full red lips and white teeth, imagining what that mouth would feel like when it slid over his sex and sucked him dry. Soon, he promised himself. Soon she'd put him in her mouth. Soon they'd be together forever.

Maggie worked late into the night. A school bus had been involved in an accident earlier that day. Four children, all under the age of eight, had been seriously injured when the driver had plowed head-on into a utility pole. Maggie spent the day at her desk, and along with the station's crew, anxiously awaited information on the children's condition. A sigh of relief could be heard throughout the entire station as it was learned that all four children, although suffering serious injuries, would pull through.

Only then did the media turn their attention to the driver. Only then was it learned that the driver hadn't been drunk, as was at first supposed. Her odd behavior, slurred speech, and subsequent collapse had been the result of a minor stroke brought on by an undiagnosed case of diabetes. Considering the possibilities, Maggie could only offer up her thanks that the accident hadn't been far worse.

It was midnight before all the facts were in and Maggie finished up the story with a one-minute spot between *Nightline* and the *Late Night Movie*.

* * *

Jim Carpenter jiggled the lock on his apartment door and sighed. Beverly had locked him out again. Damn, but women were unreasonable creatures. Didn't they understand that a man needed a few hours with his friends to unwind, to bullshit and complain about problems that could never be solved? Why couldn't she understand that sitting in the neighborhood tavern, having one or two with the guys, didn't hurt anyone? "Beverly, let me in," he pleaded.

No answer.

Jim had been married long enough to know that begging, especially from the wrong side of a locked door, would lead exactly no where. When Beverly was in one of her moods, probably caused by PMS, she didn't care if he slept on the floor in the hallway all night. If he didn't make it home for supper, and he didn't at least once a month, the door was dead-bolted from the inside. He sighed, knowing he had no alternative but to come in through a window again. Damn all women to hell. Tomorrow he was going to talk some sense into the one he'd married. Tomorrow he was going to let her know just who was the boss in this house.

Jim murmured something about being the king of his castle as he stood on a discarded box and reached for the fire escape. It took some effort, his equilibrium not being what it might have been, but he managed to pull the ladder steps down. God, he was likely to break his neck. If he did, it would be Beverly's fault.

Jim started up the steps. He was dizzier than usual tonight and had to stop a few times to get his bearings. He frowned. Was that the second floor? Jim looked down into

13

the dark alley, between the two apartment buildings. He could see nothing below but the deepest shadows. He blinked as he tried to think. No, this wasn't the second; it was the first. The next one was the second. Jim grinned. He wasn't so drunk that he'd forgotten how to count. One more to go and he'd soon be tucked comfortably in his bed.

Damn, the window was locked. Jim figured he was in for it tomorrow. When she locked the door and the window, that meant she was really mad. He breathed a sigh. He didn't want to fight. He loved Beverly, but couldn't she understand that a man had to let off a little steam with the guys once in a while?

Jim knocked on the window and waited. Nothing. "Beverly," he whispered as he knocked again. Still nothing.

Now a man, any man, even a nice one like Jim Carpenter, could be pushed only just so far. After that, well, he wasn't about to be locked out of his own house. Jim took off his jacket, never feeling the cold, and wrapped it around his hand. It took three tries, but he finally broke the window, unlocked it, swept aside the glass, and slid inside.

"Goddamn," he groaned, as his shin caught the edge of a chair. Beverly had been moving furniture again. Why wasn't she like other women, who just vacuumed under things? Why did she have to moved everything at least once a week? Usually it took him at least that long to get used to everything and then she went and moved it all over again.

Jim limped toward the bedroom, with only the light of a full moon to guide him on his way. "Bev," he said into the darkened room. Nothing. Maybe she was sleeping with Junior. Jimmy was sick, wasn't he? Sniffles, he remembered, just as his body fell across the bed.

Maggie was bone weary. Because of the accident, she had gone into work hours earlier than usual. The combined worry over the children and the long hours had left her limp with exhaustion.

It had become a habit, since Chris Johnson knew, as did most of her friends, the problem she was having with Henry Collins, for him to escort her to her door whenever she worked late. Chris was the station manager of KFLI, Ellington's small, independently owned television station some fifty miles or so east of Colorado Springs.

Chris had come to Ellington some six months ago. Almost from the first day of his arrival, he and Maggie had begun to see each other on a social basis. Lately their dinner dates hadn't ended until the following morning. Maggie was beginning to believe that something good and strong might come of their relationship. Chris knew about Henry, and the fact that she was being stalked by some wacko didn't seem to bother him any. He wasn't the least bit afraid to get involved. As a matter of fact, over the last few weeks, he'd been hinting that they move in together. Maggie was tempted, but she didn't want fear to enter into her decision. If she was going to live with Chris, she wanted to make that decision out of caring for the man, not for the safety he could offer her.

Chris knew she was tired. He hugged her close and leaned down to brush his mouth gently over her lips. His eyes smiled. "You want to offer me a drink?" His words said one thing, but the look in his eyes meant something else entirely.

"I don't know, Chris. I'm awfully tired."

"I know, honey. I was thinking maybe you could use someone to hold you tonight."

"That's all?" she whispered, as she rubbed her face into the warmth of his neck. "Just hold me?"

Chris felt a stirring deep inside his gut at the unconsciously sensual movement. "Well, holding was all I had in mind, but I reckon I can help a lady out when she's in need."

"I'll bet you can." Maggie grinned at his teasing. As always, when she was with Chris she felt safe, and when she felt safe, her guard lowered to reveal a tantalizing smile and delightful sense of humor.

Maggie unlocked her door and reached for the light switch as the two of them stepped inside. "And just what kind of help are we talking about?"

"Well, I . . ." Chris stopped talking when he heard Maggie's gasp and felt her stiffen at his side. "What? What's the matter?"

Maggie felt her knees wobble and her heart race to madness. A pulse throbbed in her throat, choking off her breath. In her ears it deafened her to anything but the pounding of her heart. "My window is open."

"Maybe you left it . . ."

"It's broken. Look at the glass." Her words were a low whisper as the horror came back in a rush, leaving her trembling with almost debilitating weakness. No, not weak. She wouldn't let him make her weak. She couldn't live forever in shivering fear.

"Maggie, you don't think he's still here?"

"I don't know." With trembling hands, Maggie reached into her purse and pulled out her gun. She clicked off the safety.

16

"Put that thing away before you kill someone."

"Killing someone is exactly what I had in mind."

Jim Carpenter stumbled into the bathroom. In a bleary-eyed sweep, he took in the new towels, the perfume, and the wicker accessories and cursed. This had to have cost him a damn fortune. What the hell was the matter with Beverly? *She* knew he didn't have this kind of money. What was the matter with the bathroom the way it was? He was going to have a talk with Beverly, the minute his mind was clear. The minute he . . . Jim groaned as he somehow slammed up against the door. How the hell had that gotten in his way?

Jim muttered a low curse as he came from the bathroom. A second later the overhead light came on, causing him to blink with surprise. Hardly an instant passed before the sound of a discharging gun sent him scrambling beneath Maggie's bed. "Don't shoot," he screamed, instantly forgetting his promise to show his wife who was boss. "Beverly, for God's sake, all I did was have a drink with the guys!"

The shot and the dive under the bed had not cleared Jim's mind enough for him to finally realize he had somehow miscounted and entered the wrong apartment. It was the deep blue carpet that did it! Beverly hated dark colors. Even if she'd had the time and money, she would never have recarpeted the room in dark blue. It was at that moment that Jim Carpenter silently vowed never to take another drink for the rest of his life, if only he'd be allowed to live through this night.

Chris was the first to shake off his shock and regain the ability to speak. "Jesus, Maggie," he gasped, "for Christ's sake, you almost shot him!"

Maggie hadn't been able to stop her finger from

squeezing the trigger. Even as the man dived under her bed, the gun went off again, and then again. It was hardly an instant after the last shot echoed in the silent room that she realized the man she'd shot at wasn't Henry Collins, but Mr. Carpenter, from downstairs. She frowned at the thought. What in the world was Mr. Carpenter doing in her apartment, coming out of her bathroom?

It took a few minutes, but Chris wrestled the gun from Maggie's stiff fingers and then finally pulled the terrified man from under her bed. By the time they entered Maggie's living room, it was apparent from the banging on her door that someone had called the police.

A half hour later, Deputy O'Mally shot her a glaring look, silently communicating his displeasure as he listened to a follow officer tell of the night's happenings.

Maggie couldn't hold back the words when he finally approached, "It's easy for you to condemn, isn't it? But what would you have done if it had been your wife, or your sister?"

It took only a second before O'Mally nodded, realizing he just might have shot the jerk himself. Luckily for everyone, the lady had less control than she'd first imagined. Her discharging gun had lodged three bullets into her ceiling, rather than into the terrified drunken fool who sat on her couch, shaking still.

It was almost an hour before everyone left. The police were satisfied that it had all been a misunderstanding. Mr. Carpenter had not meant to break into her apartment. They weren't pleased that Maggie had discharged a gun without first asking questions or waiting for an explanation, and despite their grudging understanding, had left her with no doubt that the casual use of her gun could have ended in tragedy. Since Colorado allowed her the

18

right to protect herself, they had no choice but to leave her with the weapon.

Mr. Carpenter was, no doubt, at this moment being comforted by his wife, in his own bed at last, while Chris and Maggie sat on her couch, sipping from cups of decaffeinated coffee. They went over the night's events and Maggie's final decision. "Honey, that's not the answer. Running never is."

"I'm not running. I just need to get away for a while." And then she added honestly, "My nerves aren't what they used to be."

Chris could see that much for himself. Any woman would suffer under the kind of tension that was forced upon her. But Chris figured he knew better than most the solution to her problems. "Let me move in. Once I'm here . . ."

"It won't make any difference, Chris." She looked at him, her blue eyes pleading for understanding. "He's never going to give up. Just listen to the tapes and you'll know he won't."

"He no longer threatens. Maybe . . ."

She shook her head. "He's waiting for me to relax my guard."

"Maggie, if he knew you were involved."

"If he did, things might get even worse."

Chris's mouth twisted into a grimace of disgust. "I suppose Sandra told you that."

"I know you don't like her, but she knows what she's talking about. She's the best in her field." Working on a murder investigation, Maggie had had cause to interview Sandra Black some three years ago. Since then the TV anchorwoman and the psychiatrist had become the best of friends.

It was easy enough to see that Chris wasn't at all happy at the thought of Maggie's leaving. She didn't want to hurt him, but she had to get away. She had to think things out in order to decide what to do next. But most of all, she had to put this terror behind her, even if it was only for a little while. Maggie put her cup down and came into the warmth of his arms. Snuggling close, she promised, "Don't worry, I won't be gone long."

The next day, she called her father's home, not at all surprised to hear her sister answer. "Pat? It's Maggie."

"Hi, Mag. How ya been?"

"Good. And you?"

"Honey, you don't want to know. Andy is flat on his back again."

"Oh, I'm sorry."

Maggie could almost see her sister's shrug. "He'll be all right, but for every week lost, we fall three weeks behind on our bills."

Maggie smiled at her sister's exaggeration. Pat *did* have a tendency to dramatize any situation. Andy was a doctor. He and his partner had a thriving practice. Maggie knew there'd be no tightening of belts in that family.

"Ah—look, Pat, I was thinking about coming home for a while. You think that would be all right with Dad?"

Pat laughed. "Of course it's all right," she said, without bothering to ask their father. "Is something wrong with your job?"

"No, my job is fine. I just need a vacation."

"Maggie, something *is* wrong, isn't it?"

"I told you, nothing's wrong. I just need a break."

They talked for a few more minutes, discussing her

father's obvious involvement with the widow Perkins who lived three houses down the block, before Maggie promised to get back to her sister on exactly when to expect her.

Chapter Two

Maggie hung up the phone, unable to repress a shiver as a chill of foreboding ran down her spine. No messages. He should have called. If he was still in Ellington, wouldn't he have called? Maggie frowned at the thought and forced her panic aside. She was being ridiculous. It served no purpose to imagine all kinds of horrors.

The last few days had been particularly upsetting. Because of the episode with Jim Carpenter, she was a bit more jittery than usual. What she needed was to calm down and get a tight rein on her control.

Maggie took a deep breath, trying for a calmness she couldn't quite feel. Of course he was still in Ellington. Where else would he be? He couldn't have followed her. He couldn't have known she was leaving town or where she was going.

Maggie nodded at her thoughts, knowing she was right. There was nothing to be afraid of, nothing to fear.

She reached for the phone again and dialed Chris's number. Maggie couldn't hold back her sigh of pleasure and greedily welcomed the rush of warmth at hearing again his familiar deep voice.

"Hi, honey. Is everything all right?"

She'd been gone only one day, yet just hearing his voice caused an incredible wave of homesickness. Maggie could well imagine his smile, the lazy, loose way his long fingers held the phone to his ear, his legs stretched out before him as he sat upon his couch, the couch where they'd twice made love, so anxious for each other that they couldn't wait the few seconds it would have taken to walk into his bedroom. She could almost see his flash of white teeth upon hearing her voice, his clear blue eyes, his blond hair, his handsome features.

Maggie pushed aside the aching loneliness and smiled at his obvious concern even as she wondered why it had been so important that she leave. If she were home now, they'd be snuggled together on her couch, watching a late movie, sipping from glasses of wine, knowing they'd soon retire to her room, where Maggie could lose her fears in his gentle loving.

A moment later, she shook off all thoughts of regret, knowing she'd done the right thing in getting away. The tension had been too great. It was cutting into their time together, robbing them of the pleasure they should have known. There was no other way. She'd needed to put some space between herself and Henry Collins. "Everything is fine. I told you there was no need to worry."

"I know, but I'd have felt better if you'd listened to me."

Chris had wanted her to fly. Maggie had insisted she drive, knowing she couldn't live in California without a car for an entire month.

"Where are you?"

Maggie had taken route 25 north to 80, which would bring her through the southern part of Wyoming, into

23

Utah and then Nevada, and finally, Reno, which was about a hundred miles from her father's home. She had already driven the thousand-plus miles in two grueling days, but decided she was in no particular hurry this time. Since she had taken a month's leave of absence, she meant to see a bit of the country side and make the drive in three, possibly four days. "I'm on 80, somewhere around Rock Springs, Wyoming." According to her map, Maggie figured she was approximately eighty miles east of the city.

Chris heaved a sigh.

"Now, don't go worrying. I've done this before." The fact was, Maggie, who had no love of flying, had made the drive three times before.

"I know, but it's winter. Suppose it snows?"

"The interstate is always the first road cleared. I'll be all right."

"Call me tomorrow night. Promise."

"I promise.

"Ah—Chris, would you do me a favor?"

"Anything. You want me to bring something with me next week?" Chris was flying in next weekend to meet her family. Things were moving along, to Maggie's way of thinking, at a slightly hurried pace. Chris had asked her to marry him the night before she left. She hadn't said yes, at least, not yet. Instead, she'd asked that he wait until this business with Henry Collins was over.

Maggie wasn't sure she loved Chris. Granted, she felt something very special for him, but was that love? Perhaps. It had been only one day and she was already eager to see him again.

"No, I want you to look Henry up, make sure he's still in Ellington."

24

There was a moment of shocked silence, and then, "Christ, Maggie! You don't think he followed you?"

Maggie yanked the phone from her ear and frowned at the shouted response. "No. I don't think he . . ."

"Jesus!" he cut her off, as horrific thoughts came to plague him. "What the hell is the matter with us? Why didn't we think of this before?"

"Chris, it's probably nothing."

"What's probably nothing?" A minute passed.

"What?" he demanded again.

"I called my machine. There were no messages."

"What does that mean?" If his tone meant anything, Chris was close to panicking. "God, it means he's following you, right?"

"It could mean that the police have scared him off. It could mean that he's finally given up."

"Maggie, I want you to turn your car around and come home *right now.*" Apparently, he did not agree with either supposition.

Maggie knew he was worried for her welfare and took no offense at the direct order.

"On second thought, I want you to stay right where you are. I'm coming to get you."

"Don't."

"What do you mean, don't? You could be in serious trouble."

"I'm not. I'd have noticed his car. He's not following me."

"You're not sure of that, or you wouldn't have asked me to look him up."

Silence.

"Maggie, please. Listen to me."

Maggie shook her head, denying there was cause to be

25

concerned. "Chris, calm down. You're getting upset over nothing."

"Nothing? The guy is a nut."

"Right, and I won't allow a nut to take control of my life." The truth of the matter was, she couldn't allow anyone that right. For just an instant she wondered which was worse, the occasional sense of suffocation she felt in Chris's protection, or the terror she felt at Henry's threat. Maggie shrugged aside the thought. All she knew for a fact was that she had to get away, even if she chanced putting herself in still greater danger. To save her sanity, she had to.

"Is that why you're running?"

"I'm not running. I just needed to get away for a while."

"Maggie, please."

"I don't want to argue."

Chris knew Maggie well enough. His insistence was getting him nowhere. He could almost feel her backing away. "Don't hang up."

"I'll call you tomorrow night."

He forgot the need for self-control and blurted out, "Stay where you are. I'm coming after you."

Maggie repeated, "I'll call you tomorrow night," just before she broke the connection.

She shook her head, feeling a deep sense of regret. She shouldn't have called. At least, she shouldn't have mentioned the fact that Henry hadn't left any messages on her machine. Instead of soothing her nerves, her conversation with Chris had only left her more upset than ever.

She breathed a tired sigh, blaming her extreme emotions on exhaustion, knowing it was easy to grow upset when you were tired. Even though she'd taken her time, stopping often to rest, the drive had been hard—harder still when one took into account the chaotic emotions she'd suffered lately.

After bathing, she dressed in a cotton nightshirt and stretched out upon the bed, where she tried to think through this impossible situation.

Yes, she was afraid; but she could feel that fear lessen with every mile that separated her from Ellington and Henry Collins. Logical thought was beginning to take over. She could look at her situation with a clearer mind, a mind free of fear.

Henry's unwanted attentions did instill a certain amount of apprehension. Well, to be honest, it was more than apprehension. At times, especially in the beginning, she felt nothing but outright terror. Still, as the weeks turned into months and the months lengthened into a year, she'd found herself questioning Sandra's warnings. Maggie couldn't help but consider the fact that Henry probably had many opportunities and yet had not brought her harm. If Sandra was right about obsessive personalities, why hadn't he done something by now? What was he waiting for?

Maggie released a trembling breath. Despite his sometimes wild threats, he obviously loved her, or believed he loved her. In any case, he wanted her. It was a sickness, an obsession he couldn't control. He could drive her crazy with that wanting, but Maggie was beginning to wonder if he had it in him to bring her physical harm. Judging by the past year, she couldn't help but begin to doubt it.

Sandra was wrong. She had to be wrong.

Maggie clung to that thought, to that hope, for it alone brought her a much-needed sense of peace. She smiled as she reached for the lamp. Bringing the room to darkness, she knew she'd sleep well.

Henry couldn't have felt more rejected than when he watched Chris bring Maggie home and then wait until the following morning before he finally left. The first time it happened, he'd almost gone insane. Perhaps he had, for he couldn't remember anything until he'd landed the final blow to the prostitute's bleeding face—and then, in disgust, thrown her unconscious body into an empty alley. He nearly beat her to death, in his own car, in broad daylight, and he hadn't realized he was doing it until it was over. It was all Maggie's fault.

He'd never known a greater sense of rage. Henry hated her and the man she'd taken up with. He should have known she was nothing more than a whore. All women were whores, weren't they? How could he have been so stupid as to think her different? Why? Because she was beautiful? Maybe on the outside; but inside, where it counted, she was dirty and diseased, as cheap as the worst of the lot, and he was going to take care of both her and her boyfriend. First her. Henry almost salivated at the thought of hurting her.

He sat in a rented late-model sedan, in a far corner of the parking lot. A lighter flared as he took a deep drag on a cigarette. His dark eyes glistened with madness as they watched the door of room number fourteen. A smile touched his thin lips. She should have known better. There was no way she was going to get away from him. He loved her; he'd never let her go.

Her motel room light went off. Henry smiled again. He was a patient man. He could wait, for the day wasn't far off when he'd stand over her and listen to her pleas for mercy. On that day, before he finally killed her, he'd bring her just a portion of the pain he'd suffered. And then the moment he got back, he was going to fix that fuckin' Mr. Wonderful.

At six the next morning, after a light breakfast in the motel restaurant, Maggie drove her blue sedan out of the parking lot, along the service road, and onto the interstate. The weatherman promised only a light dusting of snow. True to his word, it was snowing very lightly. Precipitation barely dampened the road.

Maggie figured she'd make Rock Springs in two hours. If the sky hadn't cleared by then, she'd stop at another motel and wait out what could easily become a serious storm.

An hour passed and then another. Maggie frowned, unable to understand why there was no sign of the city, no sign of civilization of any sort. She shivered and snuggled deeper into her fur-lined trenchcoat. The car's heater blasted a steady gust of hot air. It didn't matter; Maggie was cold, and the more desolate her surroundings, the colder she grew.

The snow was falling steadily now, much heaver than the weatherman had first predicted. Maggie shot the digital numbers on her dash a look of disgust. Too little too late. Now he spoke of blizzard conditions. Now, when the storm was already upon them.

The windshield wipers groaned, struggling against the thick accumulation. It was growing deeper with every minute and more treacherous with every mile she traveled. She glanced at the mountainous landscape. White everywhere. A winter wonderland. It lay heavy upon bushes and trees, bending sturdy limps almost to the ground.

At any other time she might have appreciated its serene beauty, but not today; today it was a nuisance. It slowed her progress immeasurably.

Her car barely crawled along, slipping almost as much to the left and right as it did forward. The road appeared narrower. It shouldn't have. Maggie shot the open map laying beside her a puzzled glance. Had she somehow turned off the interstate? She shook her head. Snow covered just about every sign, but she would have noticed an exit. She didn't need a sign for that.

She was still on the highway; she had to be.

Maggie saw a sign ahead and breathed a sigh of relief. It was all right. She wasn't lost. But just to be sure . . .

Maggie stopped the car and got out. The wind sucked the breath from her lungs. She ducked her head, hunched her shoulders, and snuggled deeper into her coat as the wind slapped snow like sharp slivers of glass against her face.

She slipped and regained her balance. A sheet of ice coated the road beneath four inches of snow. Damn, what was she doing wearing high-heeled boots in this kind of weather? She struggled against the wind and the slippery footing, but reached the small sign at last. With her gloved hand she wiped away a coat of white powder and she gave a soundless cry of dismay. No wonder this area had seemed so desolate. No wonder there were no stores, motels, or gas stations. There was nothing but miles of snow-covered woodland because she'd somehow left the highway.

She had to go back; she had no alternative. Who knew what lay ahead? Who knew when she might come across the next town?

Maggie moved toward the car, slipped again, and fell. Cold, wet powder covered her face. It hampered her breathing. Maggie wiped away what she could and came to her feet again. One side of her was heavily coated with snow as she finally fell into her car and breathed greedily of the warm air inside.

Her body trembled uncontrollably, whether from nerves or cold, she couldn't say. She tore off her leather driving gloves and held fingers that were already stinging before the warm vents. Lord, had anything ever been so cold?

Maggie shivered as the snow on her hair and skin melted and a cold trickle slid inside her coat at collar and wrists. Her boots were filled with the stuff, her ankles stinging from the cold.

Maggie emptied her boots, replaced them, and dusted away any snow that still clung to her coat. A moment later she was driving on. Just a bit further, she promised herself . . . just far enough to find a safe place to turn around.

Maggie smiled with relief as she came to an unmarked intersection. There were no stop signs. No signs of any kind, in fact. She dared not continue down what was obviously a country road, for Maggie knew it could go on for another hundred miles before she came across anything.

At her snail's pace, Maggie figured she was an hour or so from the last truck stop. She hated to turn back. If Henry was following her, there was a good chance she might run right into him. Only it didn't matter; she had to go back. She had no choice.

Very carefully she drove through the shin-high accumulation, bringing the car into a wide U-turn. Momentarily out of control, the car slipped sideways. Maggie cursed the fact that she had no snow tires, but the truth of the matter was, beneath the snow was a solid sheet of ice, and even snow tires couldn't have helped all that much. What she needed was a four-wheel-drive vehicle. What she had was a serious problem.

She saw it coming and knew there was nothing she could do to stop. She tried to pull the car out of the turn, but the wheels seemed to have a mind of their own. The car continued on, sliding sideways, coming to a groaning stop only when its front wheels dropped into a deep rut that ran alongside the road.

Maggie felt a wave of breathless panic. *No! Oh God, please. Not now! I can't be stuck . . .*

But she was.

Maggie, in a panic, slammed the car into reverse and listened as the wheels spun uselessly over the ice. She gave a soft cry of alarm as the spinning wheels caused the car to drift to one side, lodging itself deeper into thick, wet white.

"Now you've done it. Now you've really done it," she groaned aloud. Maggie put the car into park and sat very still, trying to gather her wits. Her first impulse was to slam the gears into reverse again, but through sheer force of will, she managed to fight off the tendency to panic, knowing it had so far served no purpose.

Her next thought was to get out and run, but she again squashed the inclination. Running wildly down a lonesome country road in the midst of a full-blown blizzard wasn't likely to do much of anything but get her into even more trouble.

No. She had to think. *Use your head, Maggie. Think!*

Maggie sat very still and took deep, calming breaths. She waited for the panic to subside, waited for her mind to clear itself of the budding hysteria. A few minutes later she realized she had little alternative. She could either wait out the storm and pray for help to arrive, or leave the car and walk back the way she had come.

It was an easy choice to make. Considering the fact that she was hardly dressed for a few hours' trek through she wasn't sure how many inches of snow, the safest thing, the only thing she could do, would be to stay with her car.

Maggie glanced at the dials on her dashboard and sighed with some relief. She had three-quarters of a tank of gas . . . if she was careful. If she used the heater sparingly, and the storm didn't last for days, she just might come out of this mess alive.

Trying to bolster her spirits, Maggie forced a smile and settled down to wait. Eventually someone would come by. The trucks that cleared the highway would later do the same to the side roads. The highway patrol, or a nearby rancher . . . someone would find her. Hopefully, not before it was too late. Maggie shook her head. She wasn't about to die. Not if she had anything to say about it. Not if she was very careful.

As she'd expected, the storm grew worse as the day went on. Every hour Maggie opened her door, stepped outside, and with the sleeve of her coat, wiped away what she could of the snow. She couldn't allow it to cover her car and blend the dark color into the white scenery, disguising it from any passerby, any would-be savior.

It was close to noon when Maggie realized she'd had

only a cup of coffee and a piece of rye toast for breakfast. She shook her head in disgust, knowing she hadn't even a candy bar to nibble on. Nothing but a styrofoam cup, half filled with cold coffee.

Before settling down to wait out the night, Maggie went through her luggage. She changed from jeans and high-heeled boots into a sweatsuit and then pulled yet another over the first. She wrapped her cold feet in fluffy slippers added two sweaters and then replaced her coat. She was warm. Almost comfortable, in fact, especially when she pushed her hands under her coat. It was bitter cold, but dressed as she was, there would be no chance of hypothermia setting in.

By midnight, Maggie had finished what was left of the coffee and filled the empty cup with snow. At least she wouldn't be dying of thirst.

How many days could a body live without food? She'd heard of people surviving a fast that had lasted for weeks. Maggie grinned. She was going to eat to her heart's content, the minute she was rescued.

She dozed and awakened to icy cold. The wind howled around her car. The cold, forlorn sound sent shivers down her spine. She started the car, silently urging the engine to hurry and warm up.

Once the worst of the chill was gone, she turned off the motor. It was an exercise in futility, for the wind was unceasing and the car grew almost instantly cold again. The night had never seemed so long or so lonely. She fought to stay awake, lest she miss the opportunity to be rescued. Suppose someone came along? Suppose they did, and she slept through it all? No, there would be plenty of time to sleep tomorrow.

The weatherman promised the snow would end by

morning. But another storm was fast approaching, due to arrive tomorrow night. Once it grew light, she would clean off her car. Surely someone would come by; someone would save her.

In the small hours of the morning, Maggie dozed.

The sound was coming from far off. She could hear the engine roar and tried to hurry out of its path. She couldn't. It was always the same in dreams. When you needed most to run, your legs wouldn't move.

The sound was louder, and with the wind came an odd scrapping. Maggie couldn't recognize the sound. She knew it, but at the same time, she didn't. What was it? Maggie tried to identify the sound. Had she ever heard it before? She struggled to answer her question, and when she couldn't, she struggled to come out of the dream. She couldn't do that, either.

Her heart was pounding, louder than the scraping, now. Louder than anything she'd ever heard before.

And then the frightening sound began to fade. It was moving away, and with it, her heart calmed its pounding. What had there been to fear?

Maggie's eyes blinked open. Silence. Was it the sudden, empty silence that had awakened her?

It was cold. She was damp with sweat. Again she started the car. It was light, and yet it wasn't. The car was engulfed in shadows, and Maggie realized the snow had blocked out much of the day's light. She turned on the wipers. Nothing happened. Was the snow so thick?

Maggie rolled down the window and gasped as her lap filled with cold, white powder.

Lord, how deep was this stuff? She closed her window and tried to open her door. Nothing. She strained against it. Still nothing.

Maggie replaced her slippers with her boots and scrambled over the console into the passenger seat. She breathed a sigh of relief as the door opened, but her sigh grew into a gasp of surprise when she came to her feet only to feel them slide out from beneath her.

With a stifled cry, she ended up half under the car. Maggie lay there for a moment, cushioned in soft, cold white.

Accumulated snow lay a good two feet thick upon the roof of her car. She looked toward the road and groaned her disappointment. The road crews were out. A truck had come by and almost buried her car beneath a small mountain of snow. It was the truck's engine she'd heard.

Maggie forced back tears of panic. If they'd come once, they would come again. She hadn't lost her only chance of getting out of here. The next one she'd hear in time.

Maggie held to the door for support. High-heeled boots, especially boots that came only a bit above a woman's ankle, weren't exactly appropriate for snow more than two feet deep. In a second they were filled with snow. Maggie ignored the discomfort.

She slipped, fell, and somehow came to her feet again, only to fall once more. The last fall caused her to roll down the manmade hill of snow and Maggie found herself lying along the side of an icy road. A road that had been recently sprinkled with sand.

"Where were you last night?" she muttered, knowing her car wouldn't have slipped in the first place if the road had had this kind of traction.

The sun was strong. It glared a blinding light upon the snow's surface. Maggie squinted and then scowled as she realized her car was still running. She hurried back and turned off the engine. There was no guarantee when she'd be rescued and no sense wasting gas in the meantime.

An hour later clouds covered the brilliant sun and the snow came again. The first chance she got, Maggie was going to kill the weatherman. It was mid-morning and it was snowing. He'd promised it wouldn't start until to-night. She'd had her heart set on being found before the snow started again.

Thank God she hadn't given in to the impulse to walk back. She'd be caught in yet another storm, and this time, without the protection of her car.

By three o'clock it was dark and snowing heavily again. Maggie figured she'd be spending another night in her car. Her stomach growled at the thought.

She cleaned away what she could of the snow before slipping again into the car's cozy if temporary warmth. A minute didn't go by when she stopped praying. Surely God would hear her. She was twenty-four and couldn't remember asking him for anything before. If you didn't count the Barbie doll when she was eight, this was the first time, and she'd never needed his help more.

Send someone. Oh, please, God, send someone.

Hours later she heard the sound of a car. She almost cried for joy. She flicked on her emergency lights and begged, "Please. Let them see me. Please."

A white blur was groping its way through hip-high snow, and then, like a miracle, a gloved hand was knocking on her window.

Tears of relief slid down her cheeks. It was all right. Everything was going to be all right.

Only it wasn't.

During the next hour, Maggie would have cause to wonder if anything would ever be all right again.

Chapter Three

Maggie tried to fight the nearly paralyzing fear, but she was helpless against the stark terror, as the man she'd only seen in pictures—and once, in a police station, behind the protective screen of a one-way mirror—slid into her car. She thought, then, minutes too late, of her foolishness in not locking her door, in not bringing the gun that lay beneath her seat to her lap.

Henry Collins sat in the passenger seat, oddly comfortable, as if he truly belonged there. He waited a long, breathless moment before turning toward her. And when he did, his heart knew no greater glory. He'd remember this moment always, remember it as the first time, close up, that he saw her in the flesh. She was prettier, he thought, in person. Beautiful, in fact. More beautiful than any woman he'd ever known. Henry Collins never took into consideration that he truly did not know this woman. He believed he did, and for him, that belief was enough.

He smiled warmly, feeling bigger, taller, than his five foot eight inches, for the first time in his life, in total control of his world. There was nothing he couldn't do, nothing he couldn't have, now that she would finally be his.

She sat behind the wheel, saying nothing. In the deeply shadowed interior, she appeared small, not in height, perhaps, for he'd seen her from a distance often enough and knew she stood almost as tall as him. No, she wasn't short. She was slender, sort of small. What was the word? *Petite*. That was it—she was petite.

He'd seen her maybe a thousand times on television, but television could never compare to this. He'd never been this close to her before, and being this close, close enough to actually touch her, nearly took his breath away.

Henry's heart thundered with excitement. He'd known this moment would come someday. He'd dreamed it, breathed it, lived it, and at last it had come. She was very quiet, perhaps a bit stunned, though she shouldn't have been. She should have known, as he had, that he'd find her, that they'd be together. Gently, very softly, he broke the silence that lay between them with the most terrifying words Maggie ever heard: "Hello, sweetheart."

"I . . . I . . ." Maggie stumbled over her words, trying desperately to remain calm, to keep at bay this nearly overpowering need to scream. She knew it would be a miracle if she lived beyond this night, knew it as certainly as she knew her own name. That she'd be raped was a given. It was a ghastly thought, and yet Maggie believed she could manage to withstand that horror. Others had managed as much, and she thought herself to be no weaker than those brave souls. The question she faced wasn't would she or wouldn't she be raped; the question was, would she live through it? Now that this dreaded moment was actually upon her, Maggie could only wonder if she was strong enough to hold to her wits and use

39

them to best advantage. Could she, please God, get through this alive?

"Henry, what are you . . . How did you . . . ?"

Henry Collins laughed. "You didn't think I'd find you, did you?"

"I was hoping someone would." *But not you, oh God, never you!*

"Why did you leave the highway?" he asked, the words soft, inquisitive, almost gentle. "I almost lost you. Did you do it on purpose? Did you know I was following you?"

"N . . . n . . . no. I didn't know. I didn't mean . . ." Maggie tried to keep her voice steady, but it was beyond her power. She'd never been so afraid in her life, and there was no way that she could stop him from realizing that fact.

Whatever Maggie had been about to say was suddenly cut off as Collins's hands reached for her throat and closed tightly, horrifyingly, around it. The attack came with no warning, no change of manner or tone. It was sudden and unexpected, and Maggie knew with a certainty that these were her last few minutes on earth. She thought she should be afraid and she was, but not nearly so afraid of dying as of words that held no anger or rage, but were somehow whispered, despite their menace, in an almost loving fashion. "I should kill you, bitch. I should kill you for trying to run away."

She was nothing but a whore, just like every woman he'd ever known. His fingers tightened around her throat as he grew more sure of that fact. He had watched her every night, watched her smile when he opened his pants and displayed his cock for her eyes alone, when he whispered the things he wanted to do to her, when he stroked his sex into a huge erection, all the while promising it

40

would be hers soon. She'd loved it. Her smile had told him she loved it.

Women were bitches, every one of them. They smiled and teased, knowing it would bring a man to them, and when the man came, they made believe they weren't interested.

And this one was the worst. She led him on, teasing him with her beautiful smiles, daring him to come to her, only to run when he did.

What was a man supposed to do? What did a woman want? He would have done anything for her, anything.

Henry might have known a sense of calmness, of sure-ness, if she'd struggled. If her nails had clawed at his hands. If she put up any kind of resistance. But she didn't struggle. She didn't do anything but simply and calmly watch him kill her. No one had ever done that before. The others had put up a struggle. They had been afraid to die. And because she wasn't, Henry knew it was a sign. He'd been mistaken; she wasn't like the others. She wasn't anything at all like the others, and she didn't deserve to die.

Maggie never realized the pain. All she knew was that she couldn't breathe and that she had an overwhelming temptation to allow his murderous intent, to give in to the blackness, to forever leave the fear behind. To succumb, to allow, to know at last a measure of peace. And then she knew she couldn't. It wasn't in her to weakly submit. She'd fight him. She'd fight him always. She had no other choice.

The attack had come about suddenly, unexpectedly, and then, just as suddenly, before the blackness that had lingered at the edges of her consciousness thickened, growing even more dense, more inviting, before she had a chance to fight him, she was free. At first she didn't realize she was breathing, didn't realize that the blackness that had been slowly edging out her life was gone. "I wasn't," came a strangled whisper, as she took huge gulps of air into starved lungs.

Henry frowned, wondering if he'd heard her right. "You weren't?"

Maggie took a another breath, wondering how it was that she'd never before noticed the luxury in that thoughtless, reflexive act. She swallowed and shook her head. "I wasn't, Henry," she said, her voice harsh and grainy. A trembling hand came to her throat as if to ease the pain. "My father is ill. I was going home for a visit." Maggie could only wonder where the lie had come from. How had she managed to remain so calm, to keep her senses about her even as this madman took yet another route in his insanity?

"Oh, I'm sorry, sweetheart. I didn't mean to do that."

The sudden switching of temperaments, from cloyingly tender to violent, was perhaps more terrifying than the actual confrontation itself. It made a chill race down her spine. She didn't know what to say, what to do. A wrong word, an innocent action, might send him into another instant maelstrom of madness. She trembled at the thought, knowing somehow that his next attack would be worse, perhaps even more than she could bear.

She wanted to scream, to cry, to wail her horror, to beg for reprieve, to explain that she didn't know how to appease, what to say, what to do, but she did none of these. Instead, she took a deep breath and smiled, even though her lips trembled with the fear she knew. "It's all right," she managed, in a voice still unrecognizable. She wasn't sure she'd ever be able to talk above a whisper again. But now wasn't the time to worry over the pain in her throat. Now was the time to think. *Think, Maggie! You might win, even over cunning madness, but only if you think . . .*

"Yes, it's all right," Henry said, as he took her hand and pulled her toward him. His touch was gentle this time. Gentle, if you didn't count the fact that he pulled her over the console, careless of the bruises it caused her legs and bottom. "Everything is all right now," he said, as he settled her upon his lap, "now that I've found you. Everything will be just as we always planned it."

No questions were asked. He'd stated what was, to his way of thinking, a fact, and Maggie nodded, knowing he expected something in the way of a response. His softly spoken words might not have totally penetrated her fears, but still Maggie realized he was gentle at the moment, and she had to keep him that way—no matter what it took.

He held her hand to his chest. She could feel the beat of his hated heart and wondered how it was possible to know more disgust. Maggie fought back the sudden and ridiculous urge to fight him, knowing she could not win out against a man's strength. Instead, she took a deep, fortifying breath and swore that in the end she'd beat him. She'd beat him with her wits. "Can we get out of here, Henry? Can you take me away?" Maggie knew she had no chance to escape while they were lost in this mountainous wilderness, beneath thigh-high accumulations of snow. She had to get back to civilization. Only then might she find help; only then could she make good an escape.

"Yes, sweetheart. I'll take you out of here, but first, take off your clothes. I've been waiting a long time."

Maggie knew a moment when cold fingers of fear clutched at her belly and chest. She'd read that expression on occasion and thought it perhaps a bit overdramatic on a writer's part, but now she knew it as fact. She felt colder than cold as a numbness took hold of her. She knew her words would have no effect, but found it impossible to hold them back. "It's cold, Henry."

Henry laughed at that. "Don't worry. I'll keep you warm." He didn't give her any further chance to argue the point as he ripped at her coat and flung it aside. He reached then for her neck. "Wait," she said, but he didn't listen. He grabbed both sweatshirts and pulled—trying, Maggie supposed, to tear them from her body. She thought she'd strangle to death before the material gave. Finally Henry seemed to realize as much. He cursed and then wrenched both shirts over her head, leaving the top part of her body clothed only in a bra.

This was it! This was the moment that would change her life forever. Maggie had never known such helplessness. There was nothing she could say, nothing she could do but allow the abuse and go on from there.

She never felt the chill of the air. She ignored the pain at her throat, the scratches his nails had left behind, and the bruises she'd see tomorrow, if she lived to see tomorrow. She ignored it all, for her thoughts centered unerringly on the gun. If only she could reach it. If only he gave her a chance to reach it . . .

The lacy material of her bra was no match for his strength. He seemed to find some enjoyment in the fact that he easily tore it away. He smiled, and then, at the sight of her near nakedness, took a deep, unsteady breath.

Maggie couldn't control her shudder of revulsion, but thank God he misunderstood the reason behind it. "I'll warm you, sweetheart. I promise." His hands were on her, cupping her breasts, holding them to his view, despite the fact that he could see little more than shadows inside

44

the car. "Don't worry. You'll be warm in a minute." And then, "Turn on the light. I want to see you."

"Henry, I . . ."

Suddenly he pinched her nipples so hard, so viciously hard, that Maggie could only wonder how she managed to fight back her scream of agony. She thought it nothing less than a miracle that she was able to speak at all, and yet she managed to gasp, "Wait a minute."

She turned, panting, trembling, nearly out of her mind with fear, as she leaned over and around the steering wheel, on the pretext of reaching for the interior lights. She held one hand to the wheel for support while the other groped in the darkness under her seat for the elusive gun. A fingertip touched its barrel just before she was wrenched upright. "I'll do it," he said, as Maggie fought back tears of frustration and despair.

The lights came on and Maggie could see the madness she'd only heard and sensed before.

Henry's eyes widened at the sight of her nakedness. "Beautiful," he said, turning her more fully toward him. "I knew you'd be beautiful."

Maggie could hardly breathe. When had she ever known such fear? Her heart pounded so loudly, so hard, it nearly strangled her as she tried to think. How was she supposed to act? She didn't know what to do. Did he want shyness? No, he might abuse her all the more if she pleaded for darkness. Hadn't he pinched her brutally when she hadn't immediately turned on the lights? Did he want boldness, then? Perhaps. Maybe she could get him to relax his guard if she pretended to like what he was doing.

"I'm glad you turned on the lights, Henry."

45

Gray eyes narrowed as they left her nakedness to meet her gaze. "Why?"

"Because I wanted you to see me."

Henry's mouth twisted into a sneer of disgust. "Don't talk like a whore, Maggie," he said, just as he landed a powerful blow to her left eye. Maggie's head snapped back and she moaned at the sudden and unexpected punch, but Henry took no notice. "You're not a whore, are you?"

She moaned the word "No," but Henry didn't hear it. She saw lights flash behind her eyes. Her head was buzzing, or was it her ears? She felt her bottom lip split at yet another punishing blow and then another and then another. She'd made a mistake, a serious mistake. She'd have to try something else, but she couldn't do anything while he continued to hit her. *Oh God, please make him stop. Please, give me another chance!*

And as if God had heard her plea and instantly answered, her punishment ended. Maggie thought she'd thank God later. She couldn't take the time to think on her bruises and pain, either. Right now, she had some serious reasoning to do. She had to make sure he didn't hit her again. She had to.

His voice was breathless as he looked over the damage done, at the blood that seeped from her cut lip, at the skin around her eye, already discoloring and swelling. "*Now* see what you made me do."

Damn her to hell! She sounded just like a whore, just like all the rest. They disgusted him with their lack of modesty, their moans and sighs of pretended enjoyment. He knew it was all an act. He knew they didn't mean the things they said. And whenever he could, he'd made sure

46

they would never say them again. Henry sighed his disgust. He'd thought she was different. He'd thought . . .

"I'm sorry, Henry. I didn't mean it." She swallowed and breathed heavily through her pain. "I . . . I . . . thought you *wanted* me to say that."

Obviously puzzled, Henry looked at her. "You mean you were trying to please me? Is that it?"

Maggie nodded, terrified to do or say anything that might bring on another bout of violence.

Henry closed his eyes and breathed a sigh of pleasure. She was different. He'd known she was different from the others. He chuckled softly. "I love you for that, Maggie. I've always loved you. You know that, don't you?"

She nodded again.

"You love me, too, don't you?"

Maggie took a shuddering breath. She didn't have to force the lying nod. She'd have done anything, said anything.

"Then show me, sweetheart. Show me how much you love me."

Maggie only wished she knew what he wanted. If she dared make an advance toward him, she chanced yet another flurry of blows. No, the last had almost knocked her senseless, and it was imperative to keep her senses if she ever hoped to win out here. "I don't know what to do, Henry."

Henry smiled the smile of the insane and grew suddenly so gentle it sent shivers of fear throughout her entire body. He spoke as if he were giving a lesson to an innocent in the art of loving. "First you kiss me, sweetheart, and then you open my pants."

Maggie felt her stomach lurch. She almost gagged at the thought of performing oral sex on this monster; she

47

could only assume it was oral sex that he wanted. Maybe it was better to die and get it over with. Maybe . . . no, it wasn't better to die. It wasn't ever better to die.

She'd give him what he wanted. She'd give him anything he wanted, and then, the first chance she got, she was going to kill him. Maggie leaned forward and place a light, sweet kiss upon his lips. She winced in pain, thanks to her bleeding lip, but managed, "Like this, Henry?"

"Oh, sweetheart," he breathed, in obvious bliss.

Maggie fought aside the reflexive gag at the stale breath. Between cigarettes and a none-too-clean mouth, he was disgusting. Everything about him, from his madness to his less-than-clean body, was disgusting. And Maggie had no choice but to make love to him.

She kissed him again and again. Her mouth was killing her, more so at every brushing of her lips against his. She thanked God that he appeared to want no real intimacy in her kisses, but seemed more than satisfied as she kept her mouth closed.

His head had fallen back as he allowed the pleasure, and then, as his breathing grew ragged, he whispered, just like she knew he eventually would, "My pants, Maggie . . . open my pants."

Maggie had no need to act the shy virgin here. She dreaded this as much as she'd ever dreaded anything in her life. She never realized her hesitant fumblings only served to give him a virginal impression. "Don't be afraid, sweetheart. I've dreamt of this for so long," he whispered.

He guided her to kneel on the floor of the car, between his legs. Cold and miserably afraid, she knelt in the cramped position, the dashboard digging into her back. "I . . . I . . . don't know," she said, knowing, of course, that he wanted to tell her how. *Please*, she begged in silence, nearly reaching the end of her limit as he trapped her between his legs.

"Touch me, love me, sweetheart."

Maggie shuddered again, knowing only fear. He wanted her to love him, to touch him, to put her mouth on him. If she refused, she chanced another brutal attack; if she did as she was told, he'd no doubt believe her too bold again. Either way, it would be a miracle if she managed to escape this moment unscathed. Her skin crawled at the thought of touching him, and yet, if she refused . . .

"What are you waiting for?" His voice was suddenly hard, the breathless need somehow gone as a thread of annoyance sent a chill down her back. "You want to do this, don't you?"

She nodded. Knowing the punishment that awaited her, she blindly, mindlessly, reached for him . . . but it was too late, she'd hesitated too long. A sense of doom overcame her, for she instinctively knew nothing she could do would appease him now.

Henry was visibly disturbed. He began to mutter curses and threats, and Maggie felt a sense of real panic. What could she do? How could she calm him? How could she stop what was sure to come?

"Bitch! You did that on purpose." His mouth twisted with disgust as his hands wrapped themselves in her hair and pulled until tears made her eyes smart. "You're just like the rest. You want to see a man beg for it."

Maggie knew a fleeting thought that he wouldn't rape her, after all; that he couldn't manage an erection and his failing was now to be laid at her feet. No, he wasn't going to rape her, but the alternative was even more terrifying.

God, if only her car didn't have a center console. If only

she could have reached her gun, which lay beneath the driver's seat.

Desperate now, she cried out as his fingers reached for her breasts and bit deep into the softness. "No, Henry. I don't know, is all. I don't know what to do."

Henry laughed, the sound maniacal. "Every woman knows what to do, liar!" His fingers dug deeper, his nails biting into her skin.

She'd said she wanted him, but she didn't. She'd lied. The whore had lied. Henry shuddered his disgust. She knew how to please a man; she knew how to touch him, kiss him. She was a whore, and all whores knew. She was going to suffer for this, for causing him to lose the pleasure.

A mad light glittered in his eyes as his mouth curved into a sneer of hatred. "You bitch," he said, as he hit her so hard that Maggie felt something snap in her neck. She never noticed that her head slammed against the dashboard as blood gushed from her mouth.

From beneath the dashboard, something sharp cut into her back as she was dragged from the floor. Suddenly, she was flung over the console. Her head hit hard against the door. There was no need to hold her in place. Maggie was so stunned by the blows, she couldn't have moved. The console was digging into her hips, the gearshift into her side. But Maggie never felt what was in comparison a minor discomfort, for he began to hit her again, each blow harder and more damaging than the last. He knelt on the seat and leaned over her, tearing at her pants even as he bit her unmercifully.

She'd been wrong; he *was* going to rape her. Maggie knew only a cold sense of certainty at the fact.

She couldn't hold back her screams of torment, and the

screams seemed to excite him as nothing else had. He laughed madly as his teeth sank deep into her soft flesh.

It was then that Maggie knew she wouldn't live through this night. Despite her best efforts, she was going to die. If she reached for her gun now, he'd probably turn it on her. Only it no longer mattered. She'd die, but at least this horror would end.

Henry, otherwise occupied, never realized her intent as her hand reached under the seat, fumbling for the weapon. And then came a very loud, very startling sound, just before he collapsed heavily upon her chest. The loudest sound she'd ever heard.

It was only then that Maggie realized the gun was in her hands. She blinked in amazement. She'd fired the gun a number of times at the shooting range, and yet it had never sounded half so loud.

And then her thinking seemed to shut down and she worked purely on instinct. From somewhere far away she realized his weight and knew the man atop her was dead, that his blood was running all over her chest, temporarily warming her against the car's chill air. His urine did as much to the lower half of her, for in death, his body gave up the last of its control. But she didn't think on that fact; she couldn't. All she could think of was to get away . . . to get as far away as possible.

Maggie didn't want to touch him, she didn't want to look, but she had to throw him off her. She had to, if she ever wanted to get up.

Her hands were covered with his blood, but she finally managed to squeeze out from under him. She was on the floor again, pulling from beneath his body her blood stained coat. She didn't think to put her sweatshirts back on. She never saw them crumpled upon the floor, in any

51

case. All she could think of was to get out, to leave this horror behind.

She opened the car door to a gust of cold, clean air, the best air she'd ever breathed, and fell into a mound of icy snow. She shuddered her relief as she rubbed her half-naked body against the wintry powder. Nothing had ever felt so good. She turned onto her back, careless of the injury she might cause to her skin, trying to erase from both body and mind the touch of him, the smell, the ordeal she'd just suffered through. She choked on her tears, tears she hadn't until this minute realized she'd shed. She thought perhaps she was hysterical, but she couldn't stop. Again and again she took huge mouthfuls of snow. She rubbed snow over her teeth, her tongue, trying to take away the scent, the taste, the memory. He hadn't raped her, but he hadn't had to. She'd never felt so dirty and wondered vaguely if she'd ever feel clean again.

And as she wondered, her fears began to ease. Her heart began to resume once again to its normal rhythm. She realized she was cold . . . terribly, terribly cold. Only the cold felt good, almost soothing, as it numbed her pain. Perhaps too good ever to leave . . .

She didn't want to look for her coat, but somehow the need to survive came to take hold and she did.

She forced herself to look in the car. It was there. She'd dropped it on the floor in her desperate need to get away.

She pushed her shaking arms into the sleeves. She never felt the bruises, never thought of the destruction he'd caused. All she could think of was to put this horror behind her. The fur lining, damp in spots from his blood, soothed and warmed her trembling body. She never realized she stood knee-deep in snow with only her slippers for protection. She began to back away, even as she searched through the dark for his car.

She fell a number of times in her haste, but finally reached his car. She was covered with snow and trembling with cold and maybe shock, but it didn't matter. She was free. Free of him, free of the horror.

Behind the wheel now, she fumbled for the keys and then cried out her despair as she realized they weren't in the ignition. She'd have to go back. Dear God, no! She had never dreaded anything more in her life. She shivered in disgust at the very thought of seeing him, of touching him again.

She rested her head upon the steering wheel and sighed. She had no choice but to search through his pockets.

She returned to her car, calmer, now that she'd had a moment to compose herself, and searched through his pockets. She offered a prayer of thanks when her fingers touched the keys.

The roads were cleared from last night's plowing, but snow was beginning to accumulate again. Maggie managed to turn the car around, sliding only a bit, and headed back the way she'd come.

Chapter Four

In a truck stop, an hour or more south of Maggie's snow-bound car, Mike Stanford hunched over a table and cradled a mug of hot coffee in the palms of his hands. He sat alone in a booth. Large windows to his right allowed him to view the ever-worsening storm. On his left, separated from him by a narrow aisle, stood a row of tables.

On the table beside his cup sat a battered Stetson. Mike wore the usual costume of many men living west of the Mississippi—a plaid cotton shirt, a fleece-lined denim jacket, tight jeans, and cowboy boots. On his tall, lean frame, these everyday work clothes looked better than on most.

From his lonely station, Mike watched the waitress laugh at one of the trucker's suggestive remarks and tease him with a brazen comment in return. He'd known Stacey for a long time, had gone to school with her younger sister, actually. Stacey didn't look it, but she had four kids, as well as a little granddaughter that was as cute as any kid had a right to be.

Mike smiled at the teasing, knowing it was nothing more than meaningless chatter, at least on Stacey's part.

She'd been married to Chuck Parker for something like twenty years. Chuck was a man bigger than most and so goddamned ugly that he often joked that one look at his face could make a grown man cry. The thing was, Stacey didn't seem to mind.

Once, while at a party and maybe having had one too many, she told anyone who was interested in hearing it that when the lights were out, it didn't much matter what a man looked like. What mattered was what he had to offer a woman, and to hear her tell it, Chuck wasn't big only in height. At her tribute, Chuck had blushed, and said very softly, "Stacey," which only convinced everyone that she'd spoken the truth. She'd laughed, but there was a special soft look in her eyes. And then that look had turned purely wicked the most wicked Mike had ever seen. From that day on, the women around here had looked at Chuck in an entirely new light, while the men had laughed and slapped him on the back at almost every encounter—in awe, Mike figured, if not in simple envy.

Mike shifted, slightly uncomfortable at his thoughts, and wondered why he was thinking along those lines. And then he realized it had been a while since he'd visited with Lanie. Mike counted back. It had been almost two months.

After leaving his parents' place, he should have headed for town rather than his ranch. Now the weather had grown much worse. Now it was too late. *Damn.*

First he'd had the flu, and once he'd recovered from that, there had been so much to catch up on, he hadn't time for more than work. For weeks he'd been either too sick or weak and then too busy to go to town, and when he'd finally had a chance for a little fun, there had been his parents' party. A party that had lasted just about all weekend. His sister had done most of the planning, but just about all the real work had been left to him. She had done the inviting and had ordered the food, but it had been left up to Mike to get the food there. And of course, since Susan usually forgot something, Mike had had to drive the thirty miles from his folks' place to town for the beer and haul it all the way back at the last minute.

Mike smiled. His parents had left yesterday, and Mike figured just about now they were stretched out on a beach in Maui, beginning a month's vacation. Mike and Susan had paid for this long-put-off honeymoon. Mike was happy to do it. After all his folks had gone through on his account, he figured he owed them at least a month of happiness.

Five years before, Mike had been convicted of murder. His family, but especially his mother and father, had stood by him, believing him when he'd said he was innocent. And he'd only made it through the mess that had become his life at that time because of them. Too bad he couldn't say the same for his ex-wife.

Of course, he'd long since realized that it wasn't Cynthia's fault. He couldn't hold it against her for not standing by him. After all, she had been and still was a young woman. A young woman staying faithful and facing twenty years alone was more than any man had a right to ask.

Still, it was only a week after he'd begun his twenty-year-to-life term that he'd received the divorce papers. And he hadn't been able to trust a woman since.

His ex-wife lived in California now. She was married again, and Jimmy, their son, lived with her. Mike got the boy every other Christmas and a couple of weeks during the summer months. The arrangement was hard on both father and son, but especially on Mike, since he would have preferred to see his son a lot more often. Still he figured things had worked out better than in most divorces. At least he and Cynthia could communicate.

It had taken a long time for the sorrow and anger to pass. At the time, Mike had figured no man had more of a right to those emotions. The day he'd been served with the divorce papers, he'd thought seriously of ending it all.

If it hadn't been for his mother and father, he might have done just that. The truth was, he couldn't bring himself to add to their disappointment. For a whole year they had come every visiting day, and the two of them had been there the day the state had dropped the charges, and waiting to take him home the day he got out. Mike smiled. He was glad Susan had thought up the thirty-fifth wedding anniversary surprise party, as well as the far too long delayed honeymoon trip. He imagined them now, enjoying themselves on the first trip they'd ever taken, and knew there was nothing he wouldn't do for them.

Mike motioned a waitress for a refill and then glanced at the headlights coming in from the road. The car was moving too fast. Didn't the driver realize that ice lay beneath the snow? What the hell was the matter with him?

Mike's body tensed as he watched the car roll closer, closer to the café. He breathed a sigh as it came to a stop hardly two feet from his Cherokee Jeep. Damn, but that was playing it close. Too close.

The parking lot was brightly lit. Despite the storm, the lights outside illuminated the entire lot, and the whiteness of the snow only magnified that light, making it appear almost as light as day.

Mike watched the green sedan's door open and

frowned as a furred foot came into view. What the hell? Was someone wearing slippers? In this storm?

A woman swayed as she came from the car, shut the door, and leaned momentarily against the vehicle as if trying to get her bearings, or perhaps waiting for enough strength to make the distance between her car and the café's door.

She appeared to be drunk, and Mike cursed the idiocy of driving under the influence, especially in this weather.

And then he realized she wasn't drunk. Despite the distortion caused by the glass window, harsh lights, and falling snow, Mike could see she was in some trouble. He frowned, his dark eyes narrowing as he strained to see more clearly. Her left eye appeared to be swollen almost shut, while, if he wasn't mistaken, blood coated her mouth and chin from a cut lip.

She pushed herself from the car and staggered toward the café. Mike stiffened, for just then a gust of wind blew her unbuttoned coat open. She was naked beneath it except for her pants. That in itself was startling enough, but what was even more startling was the blood that smeared her chest. It was easy enough to imagine from the way she walked that she had suffered a multitude of injuries.

Mike got to his feet. He didn't think on his intent. He only knew this woman needed help.

Maggie, unaware of the state of her dress, staggered toward the beckoning light of truck stop's café while blinking back tears of relief. She was moving on pure adrenaline, no doubt suffering some shock. Still, she knew she had to find help. A man lay dead at her hands. She had to find someone, talk to someone about it.

Maggie entered the café. Her coat was still open, but

with no gusts of wind to disturb it, the edges lay against one another. No one but Mike realized she was naked beneath it.

No sooner had she entered the café than Maggie saw him standing at a table by himself, away from the crowd of truckers and waitresses who stood or sat to the right of the large, open room. Maggie never hesitated. She moved toward him and without asking permission sat uninvited at his table, her back to the rest of the café's inhabitants.

Mike said nothing as he watched her almost fall into the booth. The window hadn't distorted as much as he might have hoped. Her coat was covered with blood, one sleeve in particular.

Her face was battered. Some son-of-a-bitch had really done himself proud, the way he had worked this woman over, he thought in disgust. Mike was a man who rarely used violence. He'd found that a man could usually talk himself out of almost any situation. So it came as some surprise that he realized a sudden need to return the favor. He felt his hands curl into fists and knew a longing he hadn't felt in a very long time.

"Call the police," she said, before he had a chance to say a word. "Please."

"Are you all right?" Mike sat down opposite her.

Maggie forced herself to think about that before she nodded slightly and said, "I think so."

"What happened?" The truth was, it was easy enough to see exactly what had happened. The question was asked almost as a reflex.

"I killed a man."

Jesus! Mike hadn't expected to hear that! He'd thought she'd tell him that her husband had caught her with a lover, or something. He'd thought maybe she'd tell him her man was jealous and had slapped her around, although he could see it was more than that. He'd never expected to hear that she'd killed someone.

"What? Are you sure? What happened?" Mike asked all three questions without giving her a chance to answer one.

"It was Henry," she said, as if taking for granted that he knew who Henry was. "He found me." She shook her head and Mike thought she might cry, but she didn't. She took a deep, steadying breath, and eyeing his coffee cup, asked, "Could I have some of that?"

He instantly pushed the cup toward her and watched as she brought the cup to her damaged mouth with trembling hands. She made a face at the taste, or maybe it was because of the bloodied condition of her lips. In any case, she managed to down every drop. She took another breath and muttered, to no one in particular, "I thought I had gotten away." She shuddered then and said, "God, I'd prayed, I'd hoped."

There were bright red marks at her throat. The scratches were bleeding in places. Whatever had happened, whatever she'd done, Mike figured the bastard must have deserved it.

"Wait right here," Mike said, as he got to his feet and headed for the phones. He called to the waitress, "Stacey, bring two cups of coffee to my table, will you?"

Mike dialed Jim Forster. Wyoming might be a big state, but there weren't so many people living in this area that Mike didn't know every cop personally. He'd gone to school with Jim. It was Jim who'd reluctantly picked him up after the dead woman had been found and Mike had been identified as the murderer.

Mike hadn't held it against Jim. He'd known even then

60

that Jim had only been doing his job. At the time, because of a witness swearing a man of Mike's description had been there, Mike knew Jim had had no choice.

The call went through, which in itself was a miracle, considering the storm. A voice on the other end answered, "Police."

"Jim Forster."

"He's not here."

"When will he be back?"

"There's been an accident out on 80. A bus hit a truck and they both went off the road. It's a mess. He won't be back for a while."

Mike digested this information. It might be hours before Jim could come. What the hell was he going to do in the meantime? He couldn't leave the woman here, could he?

Mike glanced through the glass and watched as a trucker left the crowd at the other end of the room and started toward the woman. Her red hair, hanging beyond her shoulders, all mussed and curling, disguised the damage done to her. Mike figured the man hadn't seen her enter and was now thinking maybe getting stuck in this storm wasn't the worse thing that could have happened to him.

"Tell him to call Mike Stanford when he gets back, will ya'?"

"Sure. Has he got your number?"

"He's got it," Mike said, just before he broke the connection and returned to his table. Mike slid into the booth at the woman's side. The trucker never saw his glare, his gaze, moving over the woman, and the blood that covered most of her clothes. She directed her gaze toward the cup of coffee on the table, so he couldn't see much of what she looked like, what with her hair falling forward, protecting her from his view. But she'd forgotten her opened coat, and the trucker got himself an eyeful before Jim realized the direction of his gaze and brought Maggie's coat together.

Mike cursed the fact that his fingertips had brushed against her. He hadn't meant to touch her, and he certainly hadn't meant to feel what he was feeling. Damn, the first chance he got, he was going to Lanie's place. "What the hell happened?"

"She had an accident."

"Is she all right?"

"Yeah, she'll be all right, thanks." Mike could only wonder if he spoke the truth. The woman beside him was shaking like a leaf. He wondered if maybe most of the blood that covered her wasn't hers. Maybe it was. Maybe she was bleeding under that coat. Maybe she'd lost too much and was going into shock.

The trucker walked off and Mike leaned toward Maggie, his arm around her back. "Listen to me—I've got to get you to a hospital."

Maggie looked at him for a long moment, her mind lost in the horror of this night. She hadn't heard anything he'd said. She frowned, wondering who he was. Had she ever seen him before? Yes, she thought, he was the man she'd asked to call for help. "When are the police coming?"

"That's the problem—they're not."

"What?" Maggie felt a moment of confusion. Hadn't she told him what had happened? Maybe she'd only thought she had. "Didn't I tell you . . ."

"You told me," Mike said, cutting her off. "There's been a pretty bad accident. They won't be available for a while."

"Oh," she said a bit vacantly, and Mike wondered if she understood what he'd just said.

"You need to go to a hospital."

"No." She shook her head and then moaned at the pain the movement had obviously caused. "I'm fine."

"You're not fine, ma'am. You've been hurt."

"I need to sleep."

"You might be going into shock."

"No, really—I'm fine. Could you take me to a motel?"

Mike sighed. The weather was bad, the roads were worse, but Mike knew his four-wheel-drive could get him home. What he didn't know was what he'd find if he started down the interstate, looking for a place for her to stay. He couldn't leave her, in her condition. Maybe he should try to make it to the hospital. Maybe he shouldn't listen to her pleas. Damn. He shouldn't have stopped on the way home for coffee. *Damn*.

"Let's go," he said, while coming to his feet and dropping a few bills upon the table.

Maggie hadn't the strength to fight him. She didn't want to move, didn't think she could move; but his arms were around her, guiding her from the booth.

He placed his body before hers, blocking her from the view of now inquisitive eyes.

They were outside and he was helping her into a car, or a truck, Maggie couldn't tell which. "Where are we going?"

"I'm taking you home."

Home. Wasn't that a nice word? Home . . . Maggie thought she'd never heard anything so sweet, so inviting, so safe.

"But first we're going to stop at the hospital."

Maggie never heard the words. She was still thinking

63

about "home." She had to. If she didn't, she might think again of the horror.

Twenty minutes later, Mike pulled the Jeep to a stop outside the emergency room. The hospital was quiet but for a woman in labor who was struggling against incredible pain and building panic as a secretary calmly took information from her.

Calls had been made and doctors and nurses were preparing for the victims of the accident out on route 80, but so far, none had arrived.

Mike carried Maggie into an examining room and laid her upon a narrow bed. The nurse sort of edged him aside as she said, "Wait outside." And then, "Are the rest coming soon?"

"I don't know." Mike knew they thought she was one of the accident victims. He didn't bother to correct her. Later, he thought, would be time enough for questions and answers.

The nurse pulled Maggie's coat aside and gasped at the bite marks that covered her breasts. It took only a second for her to realize that this woman hadn't been in an accident. "What happened?"

"A man . . ." Maggie couldn't finish. Her throat grew tight as she watched the nurse's blue eyes fill with sympathy.

"The guy who brought you in?"

"No." Maggie shook her head and moaned. Why couldn't she move her head without pain?

A half hour later, all hell broke loose as the first wave of victims were pushed by paramedics from ambulances through the emergency room doors. Mike fidgeted, wondering if he shouldn't just leave. He knew the police would eventually show up, take her statement, and do what had to be done. It was none of his affair, after all, and he'd done all he could to help her. There was no reason why he should stay. Still, for some reason unknown even to himself, Mike made no move to leave.

Twelve people had been brought inside and another eight lined the hall on stretchers. With her coat wrapped tightly around her, Maggie left the examining room, leaning against the wall as she walked toward him. Mike was instantly at her side. "Are you all right?"

After cleaning and bandaging her injuries, the nurse had sent her to X-ray. The verdict—a slight concussion. Maggie told Mike as much.

"Should you be admitted?"

"No. Let's go."

It wasn't until they were in his car and heading down the road toward his ranch that Mike thought about the bill. She hadn't stopped at the desk, and Mike hadn't even thought of it. "We forgot about the bill."

"I'll go back tomorrow. Could you take me to my car?"

"I don't think you should drive."

"My bags are in it. My purse. I need . . ." Maggie couldn't finish. She was exhausted. All she could do was moan as her head fell gently back against the seat. She closed her eyes, grateful for the escape of sleep.

Mike headed for the café again, having no notion that the car she'd arrived in wasn't hers.

The car was empty, the trunk as well. Mike frowned.

A moment later he was shaking her shoulder. "Ma'am, there are no bags." He shook her again. "Ma'am, can you hear me?"

Maggie stiffened as she awoke to a man who was leaning over her. She opened her mouth to scream, but in the next instant she realized it wasn't Henry. Henry was dead, thank God. Henry could never hurt her again. "What?"

"The car is empty."

Maggie blinked, and then noticed the bright lights. "Where are we?"

"At the truck stop. At your car."

"That's not my car. My car is about an hour north of here."

Mike breathed a sigh of disgust. He didn't know whether to believe her or not. Maybe she was mistaken; maybe her concussion had caused her to grow confused. "Ma'am," he said, his doubt more than evident.

"I got stuck," she explained, as she reached for his coat sleeve, her tight grasp clearly indicating her urgency. "The car is almost buried under snow. The plow . . ."

"How the hell am I supposed to find it?"

"It's on route 18. I don't know how it happened, but I turned off the interstate."

Mike nodded. The exit was only a mile or so ahead. It wouldn't take him too far out of the way to take 18 home. "Stay awake. You have to tell me where to stop."

Maggie did her best, but the warmth of the heater felt so good. The steady gentle rocking of cushioned wheels was too much to resist. Her eyelids grew heavy and she hadn't the strength to fight anymore . . .

As it turned out, Mike didn't need her help. A car had driven this road fairly recently. The tracks hadn't yet been covered by the falling snow. And then the tracks came to a sudden end. It was then that Mike brought his Jeep to a stop. It had to be here. Her car had to be nearby.

Mike got out and searched the side of the road. He

found the car easily enough. She was right—it was nearly buried beneath a mountain of snow.

The inside light was on, but Mike couldn't see through the growing accumulation of snow on the windows. He opened the door. He had steeled himself against the sight of death. A man would be here, he thought. A dead man.

He wrenched open the door and felt a moment of confusion. The car was empty. Blood was everywhere, but the car was empty.

His gaze followed the trail of blood in the snow. It led toward the trees. Apparently the man was badly injured, but obviously alive.

Mike found Maggie's purse and one piece of luggage on the back seat. Huddled against the cold wind and falling snow, he managed to open the trunk, took out a makeup case and another bag, and put everything in the back of his Jeep.

He slid behind the wheel again and turned to find her awake and watching him, a silent question forming in her eyes. Mike shook his head. "He's not there."

"Who?"

"The man you killed. I mean, you didn't kill him. He's not there."

Maggie gasped, her eyes widening with terror. "But he has to be! I killed him! I know I killed him!"

Mike shook his head. "What did you use?"

"What? Oh, my gun."

"Where is it?"

Maggie was hyperventilating; she couldn't help it. She couldn't hold back the hysteria any longer. "I don't know. I left it there, I think." She opened her door. "I'll find it."

"Stay here," Mike said, as he pulled her back. He reached over her and closed the door. "Don't move."

He returned to the car while Maggie watched, her heart racing madly, willing Henry's body to be there. Maybe Mike hadn't seen it. Maybe . . . *oh God, please, let his body be there.*

It was too much to take in, too much. Maggie had believed she was safe at last. And now . . . she trembled as she tried to steady her breathing. Terror unlike anything she'd ever known filled her to overflowing. She expected Henry to jump out from behind every tree, every mound of snow. He was here, he was watching them; she knew it. She could feel his eyes on her. Maybe he even had her own gun pointed in her direction. She couldn't stand it. Oh, God, she couldn't stand any more of this.

She was about to hit the horn when Mike was suddenly beside her. "He's out there," Maggie said, as Mike sat behind the wheel again and closed the door. "We've got to get out of here. Please," she insisted.

Mike understood her fear. It was easy enough to imagine the man had them in his sights, especially now that Mike knew the man had a gun. He couldn't help his own shiver of fear as he turned his Jeep around and moved away from the suddenly eerie, silent site.

Neither of them saw Henry Collins lean heavily against a thick tree, blending into the dark landscape. He held a gun in his hand, aimed at the car. Henry might have pulled the trigger. If he could have gotten the car to stop swaying toward him and then away, he would have.

Chapter Five

Mike breathed easier as his Jeep lengthened the distance from the bloody scene, and easier still as he turned onto the long road that would bring him to the back of his ranch. At least the hairs on the back of his neck no longer stood up.

Someone had been out there, all right. Mike had always credited the fact that he could recognize danger before most to his being a full-blooded Crow Indian. But maybe that wasn't entirely true. The woman sleeping beside him had known there was danger out there, known it maybe before he had, and she was no Indian. Not unless Indians had suddenly started sporting red hair. He glanced at her quiet form. He couldn't tell for sure, what with her face all swollen and bruised, but her features looked good—at least her one undamaged eye did. Mike frowned, wondering what the hell difference it made. Why should he care if the woman was good to look at or not?

Right now she was in real need of care and looks didn't enter into the picture. Besides, she'd only be at his place for a night or so. After she talked to the police and her car

69

was pulled from the snow, she'd probably be on her way.

Mike brought his Jeep to a stop at his front porch. It had taken an extra half hour to come in the back way, and even though his Jeep managed the drifts of snow quite easily, the tension of driving in this kind of weather made him feel a sudden wave of exhaustion. He took a deep breath and expelled it slowly. It was late. His place was quiet, the house was dark, and he couldn't wait to get into bed. "I hope Abner remembered to feed Brandy," he said aloud, but to himself.

"What?"

He turned to find Maggie wide awake. "How do you feel?"

"Sore. Where are we?"

"At my ranch."

"Why? Why didn't you take me to a motel?"

He turned a bit in his seat. "Tell me what happened."

For just a second she wondered what he was talking about, and then, all too clearly, she remember the night's events. She swallowed and cleared her throat. "Henry . . . he . . ." She couldn't seem to get the words out. The truth of the matter was, she didn't want to talk about it. She couldn't talk about it now. Maybe not ever.

"He hurt you, I can see that. What I want to know is, why?"

"I don't know why. He's crazy. He won't leave me alone."

"You mean this has happened before?"

"No. Before, it was just stalking and phone calls."

Mike pressed his lips together and then nodded, believing he understood. "I could take you to a motel, but I don't think that would be a safe move. He's not dead, remember? We don't know how badly he's hurt. We don't know what he might do next."

"You mean, he might find me, if I went to a motel?"

Mike shrugged. "Maybe."

"The police could hide me."

Mike nodded at that. "Tomorrow, maybe. You can stay here tonight."

The woman seemed to look at him for the first time. Clearly she did not like what she saw. Mike wondered at that. He didn't think himself particularly handsome, but he wasn't scary to look at, either, and then he realized the problem: she'd been abused, probably raped. It wouldn't be farfetched to conclude that her experiences tonight would cause her to fear any man.

"I guess it's pointless to tell you not to be afraid. You don't know me, but I swear I'd never hurt you."

Maggie watched him for a long moment before she breathed a soft sigh. He hadn't hurt her yet, and as far as Maggie could see, there was no reason to expect that he would. Besides, what choice had she but to accept this man's hospitality? "What's your name?"

"Mike Stanford."

"I'm Maggie Smith. I wanted to thank you for what you did."

Mike shook his head. "Anyone around here would have done the same."

"Maybe, but . . ."

He cut her off with, "It's getting cold. Let's go in."

He waited for Maggie to nod before he opened his door and went to her side of the Jeep to help her out.

"You don't have to carry me. I can walk."

"It's no problem," he said, as he brought her to his

door. He put her down then, opened the door, and guided her inside.

Maggie hung back, afraid to enter, afraid of what she might find. "Your door wasn't locked."

Mike pressed a switch and the living room lamps took on a soft glow. "I never lock them. Most folks around here don't."

Maggie, careful of her injuries, gave a slight shake of her head. "That's not safe."

"I'll lock them tonight," he reassured her. "Don't worry."

Maggie nodded and then winced at the movement. A second later she gasped at the sight of a huge Irish setter suddenly coming toward her. Even though they no longer touched, Mike could almost feel her stiffen. "Don't worry. He won't hurt you."

The setter, his tongue hanging crookedly from his mouth, greeted his master with a whine and a few slippery dance steps. "All right, Brandy. Sit," Mike said.

"Come inside," he said to Maggie as he left her at the door and walked toward the fireplace. He was hunched down in front of it, preparing a fire, as Maggie walked to his sofa and sat.

"As soon as I get this done, I'll get your bags." He glanced behind him and asked, "You hungry?"

"I don't know."

"When did you eat last?"

"Three days ago, I think."

"Three days? Were you stranded out there all that time?"

Since her encounter, Maggie had lost all track of time. She couldn't remember how long she'd been stuck on that country road. "Two days, maybe. I can't recall."

Mike nodded as he struck a match and touched it to the crumpled paper under the kindling. "I'll fix you something."

He walked away, but Maggie's gaze didn't follow him. Instead, she watched the building fire, feeling a sense of comfort and safety she hadn't known in a long time.

Her eyes drifted closed again. God, but she was tired. What was the matter with her? Why couldn't she stay awake?

It was probably the trauma she'd suffered tonight, she thought. With her feet on the floor, she leaned sideways to rest her heavy head on a throw pillow. By the time Mike returned with a cup of coffee, toast, and scrambled eggs, she was sound asleep.

Mike thought he should awaken Jake and his wife, Miriam. Miriam could see to her, make her comfortable, get her out of that stained coat and into pajamas, or something.

But it was after midnight and this was no emergency. She could sleep in her coat tonight. Mike knew she was naked beneath it, or at least, naked from the waist up, so he wasn't about to touch her. No, she'd be fine in her coat for one night.

Tomorrow she'd be better, he supposed. After a good night's sleep, he figured she'd be able to see to her own care.

Henry was colder than he'd ever been in his life. He stood by the tree and watched the house, waiting, waiting. God, wouldn't they ever go to sleep? Didn't farmers usually go to bed early?

He couldn't feel his feet anymore. He couldn't feel his hands, either.

He wouldn't think about the pain in his head and the damaged she'd caused. It felt like half his head was gone. Henry chuckled. Half, maybe, but it seemed he only needed half.

It didn't matter. He had enough left to know he'd make her pay for what she'd done.

The blood had run down his head and into his collar and soaked his shirt. It froze against his face, adding to his shivers. He was going to get her for this. Just the thought of getting even with her made him strong again, strong enough to wait until the lights went out, until he was sure they both were asleep.

His first impulse had been to knock and ask for help. He couldn't deny that he'd been shot. He might have explained that a hunter had done it, but they, especially the man, he thought, would have called the police anyway, and he couldn't chance that.

Henry moved to the side of the house, out of the worst of the wind. He leaned against the wall and waited. While he waited, he imagined all the things he was going to do to her.

He had her gun, but he wouldn't use it on her. She didn't deserve a quick end; she deserved pain. Henry wondered how much pain the lying bitch could take before she finally died.

He was so lost in thought, he didn't notice the exact moment when the lights went out. All of a sudden he realized the house was dark. He smiled his relief. A few more minutes, he reasoned. Just a few more minutes and he'd be warm again.

He moved to a window and pressed his face against the darkened glass. The room was empty.

Against the wall again, he forced his mind to work. Had he the strength to do what must be done? It was easy enough to kill women; most women deserved to die anyway. But he'd never killed a man before. And he was so very tired. All he wanted right now was sleep, only he couldn't allow that. He'd die from the cold if he allowed that. He didn't care much whether he lived or not. He wasn't afraid of dying. He'd welcome the black nothingness when the time came, but he had something to do first.

He couldn't die until he took care of the bitch.

He thought the lights were out for about a half hour. Had they fallen asleep? Had enough time gone by?

Henry opened the door and almost grinned. Damn, it was so easy. He wished everything could be this easy.

Killing her would be this easy, he thought. Killing the bitch would be the easiest and best thing he'd ever done.

He stepped silently into the kitchen and waited a long moment for his eyes to adjust to the darkness. The drawers made no noise as he opened one and then another. He smiled as the knife glittered, silently calling for him to touch it, to take it in his hands. It was a good sign, he thought, that the knife could glitter in a house so dark. He made not a sound as he picked it up.

A moment later he put both gun and knife on the counter and began to take off his clothes. The house was warm. The warmth penetrated the cold of his skin. It felt good. Henry could smell a fire. He'd sleep by that fire tonight, he thought. After he did what needed to be done, he'd sleep for a long time.

He smiled as he shrugged out of the last of his things

and stood naked in the kitchen. Standing here made him feel good. He'd never stood naked in a stranger's house before, never realized it could make a man feel so powerful.

Silently he picked up both knife and gun just before he left the kitchen.

He was moving down the hallway toward the doors at the end of the hall. The one on his right would be theirs. That's where he'd seen the light last.

He was almost at the door when he heard the sound of a dog's growl. He stiffened and pressed his back against the wall, but that didn't stop the dog from lunging.

Henry almost cried out as the heavy animal crashed into his body, nearly making his knees buckle at the blow. He could feel the hot breath, the sharp, jagged teeth, the slimy saliva as the dog's jaws clamped over his arm, almost tearing it from its socket, digging into him, filling him with pain and terror.

In his panic, he almost dropped the gun. He tried to think, but couldn't. Perhaps it was best that he worked purely on instinct, for the knife in his other hand plunged again and again as he mindlessly drove it deep into the dog's belly. The animal whimpered softly and then fell dead at Henry's feet.

Henry trembled. He hadn't expected that. It was foolish of him. People who lived on farms always had dogs.

It took him forever to move from that spot, to regain his strength to continue on down the hall, but he managed it at last.

He opened a door. The room was dark. Henry stepped inside.

He could hear the low, even breathing. They were sleeping. He hated them for that. He hated them for being able to sleep, for being comfortable while he had been attacked by their stupid dog, while he had known only cold, weakness, and pain.

Henry reached for the light switch and flicked it on. The man muttered a wordless sound, but not the woman beside him. Perhaps she hadn't as yet fallen deeply asleep, or maybe the dog's growls had alerted her, for she gasped at the sight of a naked man in her room, and came almost into a sitting position, leaning on her elbow. Her eyes bulged with fear.

Henry smiled. He could imagine her fear. He figured he looked pretty bad, what with his arm all messed up from the dog and half his face covered with blood. Besides his injuries, he was naked. Henry was sure that was likely to scare her the most. He almost chuckled at the thought.

She opened her mouth as if to scream. Mostly he didn't care if a woman screamed. Actually, he sort of liked to see them scared. It made him feel braver, stronger, but he had no time to enjoy her screams right now. He had to get done with this business. He had to sleep.

The gun went off and the woman fell back. At the sound of the gun, the man came startlingly awake and almost leaped from the bed, but the next bullet stopped him cold. He fell back beside the woman. Henry smiled at the sight before him. They sort of looked asleep, didn't they? Henry nodded. Still, it wouldn't hurt to make sure.

He made sure, with the knife.

Then he frowned. Too late he realized he shouldn't have killed them both. The man, yes, but not the woman—at least, not right off. He should have waited to do her. He thought it might have been good to do it with her husband lying there besides them. He would have liked that.

Henry sighed. Killing them had gotten him all excited, and he needed to do it. He shuddered at the thought of doing it to a dead body. He didn't like touching things that were dead. But he could do something almost as good. Henry stood by the door, leaning against it as he worked his hardened sex over. He didn't know why, but it was good this time, better than usual. Maybe because he'd waited so long for that bitch. Maybe because he'd fixed this stupid farmer and his fat wife.

Henry turned off the light and left the room. Again he leaned against the wall. He was lucky to have found this house, this lonely little farm. There were no buildings here but for this house, a shed, and a barn. No one lived here except this man and his wife. No one could have heard the gunshots.

He needed to sleep, but more than sleep, he needed warmth. He walked toward the living room and the fire that was almost out. There were logs by the fire. Henry added three to the small flame and sighed as the room grew cozy and warm again. He'd be able to sleep now. Later, he'd think about her. Later, he'd take care of the bitch.

Maggie opened her eyes to find herself lying on a couch. She frowned, trying to remember where she was and what she was doing here, and then she remembered: she felt again the fear. Her body stiffened. And then, almost as quickly as the fear had come, the safety came as well. She breathed a sigh and relaxed as her gaze moved to the dog sleeping before the fireplace.

She was thirsty. She should get up and find the kitchen. She tried to move, but she was just so tired. She tried to stay awake, but her eyes were so heavy. It was the heat, she knew. The fireplace and the thick quilt felt so good. After days of cold, her body greedily absorbed the warmth, the comfort, and she forgot her thirst as her eyes fluttered closed again.

With one glance at a fire that had burned low, Maggie knew hours had gone by. Still, the night had yet to release its hold. She wondered what had awakened her. Had she heard something? She waited and listened, and then came the sound of a man's heavy step. Someone was moving in the dark. Her heart pounded in fear. Henry had found her. She'd thought she was safe, but Henry had found her. Why hadn't she realized that Henry would always find her? Why had she panicked? Why hadn't she killed him when she'd had the chance?

She lay there perfectly still as the steps approached, trying desperately to control her breathing. He had to believe she was asleep. He had to!

She could almost feel him lean over her, touch her. No, that wasn't true . . . he hadn't touched her. He'd touched the quilt, but not her.

She waited endless moments before he moved away. She opened her eyes just as he disappeared into the kitchen. At least, she thought it was the kitchen . . .

The house was so dark. She couldn't see much with the weak glow of the fire, but she could see enough. Beside the fire stood a poker and shovel. Maggie came from the couch, reached for the poker, and pressed her back against the wall. She stood inches from the doorway, listened to him moving around, and waited for him to come out again.

She could hear him move closer. He was almost at the doorway when he stopped. Maggie held her breath. Why had he stopped? Did he know she was standing here? Had he heard her breathing? Was he even now silently laughing at the sound of her pounding heart?

Maggie dared not breathe, dared not move, dared not think as she brought the poker high over her head.

Please, God, please! Make him come. How much longer could she stand the fear? And then, a second later, he was there. He'd stepped into the room so silently, she almost hadn't noticed. He was just suddenly there.

The problem was, he hadn't stepped far enough into the room. He was standing almost at her side. Maggie knew she'd never have a better chance. With no further thought of her options, she brought the poker down upon his shoulder.

Mike held the mug of coffee in his hand. He was just about to bring the cup to his mouth for another sip when he saw the movement, but he knew it was already too late. His entire arm went numb and the cup fell from his hand before he realized the thud his shoulder had taken. An instant after the thud came a blow to the side of his head.

For a split second he felt dazed, unable to understand why his shoulder should feel like it was on fire, and then, with one glance at the empty couch, he knew.

Maggie brought the poker back for yet another blow, but Mike moved faster than a blink as he bent low and rammed his injured shoulder into her chest, knocking her backward and down. Off balance, he followed her to the floor, landing on top of her.

Maggie tried to scream, but he'd knocked the breath from her lungs when he'd fallen on her and her scream came out a straggly sort of half-cry, half-whimper. Brandy growled, and Mike shot the dog an angry glare. "You're a little late."

The discarded poker was instantly in his hands and Mike held it across her throat with just enough pressure to assure her he was not in the best of moods. "Why? Why did you do that, lady?"

Maggie had no notion that she'd stricken anyone but Henry. Therefore she never realized it wasn't Henry upon her. It was simply too much to ask of another human being. She could no longer hold back the hysteria.

Maggie screamed a sound loud enough to make Mike's ears hurt. And they would have, if he hadn't been arguing with himself over the temptation to finish her off, here and now, just as she'd meant to do to him.

He dropped the poker and grabbed her by the shoulders. His anger was more than obvious, but Maggie, in her fear, never saw it. He shook her and her screams dissolved into wracking sobs. "What the hell are you up to?" Was it a plan? Was all this some sort of hideous plan to put him off his guard? Did she have an accomplice, maybe a man waiting outside, waiting for the chance to come in and finish him off?

Why would she do it? He had nothing of value, nothing to steal. All he owned that was worth anything was his livestock and the ranch itself.

He looked at her face for a long moment. She'd have to be crazy to allow this kind of abuse, just so Mike would take pity on her. But Mike had seen crazier things, and he wasn't taking any chances.

"No more. No more," she managed through heaving gasps. "I can't take anymore. Just kill me and be done with it."

She looked to be hysterical, but Mike wasn't about to

81

be taken for a fool again. Standing over her, he sneered at the fact that during their short struggle, her coat had come open and one breast was exposed. Was that supposed to make him forget that she had almost knocked him senseless? Was he now supposed to take her up on her subtle offering? Not likely. "Don't move. I'll be right back."

He might have told his dog to watch her, but the damn dog was so stupid, he hadn't even warned Mike of the impending attack. Even a slight growl would have done the trick. Mike shrugged into his coat and pushed his hat over the small but growing lump on his head.

It was only when he got up, only when he walked away, that Maggie's hysteria faded into stunned amazement. He was leaving! Now that he held her helpless beneath him, he was leaving. Why?

It was only as she watched him put on his coat that Maggie realized she'd hit the wrong man. Maggie opened her mouth, but before she could get a word out, the door slammed behind him.

Maggie sat on the living room floor, alone but for a dog who watched her curiously. She tried to think, to understand, but her relief at finding herself safe again was so great, she couldn't manage more than a bout of self-pitying tears.

It took a few minutes, but Maggie finally pulled herself together. She thought of the man who had just walked out of his house and wondered where he had gone. She knew he was angry. Who wouldn't be, after being struck by a fireplace poker?

Mike Stanford probably thought she was crazy. Maybe she was. Maybe this whole episode had driven her over the edge. What had he said? *What are you up to?* Maggie frowned. What did he mean by that?

Outside, flashlight in hand, Mike circled his house, searching for footprints in the snow. Nothing. Next he walked to the barn. Again, nothing. Surely if she was planning a crime, someone would be out here, someone would be waiting for the right moment to pounce.

Mike shook his head. He'd let his imagination get the better of him. She wasn't planning anything; she was exactly who she appeared to be. There had to be an explanation of why she'd hit him. Maybe he'd frightened her. Maybe she thought he was this guy Henry.

Mike stepped into his house. Every light in his living room and kitchen was on. Now what was she up to? He heard her in the kitchen.

She was half in his broom closet when Mike came up behind her and asked, "What are you doing?"

She screamed and fell into the small closet. Mike might have laughed, except that he almost fell himself, what with the way she'd scared him with that yell. "Look," he swallowed, and took a breath, "you're going to have to stop screaming every time I come near you. My heart ain't going to make it if you keep it up."

Maggie was sort of gasping as she came out of the closet. "Sorry. I didn't hear you come in."

"What are you doing?" he asked again.

"I'm looking for a dustpan and broom."

"Outside the kitchen door."

Maggie frowned.

"I don't keep my brooms in here."

"So I see," she murmured. As far as Maggie could tell, all he kept in his broom closet was dog food and a rifle.

"I keep them in the laundry room."

"That makes sense," she said, mostly to herself. She stepped into the small room that held a washer and dryer; a room that appeared to be both laundry room and catch-all for every odd item that had no real place. A snow shovel stood near the door that led outside. Beside the shovel stood a broom and an ironing board. Coiled ropes hung on the wall, as well as some sort of traps and cages. A toolbox stood in one corner, a broken lamp in another. Laundry baskets, soap powder, and bleach sat upon the two appliances.

As she'd moved off, Mike had watched her with some annoyance. The last time he'd looked, this house had belonged to him. He supposed he could put his things where he wanted them. His annoyance showed in his tone of voice. "Why'd you hit me?"

Maggie came back with dustpan and broom. She cleaned up the broken glass in the living room and emptied it into the garbage. "I thought you were Henry."

Mike had thought of that himself, but still he shot her a look of disbelief. "Why would Henry be in my kitchen, drinking coffee?"

Maggie shoved the dog food back where it did not belong and allowed him a withering glance—or one that would have been withering if both eyes had been open. With one eye swollen shut, it looked merely pitiful. "I didn't know you were drinking coffee. I thought someone was prowling around. What were you doing up in the middle of the night, anyway?"

At her question, Mike felt himself explaining, or excusing, he didn't know which, and not knowing caused his annoyance to grow. "It's five o'clock."

"So?"

"So, it's time to get up. This is a ranch, remember?"

"I didn't remember. Did you tell me you lived on a ranch?"

Mike felt a little ashamed of himself. She was in terrible shape; he shouldn't be barking at her. His problem was that he didn't much take to pain, and his shoulder and leg were hurting something awful. Still, he knew she hadn't done it on purpose—or maybe she had, only she'd done it to the wrong man. He frowned. Why was his leg hurting so damn bad?

He looked at the area that pained him and saw a piece—a good-sized piece, actually—of the cup he'd been drinking from protruding from his thigh. He made a low moaning sound. Great; this was all he needed. If this was a sample of what he could expect today, maybe he should just go back to bed and start over tomorrow.

"What's the matter?" Maggie asked softly.

"My leg."

"What?" she said, before following the direction of his gaze, and then added weakly, "Oh, God. Sit down."

Mike did as he was told, suddenly limping from an injury that until this moment had brought him no more than some minor burning discomfort. Why the hell was it suddenly throbbing?

"Where's your bathroom?"

"Through the living room."

She left the kitchen. A few minutes later she stood in the bathroom, the bright light causing her one good eye to narrow against the glare. She reached for the medicine cabinet and then gasped as she saw her reflection in the mirror. "Oh, my God!" She'd known she was hurt; she'd felt the swelling, the tightness; she'd known her lip had bled. But this . . . she hadn't ever imagined she looked so awful.

85

She returned to the kitchen a few minutes later and put the medical supplies on the table.

"What took you so long?"

"I was looking at my face. I didn't know it was so bad." She opened the bandages and salve. While she worked, she said, "If there was ever a time to rob a bank, this is it. Once the swelling goes down, they'd never believe it was me."

Mike smiled. This woman had spirit; he liked that. "Nothing was broken, right?"

"Except for my head. I suppose a slight concussion means it's cracked, at least."

At her words, Mike was reminded of his rough treatment of her after her attack. Damn, he should have remembered her condition. He should have remembered and been a hell of a lot more gentle. Eyes downcast, he muttered, "Sorry about knocking you down. I forgot about your head."

"I should have called out, but . . ." She shrugged. "I'm sorry I hit you."

He nodded.

"Pull up your pant leg."

"I can't. They're too tight." He stood and unbuckled his belt. "I'll have to pull them down."

Maggie didn't much like the sound of that, even though she knew he didn't mean anything by it. He hadn't, had he? The fact was, the trauma she'd suffered was too recent for her to take his casual words quite so casually. "Maybe you shouldn't . . ."

Her words were interrupted by his command, "Pull it."

Maggie started to shake. His pants were open, and her gaze was drawn to the bulge in his tight blue underwear. Maggie panicked. Her mouth opened in a silent cry. Oh

God, no! She'd thought she was safe. She'd thought . . .

He frowned at her odd behavior. What the hell was the matter with her now? Why hadn't she pulled the glass out? Why hadn't she even attempted to pull it out? "What's the matter with you? I can't get my pants down with a piece of glass sticking out of my leg. Pull it out. And do it fast, it's killing me."

Maggie almost moaned in relief at his angry words, words that hinted at nothing, but said their meaning straight out. She felt a little silly and knew she was thinking crazy. She had to forget what she'd gone through or be forever reminded, forever frightened, by the most innocent word. God, she had to get some control of herself.

Maggie took a deep breath and reached for the thick glass with fingers that hardly trembled at all. When she finally summoned the courage to actually pull it out, he sucked in a breath through clenched teeth, pushed his pants to his knees, and sat.

Blood oozed from the wound as she quickly covered it with gauze. "You should have this stitched."

"Maybe, but I'm not driving all the way to the hospital now. I've got work to do."

"Suppose a piece broke off?"

Mike cursed the fact that her coat was the trenchcoat variety and its collar lay closed, but low over her chest. From this position he could see more than he really wanted to. Well, more than he should have wanted to. "Just douse it with peroxide."

She followed his suggestion and then found her lips curving into a half-smile as she became acquainted with some highly unusual curse words. "You *said* to douse it."

He took a deep breath while trying to will away the last

87

of the burning pain. He might have said more on the subject if it were not for the noise in his back room and Maggie's instant and obvious fear. Mike placed a heavy hand upon her shoulder and the fear had no time to settle before it disappeared with his calmly spoken, "Easy."

The back door opened and a grizzly old man, sporting a long gray beard, stepped into his kitchen.

"Morning, Mike," the man said, paying little mind to the scene before him. Mike almost grinned at the fact that he was sitting in one of his kitchen chairs, his pants pushed to his knees, while a woman knelt before him, bandaging his thigh, wearing a coat splattered with dried blood— and Abner only poured himself a cup of coffee, acting as if the scene were nothing out of the usual, then turned, leaning his back against the counter as he took noisy, slurpy sips from the cup in his hand.

Mike nodded and in response said, "Abner." And then, "This is Maggie Smith."

Maggie smiled, but in doing so, her lip began to bleed again. Abner nodded in her direction, but said nothing about her swollen, battered face. Instead, he said to the room at large—the ceiling, mostly—"I knew it would come to this."

Mike asked, just as he knew he was expected to, "What?"

"That you'd have to beat a woman before gettin' her to stay."

Mike grinned.

Maggie smiled again and knew with just those few words that she liked this Abner.

"First of all, I didn't beat her."

"And I'm not staying," Maggie offered, as she finished bandaging his leg. "That should be all right," she said as

88

she looked over her neat job, "but you really should get to a doctor, in case there's glass inside."

Mike didn't respond. They both knew he wouldn't take her advice.

He stood and brought his pants to his waist again. He was redoing buttons, zipper, and buckle as Maggie gathered the medical supplies and left the kitchen, but not before she heard Abner grunt and then say, "That's too bad."

"Mind your own business," Mike warned.

"Did I say anything?"

"Do you ever not say anything?"

"You're too young to live alone."

Mike glanced at the empty doorway and listened for a second to the sounds Maggie made while putting the bandages away. He hoped she couldn't hear this ridiculous conversation. "And how did I know you were goin' to start that again?"

"Psychic, probably."

Maggie stepped into the kitchen again. She could almost feel the tension between the two men and wondered what that was all about. Their conversation had been low, almost whispered, so she hadn't heard anything but a final, "Shut up" before entering the kitchen again. She assumed they were talking about her; she thought it impossible for them not to be talking about her, especially with the way she looked. It didn't matter. "Where did you put my bags?"

Mike stopped glaring at the older man just long enough to say, "In the spare room."

"Where's the spare room?"

"To the right of the bathroom."

Maggie nodded. "Is it all right if I take a bath?"

89

"Sure."

She left the men to their own devices, and after taking clean clothes from her bags, stepped into the bathroom. She sat for a long time in a tub of hot water. She probably shouldn't have let her bandages get wet, but she couldn't resist the water. She'd change the bandages when she was done, and then she was going to try out that bed in the guest room.

Maggie figured this overwhelming need to sleep was due to the injury to her head, or the shock of what had happened last night. She gave a lusty yawn as she stepped out of the tub, dried herself, and slipped into her clothes. In either case, she had no choice but to give in to the need.

Chapter Six

Jim Forster sat in Mike's living room as Mike walked toward the spare room and knocked at the door. "Maggie," he said, receiving only silence in return. "Maggie, wake up."

"What?" came a soft, sleepy response.

"The police are here. Jim wants to talk to you."

Maggie moaned. She didn't want to get up. The bed was comfortable and warm, and she was so tired.

"Are you all right?"

Maggie didn't answer his question, but said instead, "I'll be out in a minute."

The two men were talking when Maggie opened the door and stepped into the living room. "What time was that?" Jim asked, and Mike returned, "I don't know. Around twelve, maybe."

Jim nodded and recorded the time in his book. Both men turned toward the sound of the door. Jim winced at the damaged done to Maggie's face. She was a tall woman, but slender and small-boned. Jim didn't know quite what it was, but she gave the appearance of being fragile. Her hair was gorgeous. It flowed loose around her shoulders in dark red curls. The tint of her skin, what part of it wasn't discolored with bruises, appeared creamy and smooth.

Mike frowned at his friend's obvious and very male interest. Jim didn't look like a cop beginning an investigation, he looked like a man who was looking at a woman. A very beautiful woman.

And Mike knew she was. Despite what had been done to her face, the fact was undeniable.

Jim stood and reached out a hand in greeting. "I'm Jim Forster. I'd like to get some information, if you don't mind."

Maggie nodded and sat at the opposite end of the couch. "I take it you haven't found him."

Jim shook his head. "There's a lot of country out here, ma'am. It might take awhile. Why don't we start with his name, his description? What was he wearing?"

"His name is Henry Collins. Call the Ellington police. They might be able to send you his picture."

"He has a record?"

She shrugged. "They had him in for questioning. Maybe they took a picture then."

"Tell me about it."

Maggie told her story. Told of the countless phone calls and the stalking that had changed her life forever. Both men listened. Jim took notes.

"What did you do?"

"I got an Order of Protection against him." Maggie offered both men a wry smile, knowing first hand how utterly useless that effort had been. "And I kept a journal, dating every phone call and drive-by."

Jim nodded.

Maggie continued on with her story, telling of shattered

92

nerves and the need to get away for a while. And then she told of being caught in the storm and somehow leaving the interstate, of getting stuck, and of spending two days, as far as she could remember, in the snow. And finally, Henry's appearance, and her terror at finding herself in the middle of a nightmare.

Jim pressed his lips together and frowned, obviously uncomfortable. "If you'd rather, I could get a police-woman to finish this. Most rape victims prefer to talk to a woman."

Maggie, careful of any abrupt movement, gently shook her head. "I wasn't raped. He forced me do some things, but I wasn't raped."

"I'm sorry, ma'am." And by the looks of him, he really was. "But I have to ask, what kinds of things?"

Maggie looked at the man, and without a shred of embarrassment, said, "He wanted oral sex."

Mike nodded at her calm composure. Good, he thought. She had nothing to be ashamed of, and he was glad she seemed to realize that fact.

"And then?"

"And when I hesitated, he started beating me." She touched her swollen lip. "He threw me over the console. He was going to rape me then, but I reached under the seat for my gun. I thought I was going to die." Maggie shuddered at the memory and unconsciously touched her chest where his bites had been the most severe. "I didn't know I pulled the trigger. I just heard the shot. It was very loud."

"You have a license for the gun?"

"Yes. It's in my purse."

"Do you realize you're not allowed to transport a gun across the state line?"

Maggie shook her head again. "I didn't know." And then she continued honestly, "But if I had, I would have done it anyway."

Jim nodded. Mike noticed he did not write the last of her statement in his book.

Jim came to his feet, the interview apparently over for now. "I'll get in touch with Ellington, see what they have."

Maggie asked, "Do you think you could call someone about my car?"

"Why?" Mike asked.

Maggie glanced in his direction. "I can't stay here."

"I think you should," Jim said. "At least for a little while. You're not going to find a safer place."

"He's right," Mike added. "The best thing you could do right now would be to sit tight." Their gazes held for a long moment before Mike realized that the sudden jolt of emotion twisting at his chest was fear at the thought of her leaving. He knew she could, very easily, find herself in danger again. She had to stay, at least until that nut was behind bars. Still, he thought it odd that he should feel so adamant about it. After all, she was practically a total stranger and none of this was any of his business.

She returned her gaze to Jim. "You said it was a big country. It might take weeks before you find him. I can't . . ."

"Maybe," Jim interrupted. "But we *will* find him. You can count on it."

Maggie nodded as Mike walked Jim to the door. The men spoke for a minute. Maggie didn't listen to their conversation; she was thinking about the fact that she was imposing on a stranger and wished she was at home with

94

her father. She'd have to call and give her family a reason as to why she wouldn't be coming back for a while.

Mike returned to the living room. Maggie noticed the movement, realized she was no longer alone, and asked, "Are you sure?"

"About you staying?"

She nodded.

"I have plenty of room."

"But . . ."

"You won't be a bother, if that's what you're worrying about.

"You hungry?"

"I'll be a bother if you have to cook for me."

"I have to get myself lunch. It won't be any trouble to get extra."

"All right," she breathed softly, and both of them knew she was agreeing not only to lunch, but to staying on for a while. "Can I use your phone? My father is expecting me. He'll be worried if he doesn't hear from me soon."

Mike nodded toward the phone on the table beside the couch, just before he left to see about lunch.

Maggie dialed her father's number. It rang three times before a woman answered. Maggie frowned. She thought at first she'd dialed the wrong number, and then she remembered her father's budding romance with the widow down the block.

Maggie answered the friendly hello with, "Frank Smith, please."

"Who's calling?"

"Maggie."

"Frank," was whispered at the other end of the line, "It's Maggie."

"Maggie," came her father's deep, pleasant voice. "I'm

cooking your favorite. Got it bubbling on the stove right now. Where are you?"

Maggie thought of the sweet, custardy rice pudding. It was her favorite, only she didn't feel much like eating anything right now. "I'm in Wyoming. I won't be able to make it there for a while."

"How long?"

"A week or two, I think."

"Why? What happened?"

"I ran into a friend." Lord, but that sounded like a lie, even to her. "She needs my help for a while. I'll explain when I see you."

"Everything is all right, isn't it, Mag?"

"Everything is fine, Dad. Don't worry."

"Is there a number where I can reach you?"

Maggie read off the number on the phone. "I promise, Dad, I'll be there just as soon as I can."

"Good, I have someone I want you to meet."

"Pat told me." Maggie winced as she forgot her injuries and smiled. "Does she make you happy?"

"Very."

"Good. Tell her I love her already. Anyone who can put up with your Irish temper is aces, in my book."

Her father laughed, and then a moment later, asked, "What about Chris? I'm supposed to pick him up at . . ."

Maggie had forgotten all about Chris and his plans to come for a weekend visit. "I'll call and let him know my plans were changed."

They spoke for a few more minutes before Maggie ended the conversation with a promise to call again before continuing on her way. Then she dialed Chris's number. His answering machine clicked on and she left a short message and the number where she was staying.

Mike returned fifteen minutes later to find her fast asleep. "Maggie," he said softly, as he placed the bowl of chicken soup Miriam had left for him and his guest on the low table. He touched her shoulder and Maggie jumped awake with a cry of fright. "I'm sorry. I didn't mean to scare you."

She took a deep but unsteady breath.

"All right?"

She nodded.

"I couldn't let you sleep through another meal. You have to eat something."

Maggie nodded again, and then frowned at her shaking hands. "I'm a little jittery, I guess."

Mike sat across from her. "Did the hospital prescribe anything for those cuts?" he asked, looking over the scratches and injuries to her face.

"No. They just gave me a little tube of something for the bites on my chest."

"Bites? You mean he *bit* you?"

Maggie didn't answer. The biting had been worse, more horrifying, than anything else he might have done. She thought perhaps she could even have withstood rape more easily than his barbaric, cannibalistic assault, for he hadn't merely bitten, he'd taken pieces of flesh with every bite. Maggie shivered at the thought, for she knew he'd swallowed them.

She didn't want to think about it anymore. She couldn't while she was eating, at any rate, for nausea threatened at the very thought of what he'd done. All thinking served to do was to remind her of the pain, the absolute horror, and her echoing screams of agony.

Her nonanswer was an answer in itself. "Damn. I knew you should have stayed at the hospital. Are they bad?"

She didn't look at him. "I don't like hospitals much. I'll be all right."

After lunch, Maggie went back to bed. She slept until dinner. And then she slept again.

The pattern repeated itself over the next two days.

Maggie awakened on the third day to find herself alone in the house. She glanced at her watch. Nine o'clock. Mike would have been up and around for hours by now. Odd, she thought that her first thoughts were about Mike. Not so odd, she countered: he'd been taking care of her for days. Why shouldn't she think of him first?

What was, in fact, truly odd was that she felt so comfortable here. She felt no fear in being alone. Maggie thought she'd made the right decision about staying on. She'd been in no shape to travel in the first place, and Mike was right: his home was safe. Somehow, she knew nothing could happen to her as long as she stayed here.

She rose from bed and looked out the window. It had stopped snowing some time ago. A few men were working a horse in the coral, while another rode into the snow-filled yard and dismounted. She couldn't see Mike, but she knew he was out there somewhere.

Maggie groaned as the water ran for her bath and she glanced into the mirror. Lord, what a mess. The swelling had lessened quite a bit. Her lips looked normal but for the cut, and she could see out of her eye again. Apparently there had been no permanent damage done, but the neat dark half-circles under her eyes were taking on a sickly shade of greenish yellow.

Maggie thought it was time for some serious delving into her makeup case. She knew makeup wouldn't cover the injury completely, but it could help. If nothing else, it would make her feel better.

Maggie left the bathroom some time later, feeling much like her old self. She'd brushed the tangles from her hair and secured the long, heavy curls with a twister. She wore clean jeans, thick socks, sneakers, and a plaid shirt. It felt good to get out of bed and into everyday clothes again, but what made her feel particularly good was the fact that she was hungry.

Thanks to Mike's insistence, she had eaten these last few days, but she'd had no real appetite and had only managed to down a few bites at every meal. Now, for the first time, she was starving. She finished all of the scrambled eggs left for her in Mike's oven, as well as four pieces of toast and two cups of steaming coffee.

She straightened up the kitchen and wandered into the living room. Sitting on the black leather couch where she had slept the first night, Maggie admired the soft golden beauty of the room. The entire house appeared to be built of pine logs. Softly glowing in their natural state, they created a homey atmosphere. A half-wall separated the living room from the kitchen. All the ceilings were beamed, and ivy plants, among others, hung along those beams.

Maggie thought everything was beautiful, especially the rugs. Bright and cheerful, they dotted the glowing wooden floors. Idly she wondered who had done the decorating.

On each side of the fireplace, shelves held a variety of reading material. Maggie got up to investigate and smiled as she noticed a number of classics, including *Jane Eyre*, of all things, along with spy novels, lots of murder mysteries, and books on husbandry.

Maggie had read *Jane Eyre* a number of times, and each time, she found something else to admire in the classic. Thinking she'd try it again, she took the book with her to the couch, made herself comfortable, and settled down for a few hours of pleasant reading.

Maggie awoke with a start to find a beautiful young woman with long black hair and the darkest eyes she'd ever seen looking at her.

Apparently the woman noticed her jump. "Sorry. Did I scare you?"

Maggie frowned. It took a second before she remembered where she was. "It's all right. These days I scare easily."

"My name is Susie. Is Mike around?"

"He's not out back?"

Susan shrugged. "I haven't looked yet. It's almost time for lunch, so I thought . . ." Susan checked her watch and then sighed. "I'd better get glasses, or a bigger watch. It's only 10:30, not 11:30."

Susan sighed and made herself comfortable in Mike's favorite chair. "Miriam told me what happened. You don't look like . . . Sorry," she said, "I have a tendency to talk without thinking first."

Maggie smiled. "Don't worry about it."

"You're real pretty, aren't you?"

"Thank you."

Susan looked more closely. "I thought I'd see bruises, but . . ."

"I covered them with makeup."

Susan nodded. "Does my brother know you're this pretty?"

Maggie laughed. "Your brother hasn't seen me with makeup, if that's what you're asking."

"I wish I could stay and watch his expression. Mom and Dad and I have been hoping . . ." Susan shrugged, but left the sentence hanging.

Maggie said nothing, not at all sure what this young woman was talking about.

"You're not married, are you?"

"No. Why?"

Susan smiled. "Just wondering," she said, so innocently that Maggie might have believed her if she hadn't noticed the gleam in her eyes. "Mike's not married, either."

Maggie understood at last the reason behind these questions. "If you think there's a romance brewing between your brother and me, you're mistaken."

"Not yet, maybe."

"Not ever, I'm afraid. I'll be leaving here as soon as they catch . . . as soon as they catch Henry Collins."

"Oh, they'll catch him, don't worry about that. It just might take some time."

Maggie nodded and Susan seemed particularly delighted at the thought. "Yeah, it might be a few weeks before that happens." She came to her feet. "Tell Mike I'll see him later. I've got to go."

Susan departed, leaving Maggie with the odd yet distinct impression that she hadn't come to see Mike at all, but to see his new houseguest. Maggie frowned; Susan was obviously interested in matchmaking. Maggie smiled at the thought. Mike was a handsome man, but hardly her type. She couldn't envision herself being interested in a rancher. Even if his looks were outstanding, and they were, Maggie wouldn't stay here a minute longer than she absolutely had to.

Later, she was in the kitchen, making a fresh pot of coffee, when she heard someone knock softly at the back door. She opened it to find a woman obviously of Indian descent and fairly close to her own age. She was holding a covered dish.

"Hi, I'm Miriam, Jake's wife."

"Hello."

Miriam smiled, a flash of white teeth against a dark complexion. "I didn't scare you, did I?"

"No. Come on in."

Miriam walked into the house and slid the covered dish onto the kitchen table. Maggie thought the woman appeared very much at ease in this house. "Mike said not to make any noise, that you might still be asleep."

Maggie knew, thanks to Susan, that the woman, and probably everyone else on the ranch, knew why she was here. She offered no explanation. "Are you all right now?"

Maggie nodded. "I'm feeling better, thanks."

"Good," Miriam nodded in satisfaction. "Mike's been worried."

"He has?" Maggie thought that strange. Why would a man . . . ? She shrugged aside the question, figuring Miriam either exaggerated or had misunderstood Mike's neighborly concern.

"Yeah, he won't let any of the guys come in here."

Maggie frowned. "Why not?"

Miriam grinned. "He said 'cause you need to get well before those baboons come traipsing through his house for coffee." Miriam chuckled and winked. "But now that I've finally gotten a chance to see you, I think it's cause you look too good and he doesn't trust any of them not to steal you away." She shrugged and then grinned again. "You know cowboys—they get a bit lonely at times. There's no telling what they're likely to do."

Maggie laughed at that, knowing she looked anything but good. "They'd have to be more than a bit lonely. If I took off my makeup, I'd scare them away."

Miriam grinned. "I brought lunch." She opened the dish. Inside was a bowl of warm roast beef and gravy. Beside it, wrapped in a linen napkin, was a loaf of hot bread.

Maggie's mouth watered. "Do you do this every day?"

"Mostly. I look after the place. Clean it once a week, do laundry, and cook lunch and supper."

"You mean, it's been *your* food that I've been eating?"

"Mike let you think he made it?" Miriam laughed. "The dog."

"Who's a dog?" came a deep voice from the kitchen doorway.

"Brandy, who else?" Miriam said, without a second's hesitation.

Both women grinned. Neither offered further information.

"Did I miss something?"

"Nope. Lunch is ready."

Mike was washing up at the sink and Maggie was setting the table when she suddenly realized Miriam was wrapping her scarf around her neck and pulling on her gloves. "Aren't you staying?"

"I already ate. See you later."

The fresh pot of coffee was ready. Maggie sat across

from Mike as they ate. "This is delicious," Maggie said, around a mouthful of hot roast beef sandwich.

Mike nodded. "Miriam is a good cook."

"Mike?"

"Umm?" he said, while swallowing. "What?"

"You told me I wouldn't be a bother."

He leaned back in his chair and looked at her intently for the first time since he'd entered his house. "What did you do? How did . . ." He might have looked surprised; the truth was, he was closer to stunned. He'd known she was attractive, but he hadn't suspected this.

Maggie realized he was referring to the bruises, swelling, and discoloration no longer in evidence. "Makeup."

"You're beautiful." Mike hadn't meant to say that. He was a quiet man who didn't often compliment women, so he was somewhat surprised to hear himself say the words.

"Thank you," she said easily, as if she heard the compliment every day. Mike figured she probably did.

Maggie returned to the original subject. "You said I wouldn't be a bother, but the men can't come in anymore for coffee."

"I brought the big pot to the barn. They'll live."

"I'm better now, so they can come back."

Mike shook his head. "No need. The barn is fine."

Maggie sighed. The man might deny it, but her presence here *was* a nuisance, to him as well as to his men. And as long as she allowed the needless pampering, things weren't about to get much better. She didn't want her presence to be any more inconvient than was necessary, and yet she was at a loss as to what to do about it. "I know my being here is a real imposition."

He shook his head. "It's no bother."

"I'll pay you for . . ."

"Maggie," he interrupted. "I don't want or need your money."

"But . . ."

"I don't know about where you come from, but out here, neighbors do for each other."

"I'm not a neighbor."

Mike shrugged. "You are now."

A moment of silence went by before Maggie asked, "What kind of an Indian are you?"

"How did you know I was an Indian?"

Mike's grin was gentle and definitely intriguing. Maggie couldn't hold back an answering smile. "Well, it couldn't be the black hair, or the dark eyes and skin. And lots of people have high cheekbones, so it must be just a wild guess."

Mike chuckled and then said, "Crow."

"How come you're not 'Mike Standing Eagle,' or something?"

"Because a great great," he shrugged, "I don't know how many greats, grandmother of mine married a white man named Stanford."

Maggie leaned back and shook her head. "I can't put it together. What's *Jane Eyre* doing on your shelf?"

Mike laughed at the puzzled look in her eyes. "You mean because I'm an Indian, I shouldn't know how to read?"

She shot him a short but withering glance before she said, "I mean because you're a man, and men aren't usually interested in that kind of fiction."

"Meaning men can't be sensitive? I thought the men of the nineties were . . ."

"Tell me the truth."

"It belongs to my sister. She left it here."

"I knew it," she said, and then, "She was here today."

"Who? My sister?"

Maggie nodded.

"What did she want?"

"To look me over, I think. She hinted at hopes for romantic involvement."

"I'm sorry about that." Mike sighed. "God, I wish people would mind their own business."

Maggie chuckled and then said, "And I knew *Jane Eyre* couldn't be . . ."

"For your information, I read it."

"Really?" Maggie's eyes widened in surprise. "Did you like it?"

Mike shrugged. "I got through it. Personally, I prefer . . ."

"Murder mysteries," they said in unison.

Both smiled.

"Where does Miriam live?"

"In the first house to the right and behind the barn. You figurin' on maybe stopping by there this afternoon?"

"Maybe."

"You should take a nap first, you'll need it."

"Why?"

" 'Cause Miriam has four kids. The oldest is only six, but every one of them is a terror."

Maggie smiled as she finished her coffee and began to clean the table. "And this from a sensitive man of the nineties? You don't like kids?"

"I like 'em all right. But I like 'em better when they don't smoke cigarettes and almost burn my barn down."

"The six-year-old?"

Mike nodded. "Little Jake. He's a good kid, except . . ."

". . . when he tries to burn down your barn."

"He thinks he's twenty-four," Mike breathed on a sigh.

Maggie smiled. "I know the type. I have a nephew who is five and tells me dirty jokes."

"Really?" Mike's eyes filled with obvious interest. "How dirty?"

"Not that dirty."

They both smiled.

"I think they're supposed to be pretty bad. He hears them from the kids in school, I guess; the trouble is, he usually leaves out an important line or substitutes the punchline from another joke." She shrugged, "Mostly he doesn't make sense, but we all humor him and laugh."

Mike came to his feet and slipped into his coat. "He'll get the hang of it."

"That's exactly what his father says."

Mike chuckled. "What does his mother say?"

"Mostly she just rolls her eyes toward the ceiling and moans."

Mike laughed and then said, "Don't tire yourself out, all right?"

"I won't."

Maggie smiled at the closed door, feeling somehow warmer and safer for the words. It was a nice feeling, knowing someone was concerned about her. Maggie frowned at the thought, feeling a measure of guilt in even thinking it. Chris had often shown his concern. Only his felt somehow suffocating, while Mike's concern caused her to feel safe. How odd.

Chapter Seven

She was standing at the doorway to his room. A gentle breeze disturbed her hair and fluttered the thin white robe she wore. White for virgins . . . white for purity.

He was afraid to move, afraid to breathe. He didn't want her to disappear this time. He couldn't lose her again.

She smiled as she came forward, her eyes lowered shyly. He could smell the roses. He always smelled roses when she was near. God, how he loved her.

She was close enough to touch, but he kept his hands on the arms of his chair, and the waiting was exquisite torture.

She laughed. She knew he wanted her. Her gaze moved to his crotch and the erection that told it all.

"Touch me, Henry," came a voice as sweet as honey. "Let's see how big we can get that cock."

Henry frowned. He didn't like that; he didn't like a woman to be so bold. He should tell her not to say nasty things. Women were supposed to be sweet and innocent, weren't they? Especially this woman. She shouldn't say bad things, or look at a man the way she was looking at him. It wasn't nice.

Henry thought she reminded him of his mother when she talked like that, always wanting to see his cock, always laughing because it was so small. Puny, she'd called it, even when it was next to bursting as she kissed and stroked it. Her little boy's puny cock, she once said.

Maggie would never say anything like that, he knew. Maggie only loved him, just as he loved her.

He wanted her to open her robe. Why did she just stand there? Why didn't she do it?

And then he realized why: she was shy. She wanted him to do it for her. She wanted him to see her, but she was too shy to open the robe herself.

Henry smiled as he reached for the tie at her waist. She was standing between his legs. He could feel the soft, whispery fabric slide over his feet. The belt came undone and the material began to slide apart. It was then that he realized the laughter. It wasn't soft; it was hard and cruel, like his mother's. Why?

He looked up into her warm brown eyes and smiled. She was the most beautiful thing he'd ever seen, more beautiful than any woman, ever. But something was wrong. Something was very wrong! What was the matter with her eye? He gasped with shock as it began to slide down her face. God, no! It wasn't! Only it was. He reached for her face, pressing the eye back into place, but his hand pressed too hard and the flesh moved away from her cheekbone. He was breathing hard now, terribly afraid as he tried to mold her back into shape, but every time his fingers moved away, her flesh began to slide again.

Half her nose was gone, leaving a small, gaping hole in the middle of her face. No! Her mouth was no longer smiling, but twisted into a sneer of contempt as it slowly rolled down her chin. Oh, please! "Henry, how's your little cock today?" came horribly from her mouth.

Henry groaned his terror. It was almost beyond bearing. Where had she heard those words? How could she have known those words?

And then he knew; this wasn't Maggie. This was his mother! No! God, please . . . he didn't want to see her again. He'd killed her. He'd killed her so many times, and yet she only came back to torture him with her evil ways.

He couldn't resist. He had to look, to make sure. Slowly he parted the white robe to unveil a blackened body, burned almost crisp. It was awful. It was disgusting. It was her. He choked from the smell.

And then she laughed. Henry didn't know how that was possible, because her mouth was sliding down her chest and still it moved. It laughed. "Look at your cock now," it said, and Henry looked down as a scream of horror bubbled from his throat.

He awoke with a gasp, his entire body covered with sweat, his heart thundering from the all-too-familiar nightmare. His hand reached, as usual, for his sex, and he breathed a sigh of relief at finding it well and just as big as always. He rolled to his side, trying to ease the pain in his chest, the fear he'd known. He hated her. God, how he hated her and her filthy kind.

His mouth curved into a sneering smile of disgust as the memories of that night came to plague as well as soothe. The night he'd silenced her dirty mouth forever.

Only he hadn't, not really. He heard her still in his dreams. Once he'd believed that Maggie could take away those dreams, but she hadn't. And now she was a part of them.

Henry rolled into a sitting position and rested his head in his hands. The grandfather clock in the hall chimed one. He had slept a long time, but it hadn't helped much. He was still tired.

He groaned as his fingers touched his wounded head. Quickly he pulled the hand away. He hadn't meant to touch it. Touching it made him weak and shivery. Henry swallowed back the nausea. He'd have to look at it. He'd have to find something—some medicine and bandages, maybe—before leaving here.

110

Henry got to his feet and moaned as the room swayed. He had to hold the wall as he moved toward the bathroom. He stepped over the dead dog and glanced at the door to the bedroom. He smiled at the silence inside.

He hadn't wanted to kill them, not really; he just needed a place to stay, and they were a danger he couldn't afford. He didn't care that he'd killed the woman. Women were dirt, they tempted men and made them do things they didn't want to do. But the man hadn't deserved to die.

Henry made it to the bathroom at last and forced himself to examine the damage the bitch had done to his head. He breathed a sigh of relief; it wasn't as bad as he'd first imagined. He could bandage it, and if he wore a hat, no one would ever know.

Henry smiled at that. If no one knew, he'd never be found.

The man who'd come for her bags had already called the police, he was sure. They'd be looking for a man whose head was bandaged. Henry laughed out loud. They'd never suspect it was him. They were never going to find him.

But he couldn't stay here. This place was too close to where her car had gotten stuck. It was still snowing, so they couldn't follow his tracks, but the first place they'd look was here.

Henry carefully cleaned and bandaged his injury. He felt better after he washed the dried blood from his face, neck, and ear. And then he entered the bedroom again. He had to find clothes, lots of warm clothes.

The man and woman were just as he'd left them. Blood had puddled and dried upon the sheets. He smiled as he

111

remembered how easy it had been to take care of them, and smiled again as he felt his strength begin to return.

An hour later, wearing a woolen hat pulled to his hairline, Henry drove the battered old pickup from the small house. The clothes he wore were a little too big, but very warm. He'd need that warmth, he thought, until he found someplace else to stay.

Inside the cab were blankets, pillows, a rifle and ammunition, along with knives and the gun Maggie had left behind. In the back of the truck was enough food to last him a month.

Henry thought he'd find himself some place to stay, although that was hardly important. What *was* important was finding Maggie. After he took care of her, it didn't matter to him much what happened. After she was dead, maybe he'd head south, where it was always warm. He'd had enough snow to last him awhile.

As it turned out, Maggie didn't visit with Miriam that afternoon after all. She'd straightened the kitchen and washed the two dishes, cups, and utensils they'd used, and by then she knew an almost numbing sense of tiredness again. Lord, when would her strength return? When would she be herself again?

She was leaning against the sink, wondering if she had the strength to make it to the bedroom, when the kitchen door opened and Abner walked in. "What's the matter?" he asked, coming immediately to her side.

"Nothing. Just tired, I guess."

"I reckon you're more than just tired," he said, as he helped her to a chair and then left her to call for help.

Maggie heard a whistle and then heavy footsteps. It felt

like only a moment later and Mike was standing in the kitchen. "What's the matter?"

"Nothing."

"She almost fainted," Abner reported, overriding her response.

"I didn't."

"You were as white as a sheet."

Maggie felt considerably better, now that she sat. "I'm wearing makeup. How could I have been white?"

Abner shot the younger man a hard glare. "Are you going to take her to Doc Bishop, or will I have . . ."

"I'll take her," Mike said, effectively taking the matter into his own hands.

"Wait a minute. I don't need . . ."

"There's a coat by the front door. Take the scarf too," Mike said to Abner. And then, to Maggie, a simple "You're going" seemed to settle, at least in his mind, the subject and any objections Maggie might have had.

Abner returned with the coat and Maggie breathed a weary sigh, knowing she hadn't the strength to fight these two determined men. At the moment, she was simply too exhausted to try. "You're wasting your time. I'm just tired."

Mike took his coat off. Under it he wore two sweatshirts. He pulled one off. A second later, he was pushing it over Maggie's head and forcing her to get her arms into the sleeves. The shirt was too big. Maggie thought it would come to her thighs when she stood. "Let's let the doctor decide that."

Mike helped her from the chair. She stood before him and allowed him to pull a short but thick coat into place. "Where's *my* coat?" she asked.

"Miriam is trying to get the stains out."

113

Just then, Maggie wobbled and he caught her to him with a low curse. "Just tired, huh? Too tired to stand?"

"I'll be all right."

Maggie refused to back down. She *would* be all right. All she needed was more rest.

They stood face to face for a long, silent moment, as if in a battle of wills. Maggie thought she was holding her own, even though she had to tip her head back a bit to accomplish a respectable glare. Only tipping her head back didn't help her equilibrium any, and she swayed again. And then, his arms tightened and she forgot all about glaring as her gaze sort of got caught in his.

Neither Maggie nor Mike noticed or remembered the older man standing there, watching the silent encounter with some real interest.

Maggie didn't often stare at a man, not even a man who looked this good. The only reason she was looking in the first place was because . . . she couldn't for a minute remember why . . .

Maggie had eyes that were milk-chocolate brown, but his eyes were darker, almost black. "Your eyes are very dark, aren't they?" she said without thought.

Mike smiled. It was then that she noticed his lashes. They were thick, long, and as black as his hair. His skin was brown, weathered from hours spent under the sun. This close, she could see the fine lines that had formed at the corners of his eyes.

His lips were thin, his jaw firm, and his hair maybe three inches too long. Maggie frowned, wondering how she hadn't noticed from the first just how attractive he was.

He put his arms around her waist, and she leaned weakly against him, breathing in the scent of fresh air and horse, along with a faint spiciness. Aftershave, she thought. Very nice.

Her mind elsewhere, she didn't notice for a minute that he had lifted her into his arms. "You don't have to carry me."

"It's easier to carry you than to pick you up after you fall."

Mike left the house, settled her in his Jeep, and then slid behind the wheel. He was driving out of the yard, careful of the bumps and gullies in his driveway, when she said, "Men aren't supposed to have long lashes."

Mike glanced in her direction, a puzzled, worried frown creasing his forehead, only to find her already asleep.

Abner watched the Jeep head toward town and the doctor's office. He grinned as he shut the front door and then slapped his ragged old hat against his thigh. A wicked gleam entered his eyes and he breathed, "Finally," on a sigh.

Henry had felt good when he'd left the farmhouse, but feeling good had lasted only until the sun had gone down and the cold had come again. He'd slept that night in the truck, the next in a barn, another in a shack that proved to be colder than if he'd slept outside.

Now, after days spent driving over these country roads, searching for a place to stay, Henry felt weak and chilled to the bone. He knew he suffered still from the effects of the gunshot. He'd thought that he was strong again, but he wasn't. He wouldn't be strong until he could sleep in a bed again and get himself a few hot meals.

Money wasn't a problem; he had more than enough of

his own, plus the thousand he'd taken from the farmer's place. Damn fools. Didn't they know that the first place a man would look would be the freezer?

Again he dismissed the thought of taking a room at the motel about five miles outside of town, the one he'd passed just before finding Maggie. He figured the cops would be watching that place. So he'd headed north, knowing he'd eventually come across a place.

What he was looking for was a small ranch, something like the last one, maybe. Once he found it, he'd ask for a room to rent. And after he got his strength back, he'd find her again.

Don Bishop had taken over his father's practice some five years ago. When people mentioned Doc Bishop, they meant Don's father. The folks around Gray Bluff still called the new doctor Donny. It wasn't that they didn't respect the man and his knowledge; they did. It was just that old habits were hard to break.

He had, of course, been advised about Maggie's experience before he began the examination. "Was it just your head?" he asked, as he pulled the blood pressure band from Maggie's arm.

He then proceeded to shine a small light in her eyes. "Mostly."

"She has bites on her chest. You might as well look them over while we're here," Mike said, as he walked toward the door, keeping his back to both doctor and patient.

"I'd know more if I could see the X-rays."

"I could run over to the hospital and get them. It wouldn't take more than a half hour."

Don nodded. "Good. Maggie can take a nap while we wait."

Mike was just about to walk out the examining room door when he said, "You'd better call ahead. They're not about to hand them over to me."

Don nodded. "Tell Nancy on your way out."

Everyone in Gray Bluff, Wyoming, knew that Nancy Carter was in love with the town's doctor. The thing that bothered Mike was that no one knew whether the good doctor returned her feelings, and Mike suddenly felt uneasy leaving Maggie in his care.

It wasn't that Don Bishop wasn't to be trusted. It was that Don Bishop was a man, a very good-looking man, far more good-looking than Mike would have liked. And since Mike had known Don as a friend since boyhood, Mike knew his reputation with the ladies was well earned. He hesitated at the door.

"What's the matter?"

"Nothing. I was . . ." He shook his head. "Never mind. I'll be right back."

Mike was back within the promised half-hour.

Don Bishop looked the X-ray over and pronounced Maggie fine; all she needed was rest.

"All I *do* is rest," she murmured in a cranky tone, having just awakened from a short nap.

"Abner found you in the kitchen," Mike reminded. "You weren't resting then."

"I washed two dishes."

"Right, but you were up for hours before you washed them."

Maggie sighed. "When will I get back to normal?"

"Don't try to rush things. It's only been a few days. Give yourself time."

Maggie nodded as she came from the examining table and slipped her arms into her coat.

They were in his Jeep again before Mike found himself unable to resist asking, "What did you think about the doctor?"

Maggie glanced in Mike's direction. He was looking straight ahead, all his interest apparently on the wide, empty road. "I don't know. What should I think about him?"

"Most women think he's good-looking."

Maggie smiled. "Are you trying to fix me up?"

"I figure you don't need my help on that score."

"Good."

"Have people tried it before?"

"A few."

"And?" he prompted.

"Let's say I have better results finding my own friends."

Meaning she had one; so Mike asked, "What's his name?"

"Chris."

"Is it serious?"

"He's asked me to marry him."

Mike frowned. "So why were you traveling alone?"

"Because I haven't given him my answer yet."

"Why not?"

"Because marriage is a big step and I don't want to be pushed into . . ." Maggie saw he was about to say something and quickly amended her statement with, "No, he's not pushing. What I meant was, I don't want to make a mistake."

"You've been married before?"

"No. Why?"

Mike shrugged. "Usually when a marriage doesn't work out, a woman gets nervous about trying it again."

"I'm not nervous."

"Just unsure."

"I'm sure that I like him very much."

Mike didn't know why exactly, but that bit of news struck him as particularly good. She hadn't said she *loved* him very much, but that she *liked* him very much. There was a huge difference.

"How come you're not married?" Maggie figured she had every right to ask a question she never would have thought to ask, since he'd done as much.

"I was."

"Divorced?"

Mike nodded. A moment of silence went by before he said, "I might as well tell you before someone else does. She left me 'cause I was in prison."

Maggie's mouth dropped open. She couldn't remember ever meeting someone who'd been in prison. At least, she didn't know if she ever had. But what she really didn't know was what to say next.

"Twenty years is a long time to wait."

"Twenty years! What did you do?"

"They said I murdered a woman."

Mike heard her startled breath and then a soft, "Did you?"

"No. They found the guy who did it a year later. But by then it was too late. Cynthia had sent the papers a week after I went inside."

"God."

"Yeah, I said that a few times, I guess."

"I'll bet you said that more than a few times."

Mike smiled. He turned toward her when he did and

because he turned he never saw the driver of the pickup truck passing from the opposite direction.

He might not have seen, but Henry did. He saw her smiling at him. Smiling just the way she used to smile for him.

Henry couldn't see, couldn't think, what with the screaming inside his head, what with this need to kill someone, something. The truck almost went out of control. He skidded and turned, but righted the vehicle somehow. Finally he brought the truck to a stop as he took huge breaths, trying to regain his control.

He watched the Jeep from the rearview mirror. He watched until it was a tiny dark speck on a sea of white, until it turned off the road, until it disappeared behind a hill.

It was then that he turned around.

Chapter Eight

"You were hurt."

Mike looked up from his meal, his eyes registering a moment of confusion at her comment, for she had picked up the conversation with no warning or further information, just as if hours had not gone by. Still, Mike realized her meaning. He leaned back in his chair and smiled. "You might say that."

"Angry?"

"A little."

Maggie smiled. "Just a little?"

He shrugged for an answer.

"And you haven't trusted a woman since."

His gaze narrowed just a bit. "Are you a shrink?"

She shook her head, happy to be able to make that simple movement at last without even the threat of pain. "TV reporter."

His gaze widened in surprise. "Really? You mean you're a celebrity? How come I can't remember seeing you before? Do you know . . ."

"Local television," she said, interrupting questions that left no room for answers, before he could ask another one.

"And no, I'm not a celebrity. I work in Ellington. It's a small town about thirty miles from Colorado Springs."

Mike shook his head, still obviously amazed, although he figured he shouldn't have been. She was a beautiful woman. And beautiful women, fair or not, tended to succeed in life. "Television is television. I never met anyone who . . ."

Maggie laughed. "I was thinking the same thing this afternoon. I never met anyone who was in prison."

"Except I wasn't a criminal, so my find is better than yours."

Maggie swallowed a piece of chicken. "Doesn't matter whether you were or not. You were still there. What was it like?"

"Prison?" He exhaled and his gaze moved just to the right of her head, his eyes unfocused, as if he was deep in thought. "Prison is a lot like . . ." He hesitated a long moment before saying simply, "Prison. It's hard to describe. Lights-out was at . . ."

"No, I don't mean schedules. I mean, what were the men like? What was it like, living with them?"

His features grew suddenly hard, unforgiving, almost dangerous, as if he remembered all too clearly, and he almost spat his response. "Animals. Most of them belonged in an asylum."

"Would you rather not talk about it?"

"It's not my favorite subject."

"Fine. Let's talk about something else, then. Tell me about Abner."

"Abner?" Mike frowned. "Why him?"

"I don't know. I think he's interesting."

"You think Abner's interesting, and not Don Bishop?" Mike couldn't have been more amazed.

Maggie grinned. "Go on, tell me."

"Abner is a pain in the . . ." Mike's words came to a sudden stop, as if he was trying to watch his language around his guest. Maggie smiled. He began again, "Abner's sole purpose in life is to bother me."

Maggie laughed. "That sweet old man?"

"Sweet? You think Abner is *sweet?*"

Maggie grinned at his look of astonishment. "I think he's adorable."

"God, don't ever tell him that! Besides, you only think like that because you don't know him."

Maggie's laughter was low and deliciously sexy. "What does he do that bothers you?"

"For one thing, he's always telling me what to do and how to do it. Besides that, he butts into my private life."

"Like?"

"Like, he's already shining up his good boots for our wedding."

Maggie blinked in surprise. "Really? He thinks we're involved?"

"No, but he thinks we're gonna be."

"Why?"

"Because you're a woman and I'm a man, and . . ." Mike didn't know what else to say, so he shrugged.

"You mean he does this all the time?"

"*Now* do you see why I said he's a pain?"

"He's a romantic. I love it."

Mike dropped his head back and looked up at the ceiling as he moaned, "Nooo."

Maggie only laughed again. "Why don't you just get married? That should put a stop to . . ."

"Because I haven't found anyone I want to marry."

"Oh. Well, that could be a problem." Oddly enough,

his problem seemed to make her feel very good. Maggie thought that was a bit strange.

"Besides, getting married wouldn't stop him. He'd just tell me how a husband is supposed to act. He'd tell me, 'A man wouldn't treat a little lady like that, boy.' " Mike shook his head. "There's nothing I can do that will shut him up."

She chuckled softly at the man's obvious frustration. "Why don't I tell him I'm married?"

" 'Cause he wouldn't believe it. He'd say, 'Then, where's her husband, boy?' "

Maggie laughed at the exaggerated husky, western twang. And then, "He calls you 'boy'?"

Mike looked at her for a long moment. He didn't say anything. He didn't have to say anything, not with that weary look in his eyes.

"Because he knows you don't like it, right?"

"No, because he knows I hate it."

Maggie thought the whole situation was delightful.

"The thing to do is to turn the tables on him, nag him into finding a wife."

"He's already buried three. I don't think it's fair to chance another. Besides, I've tried that." Maggie chuckled. "It didn't work."

"Maybe you didn't try hard enough."

"Maggie, there isn't a woman in this town, in the world, probably, desperate enough to take a beat-up old busybody like him."

Mike's words might have been a bit harsh, but Maggie saw the affection in his gaze as he spoke of the old man. "You love him, don't you?"

Mike shot her a look of disbelief. "Love that old coot? Not likely."

"Why don't you fire him, then?"

"I guess he's sort of grown on me.

"Are you tired?"

She shook her head and came to her feet. "I slept all afternoon."

Maggie was reaching for the dishes, about to clear the table, when he said, "Why don't you watch television? I'll put this stuff away."

"I'm fine, really."

She might have said she was fine, but Mike knew different. He could see just a touch of unsteadiness as she came to her feet, but she was a stubborn lady and refused to admit to any weakness. She was obviously impatient with herself for not healing faster. "Don said to take it easy."

"I am."

Rather than push his point, Mike simply picked up his own plate and began working with her. Mike washed; Maggie dried and put the few items away.

"Do you mind if I use your phone again? I still haven't gotten in touch with Chris."

"Call him now. I'll finish up in here."

Mike was preparing a fresh pot of coffee when Maggie returned to the kitchen, obviously distraught. "What's the matter?"

"His answering machine was still on, so I called work. He hasn't been there all week. They said he left town a few days ago."

"Where did he go?"

"He's coming after me."

"Why?"

Maggie related their last phone conversation and Chris's fear for her. "I didn't think he'd really come. I told

125

him not to." Her teeth worried her bottom lip, her gaze filled with fear. "Do you suppose he's . . ."

"He probably got caught in the same storm. The news said it covered most of the southern part of the state. Besides, if he was following you, he wouldn't know you stopped, so he might have already reached your father's place. And your father would have told him you're all right."

Maggie knew what he said made sense. Still, she couldn't seem to control a building sense of foreboding. Something was going to happen, something awful . . . she just knew it. "Maybe," Maggie said. "But . . ."

"Call your father. Chris is probably there."

Maggie left the kitchen again only to return a few minutes later, looking more troubled than ever. "He's not there. He hasn't called.

"Do you think . . .?" She frowned. "It wouldn't have taken this long. What could have happened to him?"

They both knew any number of things could have happened to him. Most particularly, he could have somehow met up with Henry. Yet neither dared to say it out loud.

Maggie shook her head. "It's ridiculous. The state is enormous. It would be impossible. Like finding a needle in a haystack."

"Maybe he had car trouble. Maybe . . ."

At that very moment, Chris dialed the phone from a truck stop just outside of Rock Springs, Wyoming. A minute or so later, he sighed his relief as Maggie's father told him Maggie was just fine, but worried about him. He gave Chris the number where Maggie could be reached.

Mike answered his phone. "Is Maggie Cassidy there?"

"Maggie, it's for you."

The first thing Maggie heard was, "Where are you?"

"Chris? God, I was beginning to worry. Are you all right?"

"I'm fine. Had some trouble with my car, but everything is all right now. What about you? Why aren't you at your father's place?"

Maggie told Chris what had happened, purposely leaving out the worst of it. Even then, she was rewarded with an occasional muttered curse, along with an "Oh God," or an "I told you." In the end, Maggie found herself comforting Chris. "It's all right. I'm all right now."

"I'd like to kill the bastard."

"I know. But . . ."

He cut her off with, "I'm coming to get you."

"Maybe you should wait until morning. I don't think you'll find this place in the dark."

"I can't wait until morning. I'm coming now."

"All right." Maggie glanced around the room, finding herself alone. "Hold on. Mike will tell you how to find it."

Maggie called Mike to the phone and listened as he gave directions.

"Don't go anywhere," Chris said, as Maggie took the phone back. "I'm less than two hours away."

He broke the connection, and Maggie replaced the receiver.

"Relieved?"

Maggie returned Mike's smile and said, "Very." Only somehow, someplace deep down inside, she wasn't. Not completely, anyway. It wasn't that Maggie wanted to stay here; she didn't. At least, she didn't think she did. And she was relieved to find Chris all right. But at the moment, at

127

least, she didn't want to go anywhere with him. His building anger, and the silent but obvious accusation that she'd brought this upon herself by not listening to him, left her more than a little annoyed.

He hadn't come right out and said she was at fault, of course, but he might as well have. "I'd better get my things together."

Mike nodded and said nothing as he watched her head for the guest room.

Hours later, she sat in the living room, watching the end of *Nightline*. There was no need, but still she glanced at the wall clock as its chimes rang twelve times. "I can't understand this. Where could he be?"

"It would have been easy to miss the turn-off at night. He's not familiar with this area."

"Still, he should have called.

"There's no need for you to stay up and wait with me. Why don't you . . . ."

"I'm fine." Mike wondered why he hadn't gone to bed long ago. She was right. There was no need for him to stay up. Still . . . "He probably got lost and stopped for the night somewhere."

Maggie shook her head. "He'd have called."

"He might have had car trouble again."

"Maybe."

"He's all right, Maggie. As long as he stays on 80, someone will find him. He'll be here in the morning."

"You're probably right," she said, as she got up from the couch. "I'd better go to bed."

They said goodnight and disappeared into their own rooms; Maggie to fall asleep quickly, Mike to lie there in the dark, wondering how the hell he'd gotten so used to her being here already. It had been only a few days and yet her presence added something to his home he couldn't quite name. He found himself looking forward to coming in from a hard day's work, knowing she was inside, asleep or awake, it didn't matter. All he knew was that he liked having her here.

It took him awhile, but he finally came face to face with the facts: he didn't want her to go, and there wasn't a thing he could do to stop her.

Mike was just about ready to doze off when he heard a soft sound break the silence of the night. He sat up in bed and frowned. Was someone crying? What the hell?

Mike slid his legs into his jeans, not bothering to secure them at his waist as he hurried from the room. On bare feet he covered the distance from his room to Maggie's within seconds.

"Maggie," he said softly through the closed door, "are you all right?"

He heard a murmured groan and then a startled cry before he opened the door. The light from a lone lamp in the living room allowed him to see clearly enough. She was twisting, struggling to fight off or escape some invisible foe.

Mike approached the bed. "Maggie," he said again. "Maggie, you're having a bad dream. Wake up."

Instead of calming her, his voice seemed to cause her greater distress. She grew more excited, more desperate to escape whatever it was that she thought threatened her.

Mike leaned over her, shaking her shoulder gently. It didn't help. "Maggie," he said her name again. "Maggie, listen to me."

She struck out, slapping him across the chest.

Mike sat on the edge of the bed and took her hands. He held them in his as he spoke, but nothing he could say seemed to matter. She was deeply asleep, her mind lost in the throes of horror, and he hadn't a clue as to how to bring her out of it.

Her body twisted back and forth and Mike groaned a silent curse, for the movement had caused the blanket and sheet to drop, and made the straps of her nightgown slip from her shoulders. She was more exposed to his gaze than ever. Mike could see the three bandages, but mostly he could see the soft, pliable womanly flesh that beckoned.

He took a deep breath, trying to ignore the sight before him as he held her hands to her sides. "Don't let him . . . please," she cried, amid gasping breaths and terror-ized resistance.

"It's Mike, Maggie. No one will hurt you."

"Mike, please," she said, as a part of her consciousness realized he was somewhere close by. "Mike . . ."

"Easy, Maggie," he said as he leaned closer, whispering near her ear. "Easy, darlin'."

She was running. God, why was it always so hard to run when you needed to run the most?

He was behind her. She could hear him trample the undergrowth. She couldn't see him, but she knew who he was. He'd get her this time, she knew, and when he did, it would be worse than last time. She knew it would be the worst ever.

And this time, when he was finished with her, he'd kill her.

She had to get away. She had to.

She could hear his breathing. She could hear hers as well, along with the thunder of her heart. Why couldn't she run faster? She needed to run faster.

And then Mike was there, suddenly appearing from out of the misty dark. She ran to him. but he was moving back, sort of floating

130

away, and with each step she took, he moved farther and farther from her.

"Don't leave. Please, don't leave."

"Maggie," he said. "Are you awake?"

"Mike," she gasped, and he wasn't sure. Was she awake? Did she realize what she was saying, what she was implying?

He released her hands and she reached for him. Her arms circled his neck, pulling him down upon her. "Mike," she said again, and he was sure she was awake. Almost.

Her face was buried against his throat, and Mike felt his heart begin to race madly. She didn't know what she was doing, did she?

"Maggie," he said, his voice deep and husky with need as she turned her face and began to kiss him.

He tried to pull away, but her arms held him in place. He shuddered against an overwhelming need, unable to think, unable to voice an objection as he felt her tongue move over his jaw, unable to fight the inevitability of this moment as he heard soft, sweet sounds of entreaty.

He couldn't remember how many times he'd thought about this, dreamed about this. And every time he had, he'd pushed the thought from his mind. But he couldn't push it away any longer.

She clung to him, kissing his throat, his jaw, moving beneath his weight. He wondered if she knew what she was doing. Was he taking advantage of an unguarded moment? He didn't know. If only she'd say something . . . if only he could be sure . . .

"Maggie, Maggie, listen to me," he said softly against her ear, and then he didn't care if she was conscious of the things she was doing or not, as one of her hands released his neck and slid between their bodies, into his opened jeans, to cup his sex.

Mike knew it was wrong, yet there was no way he could stop. She wanted him and he felt his body grow thick and thicker still with a wanting of his own as his hips pressed forward into her hand. "Are you sure?"

He wanted to know that she was certain before it was too late. It might already be too late.

His hands came to her face. Long fingers slid into her hair, holding her still, holding her mouth for his exploration, and he kissed her, holding back none of the longing he knew.

It was the kiss that did it.

It was the kiss that brought her startlingly and suddenly awake.

She reached him at last and cried her relief as his arms came around her. Maggie buried her face in the warmth of his neck. He smelled so good. Oh God, thank you, she said in a silent prayer . . .

He'd save her; she knew he would. She knew she'd never be afraid again, as long as she could stay in this man's arms.

Her hands clung to his neck. She couldn't let go. Maybe she'd never let go.

And then they were in a bed and he was leaning over her, whispering something she couldn't understand. Her hand moved down his body and she found him warm and eager for her.

He moaned at her touch and because he moaned, she touched him again. Caressing, she measured his length. He felt so good, so very good. She couldn't stop touching, never wanted to stop touching.

He brought her face from his neck and kissed her. God, she'd never have believed a kiss could feel so good, could taste so good . . .

Maggie blinked open her eyes. She pulled back, not at all afraid, although she thought she could have been.

132

What she felt was more like confusion. What in the world were they doing? Why were they together in bed? She'd thought she'd been dreaming. Was this part of a dream? If so, she'd never dreamt like this before. "Mike?"

It took a long moment before he noticed, but Mike felt her stiffen beneath him, felt her pull away, and then heard her ask him, in a voice that held not a thread of sleep, "What are you doing?"

Breathing heavily, Mike looked into her opened eyes and felt her hand leave his body. He groaned as he rolled from her and sat at the edge of the bed. With his face buried in his hands, he strove to bring his body back under control. "You were having a bad dream," he said, knowing his reason for being here hardly accounted for what she had discovered upon awakening. Would she be angry? Would she order him from her in her rage?

"I'm sorry."

Mike thought he probably hadn't heard right. "What?"

Maggie was not unaware of where her hand had been upon awakening. She was also aware of what that hand had been doing. She knew he hadn't placed it there. And even if he had, he couldn't have forced her to caress him.

She remembered dreaming, remembered being afraid, and then Mike had been there to comfort and soothe, enveloping her in safety. He had called out her name, asked her unheard questions, but then the dream had taken a different route. She had clung to him and safety grew suddenly into passion. Sleep had caused her defenses to drop away, and now she faced a difficult moment. "I said, I'm sorry. I was asleep. I didn't realize, I didn't mean for that to happen."

Mike nodded, never looking in her direction.

"Are you angry?" she asked.

133

"No," he said, pushing himself from the bed and the temptation he wasn't sure he could resist.

She had pulled the covers over her again, and Mike looked at her for a long moment before turning toward the door. "I know you didn't realize it, but maybe you did mean it. When we're asleep, we relax our guard and our real needs show themselves."

He didn't wait for a response, but closed the door behind him as he returned to his own room.

Maggie lay there for hours, thinking on his words. He was an attractive man. She couldn't deny that fact, but had she really wanted him? Had he been right? Had her mind used the excuse of sleep in order to touch him?

Maggie knew she hadn't. Perhaps, just perhaps, he'd attracted her more than she'd so far admitted, but she wouldn't have disguised her need for him in sleep. At least, she didn't think she would have.

Maggie rolled to her stomach. Things were getting very confusing. Maybe it was a good thing that she was leaving in the morning, before things got out of hand. And Maggie knew that after tonight, things could get out of hand far sooner than she'd ever expected.

"What the hell?" Chris grumbled at the sudden loud bang and subsequent loss of control as the car swerved suddenly toward the ditch alongside the road. It took some effort, but he managed to avoid the ditch and brought the car to a stop at last. "What else?" he asked as he turned off the engine, knowing he had no choice but to leave the car's warmth and brave the elements. "What the hell else?"

Out here, in the middle of nowhere, it was colder than

Chris could have dreamed. The weatherman might have said in the teens, but Chris figured it was closer to zero, and with the wind-chill factor, maybe twenty below. How the hell did people live like this?

Before he managed to get the tire from his trunk, he realized his hands were frozen. Damn! This trip had been a disaster from day one. First he'd forgotten his wallet and hadn't even noticed he didn't have it with him until he'd stopped for gas about a hundred miles north of Ellington. Then he'd had to turn back and get it before starting all over again. Hours wasted.

Then, on the second day, his engine had thrown a rod and he'd had to stay in a moth-eaten motel while he waited for the local yokels to find the needed parts.

He was a man of some sophistication, having been born and raised in Chicago. Still, it wasn't like him to be unkind, or critical of others, in particular, country folk. But his nerves had been strung pretty much to the limit as he worried for Maggie's welfare. Along with that worry, he'd had to fight constant delays in reaching her, because of weather, machine failure, or his own stupidity.

Damn woman, he thought, as he jacked up the car. Things were going to be different once they got married. Once he was in charge, there was no way she was going to do as she pleased.

Things were going to change, all right. She might not like it much, but she was going to listen to him, and he was going to know she was safe.

Chris was tightening the tire's bolts when the headlights of a car approached. With frozen hands, he hit his hubcap into place and stood and then wiped the dirt from his hands on a rag. As it came closer, Chris realized it was a pickup truck, not a car. He shook his head in amazement, while wondering who besides himself would be fool enough to be out on a night like this.

Henry drove back and forth for hours. And every time the truck approached, the empty road the Jeep had taken, his body trembled again with fury. He was going to get her. Nothing would stop him; nothing could, not even himself. It was too late. He couldn't change his mind now. Not after the things she'd done to him, not after she'd run off with another man.

Henry hadn't settled with the last one yet, her boyfriend from Ellington, and now he had another to add to his list. Another man who was going to suffer for daring to touch her, for daring to be the one she smiled at.

It was dark before he realized he was running low on gas. He'd have to go to town and fill up. Maybe while he was there he could get some hot food.

Henry pulled the truck into the brightly lit station. A full minute went by before an attendant came to his window. "Hi, Mister Jackson," the young man said, and then, seeing who sat behind the wheel, he continued, "You're not Mr. Jackson. What are you doing in his truck?"

"I'm the new hand. Mr. Jackson isn't feeling well. He said to stop in town for a few things."

Billy Owens looked the scruffy man over. Easy enough to do in these bright lights, only the man wouldn't look him in the eye, so he got a good look only at his profile.

There were two reasons Billy didn't believe him. One was that the man wouldn't look at him, and the second was that everyone in town knew Mr. Jackson loved this beat-up old truck. He never let anyone drive it, not even his wife or kids. Not as far back as Billy could remember. And that was at least twenty years.

From the look of doubt in his eyes, Henry figured the man didn't believe him, but unless he came right out and called him a liar, there wasn't much the guy could do. "Put in five dollars' worth."

Billy nodded and moved to the back of the truck. He figured the guy had stolen the Jacksons' truck. No big deal, as far as he was concerned, seeing as the truck was older than any around these parts and worth just about nothing. Still, he couldn't be sure, unless . . .

When he was finished, he walked back to the window and asked, "How's Helen doing? Heard she was feeling poorly."

Henry grew instantly suspicious. He thought maybe the man was setting a trap. Still, he didn't have a choice but to answer. He wished the hell he could remember what her name was. He'd seen her driver's license when he'd gone through her purse, but he couldn't remember her name. Finally he shrugged. It didn't matter. The man obviously thought the truck was stolen. So what? He'd known all along that he'd have to get rid of it soon, anyway. "She's better," he said, pushing the five-dollar bill into the man's hand, just before he drove out of the filling station.

Chapter Nine

The truck's headlights caught the man coming to his feet. The driver watched as the man rolled a tire to the back of his car. He nodded. Flat.

Henry slowed the truck a bit, peering into the darkness, trying to see into the car. Was the man alone? Did a wife sit in the passenger seat? Henry knew it wouldn't have mattered if one did. He only hoped no little kids slept in the back. He didn't want to kill little kids. He would if he had to, probably, but he didn't want to.

The road was dark, deserted, a perfect setting for what he had in mind. He needed to get rid of the truck. By now the cops would be looking for it, thanks to that stupid gas station attendant. He'd thought he'd just dump it somewhere, but that would leave him without transportation. He couldn't afford that; he had to have a car or truck. He'd never be able to get to her without it. And he was going to get to her. He had no doubt about that.

Henry passed the car and then came to a stop. Slowly he backed up.

"You need some help, mister?"

"No, thanks," the man answered, as he shoved his tire

into his trunk and closed it. He pocketed the key. "Just finished." The man began to walk toward the truck as he spoke. "You could give me some information, though. You know where Mike Stanford lives?"

"Sorry." Henry said as the man approached. "I'm new around these parts. Never heard of . . ."

Chris never heard the last few words; he suddenly realized who was sitting in that truck. Chris might have known some amazement in the fact that of all the hundreds, maybe thousands, of miles of road in this state, circumstances or fate had brought him face to face with the one man he hated beyond imagining. But Chris didn't have the time to think. His shock lasted maybe a second before he asked, "Henry? Henry Collins?"

His name was spoken in a tone so menacing it sent chills down Henry's spine.

Chris had seen the man's picture enough times. There was no way he could be mistaken, even with that straggly growth of whiskers and his collar pulled up to his jaw. It was him, all right, the man who had assaulted Maggie. Only, he wasn't going to get away this time. This time he'd know what it was like to fight someone his own size. The next thing Chris knew, he was reaching for the bastard.

Henry watched as the man came to a sudden stop and then growled a sound of instant fury as his hands suddenly reached through the window and around his neck. What the hell? This wasn't supposed to be happening. Henry had an idea to maybe do the man in and take his car, not the other way around. Why was he being attacked?

He'd said, "Henry Collins." How did this stranger know his name? Henry tried to think. Who was he?

Henry struggled, but the man was pulling him through

139

the half-open window and there was no way he could stop him. His fingers squeezed at his throat, cutting off his ability to breathe, pulling at him, careless of the fact that he was crushing his chest as his upper body was forced through the truck's window.

Henry reached wildly behind him. He had to find help. He had to stop this maniac. His fingers searched hurriedly over the truck's seat for the gun. And then it was suddenly there and he was pointing it at the man.

In a blink of an eye, blood began to pump from a hole about the size of a dime just below Chris's eye.

Henry gasped for air as the hands that had imprisoned his throat grew weak and then finally lost their hold.

In his rage, Chris hadn't seen the gun. He'd heard a very loud noise and a flash just before his head had snapped back. He thought at first that the son-of-a-bitch had somehow managed to punch him. Chris almost laughed at that. It would take more than a punch to stop what he had in mind.

And then he wasn't sure. Chris frowned, unable to understand the sudden sense of lethargy that had come over him in the midst of his rage. He knew his hold was loosening. He knew he was letting the bastard go, only he couldn't figure out why.

He was falling backward. Had his feet slipped on the snow-covered road? Maybe. Then why wasn't he dragging the son-of-a-bitch down with him? Why was he letting go?

Chris knew no pain. His mind was filled only with confusion as he dropped to the ground.

His throat free of the madman's grip, Henry almost panicked. He put the truck into gear and heard the tires

140

spin out before he realized he was passing up a perfect opportunity.

It took him a few minutes before he could force aside his trembling, his need to run, but he finally managed to think. Henry took a deep breath and then another. If he wanted to succeed, he couldn't panic. He had to stay in control. He had to think.

Ann Murphy frowned into her bathroom mirror as she fussed with her hair, trying her best to cover the half inch of growth at the roots. Damn, but she needed a touch-up. Where the hell was she supposed to find the money for it? Welfare covered only so much, and food stamps even less. She couldn't buy cigarettes, perfume, or hair coloring without cash.

Ann practiced a smile and then rubbed traces of lipstick from her teeth. She stepped back and viewed herself in the mirror behind the door. She wore a short leather skirt and her best sweater. It was snug and low enough to give Jack an eyeful. Ann had every reason to expect that he'd be more than generous tonight. She patted her flat tummy and nodded. Not bad for thirty.

She misted herself with her treasured cologne even as she swore someday she'd buy this scent in perfume at a hundred or more dollars an ounce. God, but she was sick of counting pennies for packs of cigarettes, sick of worrying if she had enough to keep herself and her small family until the end of the month.

"Mommy, do you have to go out tonight?"

Ann looked at her nine-year-old daughter, who had just entered the room, and wished she could have stayed home. It was bitterly cold out and bound to get a lot colder as the night went on, especially if Jack didn't get them a room, but planned to do it in his truck again. She sighed, wishing wishes came true; but they didn't, at least, not in her case.

"I won't be long, honey. I promise. Remember our rules?"

The little girl nodded.

"Let's hear them again," Ann said, as they left the bathroom and stopped at the hall closet. She pushed her arms into her coat.

"Don't answer the door, no matter what."

"And?" her mother prompted.

"Don't use the stove."

"What else?"

"If there's an emergency, call 911."

"Good girl. Tomorrow I'll get you something special from the drugstore."

"Can I have blue eye-shadow?"

Ann was about to shake her head when her daughter finished with, "I won't wear it to school. I promise."

"All right. Blue eye-shadow it is." She leaned down and kissed Mary's blond head.

A quick check on her sleeping five-year-old son and Ann was at the front door. With another kiss and a "Be good," she left the house and headed toward town. It was only a two-block walk, but Ann knew she'd be freezing by the time she got there. Especially since her feet, clad only in strappy high heels, were already wet and cold and she hadn't left her front yard yet.

Ann shrugged at the discomfort. Once she got to Lanie's, she'd warm up fast enough. And if Jack was there, she'd soon be warmer than warm.

In a darkened corner of an already dark tavern, one of Gray Bluff's two, Ann Murphy sat nursing a draft beer. Country-western music played as couples swayed along the dance floor. Ann hardly noticed. She was thinking about her kids. She had a feeling she shouldn't have gone out tonight. Brian had had a slight fever earlier this afternoon, and Mary had looked so sad, so lonely before Ann had even gotten out the door. Damn, how did kids manage to make you feel so guilty with just a look?

She figured there was a good chance that both her kids would be sick by tomorrow. Mary always got sick when Brian did. And that meant doctor bills. Just one more thing she couldn't afford.

Ann worked part time, and off the books, in the town's only drugstore, stocking shelves and delivering medicine to those who couldn't get out. Welfare covered the rent. Next year, she thought sarcastically, thanks to a kind and considerate government, there wouldn't be any welfare. Brian would be old enough for school, and she'd be expected to keep a full-time job. She didn't want to think about next year; this year was hard enough. This year, even with her job, there was nothing left over for life's little luxuries. All Ann could boast of owning was a TV and a phone, not even a car, and to her way of thinking, those things were more a necessity than a luxury.

After Harry had left, Ann had learned quickly that there was only one way to make the kind of money she needed.

It didn't matter that the decent folks in Gray Bluff no longer spoke to her. She needed more than rice and beans on her table. She didn't see any of the fine folks around here digging into their pockets to help.

Harry had left them four months ago. With a simple statement that he didn't want to be married anymore, he'd just walked out of her life. Ann figured his walking out had been bad enough, but leaving his family penniless was just about the worst thing the man could have done.

She'd married Harry twelve years ago, the week after they'd graduated high school. She'd never had any formal job training. She didn't know how to be anything other than a housewife and mother.

Ann smiled into her beer. Last she'd heard, there wasn't much call for either specialty around here. And she didn't have the money to go anywhere else. Most of the men in Gray Bluff who were interested in a wife already had one, and enough kids of their own. No one wanted her or her small family. Not even her mother.

Ann didn't want to think about her mother and her newest husband and their lack of compassion. She'd never cared before, so why start now? She didn't want to think about anything tonight, except getting enough money to see her and the kids through the rest of this month.

Lucky for her, she wasn't bad to look at, and a few of the men in town had a wandering eye.

Ann sighed. She could give them that, at least. She was good in bed. Harry had told her that a number of times. And since Harry had left and she'd found herself damn near desperate, others had told her much the same thing.

At thirty, she was still in pretty good shape. All right, so maybe she couldn't compete with the twenty-year-olds, but she knew things about men that twenty-year-olds didn't. She knew the way a man liked it best.

Ann watched Jack Rhodes from across the room. According to Jack, he was trapped in an unhappy marriage. With three kids, he figured he'd be stuck where he was for a while. What was a man to do?

Ann wondered why Harry hadn't felt the same.

Ann slept with Jack maybe twice a week. He was a generous man, and she was thankful for that. He'd work his way over to her table before the night was over, she knew. She only wished he'd hurry up. She didn't want to leave the kids alone too long.

Gray Bluff was too small, or too religious, or too damn cold, Henry didn't know which. All he knew for a fact was, the town didn't have whores parading themselves for potential inspection on street corners. And he wasn't happy about that.

Henry sighed his disgust as he stopped the sedan in the parking lot behind the bar. He'd have to go inside. He couldn't think where else he might find a woman, and there was no way that he was going to take care of things with his own hands. Not this time. Not after what he'd done. Henry thought he hadn't needed a woman this bad in a very long time.

It was killing her fuckin' boyfriend that did it. He hadn't realized it was her boyfriend until he got out of the truck and had himself a good look at the man. God, killing him had felt so good, he almost came while squeezing off that last shot. It always excited him when he killed, but this, this excited him more than anything he'd ever known.

Henry could only imagine how good it was going to feel when he got his hands on the bitch.

145

Ann saw him enter the dark room. Even in this dim light, he looked pretty bad. Scruffy was the word that fit best, she thought. Scruffy and small. He needed a shave, and by the looks of him, probably a bath as well. She was sitting alone, a target for any man on the prowl, and for just a moment she hoped he wouldn't notice her.

She should have known better. Her sweater was cut low and half her chest was sticking out, just about pleading for a man's hands. She'd worn the damn thing in the hopes that Jack would be particularly generous tonight, and he hadn't even come near her yet. Ann breathed out on a sigh. Yeah, she should have known better.

Again she glanced in Jack's direction. He was talking to Lanie, the woman who owned this place. Lanie was working the bar. She always did when one of her men was off. Tonight was Thursday, Tim's night off. Ann wondered how long Jack would wait before coming over. Damn, she didn't have all night.

She watched the man come toward her. He stopped opposite from where she sat and asked, "You waiting for somebody?"

Ann looked again in Jack's direction and then sighed. What the hell difference did it make? One man was much like another. They all thought they were something great, and just about none of them were. Besides, she needed the money, and Jack was taking his sweet time tonight. Maybe she could take care of this one and get back before Jack even noticed she was gone.

"Go outside. I'll be out in a minute."

Henry frowned. He hadn't expected her to say that. After all, he wasn't even sure if she was a whore or not. She might look like one, but sometimes women dressed like that and had no intention of doing anything. And this

146

one didn't talk like a whore. Usually a whore smiled at a man, said something dirty, and then told the man her price.

Henry looked as confused as he felt, until he asked, "How much?"

"Thirty dollars," Ann said, figuring thirty dollars should cover tomorrow's doctor's bill. After Jack, she'd have enough to buy the kids their medicine.

"I want a blow job along with it," Henry said. He wasn't paying a penny to any woman who wouldn't do that.

Ann shrugged. It sure as hell wasn't the first time she'd heard that. Didn't they all want blow jobs? "Fine."

Ann waited for the man to leave before she stood and reached for her coat. "You going somewhere, sweetheart?" Jack asked, suddenly standing at her side. His arm snaked around her middle as he turned her toward him. In the dark corner, his back to the room, no one could see his hand slide inside her sweater. He found her nipple and pinched it softly.

"I have to run over to the store. The kids have colds. I almost forgot their medicine."

"You won't be long, will you?" Jack asked, his gaze never leaving her cleavage, and he smiled as he tugged her sweater down a bit, exposing a pretty rose nipple.

Ann almost changed her mind. Jack leaned against her. If that bulge in his pants meant anything, he was ready for a good time. Ann liked Jack in bed. She figured he was just about the best she'd ever had. Still, thirty dollars was thirty dollars, and she'd be a fool to pass it up. "I'll be right back." Ann adjusted her sweater and pulled out of his arms. She smiled and fluttered mascaraed lashes. It was a wasted effort. Jack never stopped looking at her chest.

The man was just outside the door, waiting for her. "You from around here?" she asked, as she followed him around the building.

"No."

"I didn't think so. Haven't seen you in Lanie's before. Do you have a room yet?"

"No."

Damn. That meant they'd have to do it in his car. God, it was freezing out here, and with her luck, he'd probably want her to take everything off. Ann almost told him that Ms. Rogers rented rooms, but stopped herself in time. Ms. Rogers was one of those Bible-thumping wackos. One look at Ann and she'd probably slam the door in her face. No, they couldn't do it there. The pious lady wouldn't let her in her house. "It's going to cost you five dollars extra. It's cold."

"Fine," he said, and Ann knew, too late, she should have asked for ten.

In his car behind the bar, Ann huddled into her coat and raised her fingers to the heater's warm air. "This feels good."

The man didn't respond, but spun his wheels as he sped out of the parking lot.

"Where are we going? If you didn't have a room, we could have stayed where we were."

Again he said nothing.

Ann shrugged. It didn't matter to her any if he wanted it alongside a country road or in the middle of town. What mattered was getting back as soon as possible. And Ann figured the sooner she got started, the sooner they'd finish and she could get back to Jack.

148

She reached for his crotch and found him already hard. Good. This was going to be over sooner than she hoped.

"Jesus, it's a mess."

Mike frowned into the receiver. He'd called Jim to find out if there had been any word on Collins's whereabouts and didn't have the vaguest notion as to what the man was talking about. "What? What's a mess?"

"The Jackson place. There's blood everywhere."

"You found him?"

"That's the problem. We *didn't* find him. We found what he left behind."

"What the hell does that mean?"

"Jackson and his wife. They're both dead."

"How?"

"He shot them in bed, probably while they were asleep, and then, just to make sure, he cut their throats."

"God!"

"He gutted the dog."

Mike shook his head in stunned disbelief. "How did you know to look there?"

"We found Tom's truck on the interstate. There was a body inside."

"Who was it?"

"Never saw him before. His ID said Chris something or other, from Colorado. Poor bastard. Looks like . . ."

Jim continued to talk, but Mike's hearing shut off. Chris was dead? The man who had asked Maggie to marry him was dead. How the hell was he supposed to tell her?

"Jim," Mike cut his friend off, "I think Maggie might know the guy."

"What guy, Collins? Of course she knows . . ."

"No. The one you found in the truck."

"What?"

"I'll bring her to the station in about a half hour, all right?"

"Yeah, but . . ."

Mike broke the connection and turned to see Maggie standing less than five feet from him, her eyes wide with fright. "Who would I know? What truck?"

Mike took a deep breath before he began, "That was Jim. They found old man Jackson's truck out on the interstate. There was a man in the back."

"In the back?"

Mike nodded. "He was dead."

Maggie's heart began to pound and she frowned. There was nothing to be afraid of, nothing to fear. So why was her heart pounding like this?

The silence between them dragged on.

Maggie shook her head. It couldn't be. Mike was jumping to conclusions. Just because Chris hadn't shown up last night, he was thinking the worst. She shook her head again and in denial said, "You think . . ."

"His name was Chris, Maggie."

Maggie swallowed and wobbled a bit before she seemed to pull herself together. She stared at him, not even allowing a blink as she asked, "Chris what?"

"Jim didn't remember."

"A lot of men are named Chris. It doesn't mean . . ."

"I know, but he comes from Colorado. I think you should make sure. It could be nothing. It probably is nothing."

But they both knew it was.

150

Maggie nodded. "When?"

"I told Jim I'd bring you over in a half hour."

Maggie sat beside him, wringing her hands nervously as the Jeep ate up the miles between town and Mike's ranch. "Suppose it's him. What should I do?"

"What do you mean?"

"His folks. They live in Chicago. I don't know the number. Who will call them? Should his body be sent back there?"

"First things first, Maggie. See if it's him, and let the police take care of the rest."

"I never saw a dead body before. At least, not of someone I was close to."

"What about your mother? You told me she . . ."

"She died in a plane crash. It was a closed casket."

Mike reached for her hand and held it pressed to his thigh. "Maybe you shouldn't do this. They can find out who he is with dental charts or fingerprints."

Maggie sighed. "I'm being a baby."

Mike smiled.

"I'll do it."

He shot her a questioning look. "Are you sure?"

Maggie nodded. "I'm sure."

They entered the sheriff's office a half hour after the phone call, almost to the minute. Mike asked for Jim Forester and was directed down a long hall to the back room. The room held a half dozen desks, as well as a number of deputy sheriffs and state troopers.

Jim saw Mike enter and waved him over to his desk. "Sorry," he said to Maggie, "the place is a madhouse today."

151

"Why?" Could it be that finding one man dead alongside the road caused this much commotion?

Jim shrugged. "Gray Bluff is a small community. We're not used to crime."

Mike had forgotten to tell her about the Jackson murders, and Maggie thought the men standing around writing out reports were here because of Chris.

"He had this on him," Jim said, as he extended a wallet for Maggie's inspection.

She knew the wallet belonged to Chris. She'd given him that wallet for his birthday. Maggie opened it. Inside she found his license and nothing else. Whoever had killed him had apparently taken the rest.

Maggie nodded as she returned the wallet to Jim. "It's his."

She said nothing more as she and Mike followed Jim out of the building and into another, smaller one that had once been used as a garage. There were no windows, only bare brick walls, and Maggie thought she'd never seen a place less cherry, nor felt air more cold. There was no heat in here, and because there was no sunshine, either, it was at least ten degrees colder than outside.

In the center of the lone room stood five tables. Three of them held bodies.

Maggie shivered. Mike noticed the movement and put his arm around her waist. She looked up into his worried expression and smiled.

"You all right?"

"I'm fine."

With no further words spoken, Mike pulled back the sheet that covered one of the bodies and asked, "You know him?"

Maggie glanced at the gray-blue face and moaned at

152

the shock, at the destruction. A second later, she felt her legs wobble, and before she could think to stop it, because she'd never fainted before, Maggie merely succumbed to the darkness that threatened.

"God damn it, Jim! What the hell is the matter with you?" Mike said, in a non-too-pleasant tone as he struggled to hold Maggie from falling to the floor. He couldn't blame her for fainting. He himself felt his stomach roll sickeningly and his head grow a bit light.

"What? What did I do?"

"You could have warned her."

Jim frowned, apparently unable to understand what Mike was getting so worked up about. He'd seen bodies before. Sometimes as many as one a week in car crashes out on the interstate, only he had forgotten the shock it might be to those who hadn't. He realized what he'd done, but said in his own defense, "She knew he was dead."

"Yeah, but she didn't know he was going to look like that." Mike finally managed to lift her into his arms. "How many times was he shot?"

Jim shrugged. "I'll let you know for sure after the coroner has a look at him, but I'd guess once in the face and . . ."

"Once? One bullet caused that much damage? What did the guy use, a rocket launcher?"

"It looks like he ran over his head a few times. I hope the poor bastard was already dead."

Mike swallowed back his nausea at the thought. "His own mother wouldn't recognize him. Why didn't you tell us?"

"Sorry. I thought maybe . . ." Jim shrugged as he

pulled the sheet back into place and Mike took Maggie from the cold stench of death.

"Mike. I need to know what kind of car he was driving. Collins probably has it."

Mike only shot him an angry glare and said, "I'll call you later."

Chapter Ten

Maggie didn't awaken until she was in Mike's Jeep once again. Mike was leaning over her, securing her seatbelt, when her eyes fluttered open. "You all right?"

His face was very close to hers, and it took her a long moment before she understood his question and remembered. When she did, she closed her eyes and said, "I can't believe I fainted. I've never fainted before."

"Yeah, well, it was almost my first time, too. It was a damn stupid of Jim not to warn us."

She couldn't let go. The picture of his ruined face reappeared again and again in her mind's eye. She'd never forget the horror of crushed bone and torn flesh.

Maggie bit her lips as tears misted her eyes. Her voice was tight as she strove to control her emotions. "Do you think . . ." She couldn't go on, the answer to the question she was about to ask was too horrifying. Perhaps it was better if she never knew.

"He was already dead, Maggie."

Maggie looked quickly from the road to the man sitting at her side. Her eyes were wide with surprise. She was obviously wondering how he read her thoughts. "How did you know?"

Mike only shrugged. "It was the first thing I thought of, too." And then he returned to what was on both their minds. "Think about it. He was a big man. It wouldn't have been easy to take him down." Mike nodded to himself as his words dispelled any lingering doubts and made sense of his thoughts. "No. He was either dead or unconscious. In either case, he wouldn't have suffered."

Maggie clung to his words, praying he was right. She nodded in agreement, but said nothing more as Mike started the car and took the road that would lead them back to his ranch.

"I'm sorry you had to see that. I'm sorry I saw it myself."

"He killed Chris."

Mike shot her a quick glance. "Are you sure it was him?"

Maggie ignored the question. The wallet belonged to Chris. His license was inside. Because of the destruction to his face, she wasn't positive, but she was sure enough. "That means you could be in danger. Everyone on your ranch could be in danger."

Mike shook his head. "He doesn't know where you are."

"Chris wrote down your phone number and the directions to your place. Was that found in his pockets?"

"I don't know."

"It wasn't, or Jim would have said something."

Mike thought she was probably right about that. He scowled at the thought of Collins possibly being on his property right now, hiding, lying in wait for the right

156

moment to strike. It gave a man an eerie feeling, and not one he took kindly to.

"I'll have to leave."

"Why?"

"Because by staying I endanger all of . . ."

Mike cut her off with, "It's too late for that. Let's take it for granted that Collins knows where you are." He waited for her nod before going on. "Let's also say you left. How could he know that? Do you think he'd believe anyone if we said you were gone?"

"God," Maggie said, so softly that Mike almost missed it. "I'm so sorry you got mixed up in this."

"The police could put you in protective custody, but I don't think you'll be any safer, no matter where you are, than if you stay at my place."

"Suppose . . ."

"I'll make sure everyone knows. The men will be on guard day and night for an intruder." Mike reached for her hand and held it in his. Maggie couldn't help the feeling of security as it tightened around hers. "I promise he won't get to you, Maggie."

She said nothing more, but simply watched the miles of snow-covered greenery rush by. She thought she should feel terrified and at the very least, trapped, but she didn't. Collins was out there somewhere, a murderer, a maniac after her, and yet she felt safe. She couldn't understand why that should be, but safe was exactly how she felt.

"All right?" Mike asked, the hand holding hers tightening a bit.

Maggie smiled and nodded. "I hope you know what you're doing."

"Jim needs to know what kind of car Chris was driving."

157

Maggie told him the year, type, and color of Chris's car.

The minute they got back to the ranch, Mike dialed Jim and told him about the car. He also mentioned the paper with his phone number and the directions to his place. Just as Maggie had predicted, Jim had not found it. There was a moment of silence as Jim realized the danger to Mike's people, to their wives and kids. Jim decided the best thing to do would be to put a few state troopers in among the ranch hands. Mike did not object.

Miriam had come with lunch during their absence. While Mike spoke on the phone, Maggie set the table and divided a loaf of Italian bread that had been made into one huge roast beef sandwich into two unequal shares and made a fresh pot of coffee.

As they ate, Mike told her about Jim's plan to bring in state troopers. "One of them will always be watching."

Maggie looked up from her sandwich. "For how long?"

"For as long as it takes." Mike took a sip of coffee. "There's a lot of country out here, but Collins is eventually going to need food and gas—probably a lot sooner than we expect." Mike nodded at his own words. "And the cops are watching everything. Motels, gas stations, boardinghouses, bars. Once he comes near town, someone will report that they saw him."

Ann Murphy gave a final moan as she was shoved from the car into the cold, white silent world of snow. She'd die now, she realized, and almost smiled at the thought, for she welcomed the knowledge that death was at hand, that the hours of suffering would finally be over. That the

158

sound of his car speeding away from where he'd dumped her was the sweetest sound she'd ever heard.

She lay there very still, very quietly, waiting for the end, hoping it wouldn't be too long in coming, for her pain was intense.

He'd beaten her unconscious twice, and both times she'd awakened to find him leaning over her, ejaculating, his semen squirting into her eyes, nose, and mouth. He rubbed it over her face, then, over her half naked body.

The crazy thing was, he hadn't needed to use force. She'd been willing to do anything he wanted. Only the more willing she was, the more violent he became.

Ann might have shuddered at the thought of a man finding satisfaction only in abuse, but she couldn't garner even that much strength. Her mind drifted as the hours of torture repeated themselves in her mind's eye, like an endless nightmare. She hadn't realized a man could come so many times. She'd lost count of exactly how many times, but it seemed to her that every time he inflicted pain, he grew excited again.

She'd realized she was in for a rough time of it even before his first time, but she'd assumed that he'd be satisfied once it was over. But he hadn't been. She'd been with him all night, taking the worst abuse a woman could, and had it not finally grown light, she might be with him still.

Ann groaned at the thought. She'd rather die than suffer through a night like that again. She almost smiled at the thought, for she knew she would die in any case. Out here, alone, with no means of finding help, with not even the strength to get up, she would die by sundown.

Her ribs were broken. Ann had been in an accident once when she was a kid, and the pain in her chest and the difficulty in breathing had been exactly the same. Her eyes were swelling shut, her lips were cut and still bleeding. Her head was ringing, the only sound out here above her heartbeat.

But that wasn't the worst of it. The worst of it was the fact that he had twisted and pulled her arm so hard that he'd wrenched it from its socket. Ann thought no pain could be greater.

"How long do you have?"

Ginny Hardgrove smiled at Tommy as he pulled away from her best friend Beth Laramor's place and headed toward the mountains and their favorite place to park. It was deserted out here, miles from anywhere. There was no chance her father could find her, no chance that he'd ever know she was with Tommy. "The whole day. Dad won't expect me back until after dinner."

"And you told Beth?"

Ginny nodded. "She'll cover for me. She's going shopping over in Elster. If he calls she'll tell him I was with her."

"Gin, I'm getting sick of this sneaking around."

Ginny snuggled close to his side and placed her hand high on his thigh. She felt his body stiffen, and smiled. "It won't be much longer."

"You'll be eighteen next month."

Ginny laughed. "Right, and when I'm eighteen, he won't be able to tell me what to do or who I can see."

"Why the hell does he hate me so much? What did I do? He looks at me like I'm a criminal about to rape his daughter."

"You're twenty-five and a cowhand."

160

"God," Tommy made a face of horror. "I reckon I should be shot at dawn."

Ginny giggled. "He thinks you have no future."

"You're my future."

Ginny smiled as she nuzzled her lips to his neck. "I love you."

Tommy pulled his truck into their favorite spot and turned to her. "Marry me, Ginny. Promise you'll marry me as soon as you turn eighteen."

Ginny laughed as she moved away from him. She might be only seventeen, but she knew her power over this man. She taunted him by slowly opening her coat and shrugging it from her shoulders.

Tommy swallowed as he watched her breasts beneath the sweater sway with the movement. She wasn't wearing a bra. God!

She bit her bottom lip as she watched him watch her. Next, her sweater was pulled over her head and flung behind her.

He swallowed again and Ginny grinned. "Am I bothering you?"

"Nope," he said, and if his voice was a bit huskier than usual, neither mentioned it.

She kicked off her boots and reached for the buttons of her jeans. "You look like you might be bothered a little."

"I'm not."

"You don't mind if I get comfortable, then?"

Tommy loved it when she teased him. Loved it more than he'd ever thought possible. He wished to hell they were living together so she could tease him all the time.

"I wish it was summer. It would be better if we could do it out there," Ginny shrugged, indicating the area outside the truck, "on a blanket."

The movement caused her breasts to sway again, and the swaying caused Tommy's voice to grow even deeper. "It couldn't ever be better."

"Not even if we had more room?" she asked, as she came to kneel upon the seat and pushed her jeans and undies to her knees.

Tommy wondered why he'd never realized before just how lucky he was. He'd had his share of girls in his time, but none of them had ever been so open and honest about wanting him, about wanting sex. None of them had ever stripped down to their skin without some intense persuasion on his part. None of them had been this free and open about their wants.

"You gonna just sit there and look?"

Tommy smiled. "I like lookin' at you."

"Touching is probably better."

"Probably, but I think you have a question to answer first."

"What kind of a question?"

"I asked you to marry me, remember?"

"Oh, yeah, and I didn't say anything."

"Right."

"And you won't touch me unless I do?"

Tommy grinned.

"Blackmail is against the law, you know."

Tommy laughed as he turned sideways and leaned against his door. "So is fornication."

"Is that what we're doing? Fornicating?"

"We might, if you're a good girl and you give me the right answer."

"What's that?"

"Fornicating? Or the answer?"

"No, *that?*" Ginny said, as she pointed over his shoulder

162

and beyond their little alcove to the dark patch that lay about a foot or so from an outcropping of bushes.

Tommy turned. "Looks like a dead animal."

"An animal wearing clothes?"

"It's probably a bear."

"I don't think so. Let's look and see."

"Ginny, we were in the middle of discussing something."

"Oh, yeah, we were, weren't we?" She smiled and kicked off her jeans. Sitting opposite him, she propped her coat behind her and leaned against the door. Completely at ease in her nakedness, she smiled as she brought one leg up. Bent at the knee, she rested it against the back of the seat, leaving absolutely nothing to Tommy's imagination.

He loved it. He loved everything about her, especially the fact that he'd been her first and she'd learned this freedom in his arms.

"What were we talking about?"

Tommy grinned. "I know what you're up to, and you might as well know, I'm not that easy."

"Yes, you are," she said, and just as he came toward her, proving her right, the dark form outside moved.

Ginny gasped and Tommy turned, following the direction of her gaze. "Tommy, it's a woman. I saw her leg."

Ann lay half in and half out of consciousness, thanks to the doctor and the drug he'd given her. Her shoulder and arm were wrapped, her arm propped upon a pillow. And for the first time in hours, she felt no pain. It was bliss. Her only problem was Jim Forester. The man wouldn't stop bothering her with his questions.

"What?" she said again, for maybe the tenth time. She

163

couldn't stop her mind from drifting, and she frowned as his words pulled her from sleep.

"What was his name?"

"I don't know."

"What was he wearing?"

"Army jacket. Wool hat."

"What kind of a car was he driving?"

"White. A chevy, I think."

"Did he tell you where he was staying?"

"He didn't have a room. Are my kids all right?"

"They're fine. I brought them over to the McKenzie place. They'll be fine."

"Good," Ann said, just before she drifted off to sleep again.

Jim cursed as he watched her sleep. He'd told the doctor not to give her too much, that he needed answers to his questions. A minute or so later, Jim shrugged. She probably couldn't tell him any more than she already had. It was Collins, all right. Now, all he had to do was find the bastard. Jim sighed as he left the hospital room, wondering how the hell he was going to manage it.

Maggie laughed a wicked sound as Mike landed on Boardwalk and moaned, "Nooo."

"Pay up." She held out her hand, palm up, waiting for him to fill it with cash as she mentally added up the amount owed.

Mike looked at his side of the board and the measly few dollars that were lined up beside it. "I can't. I haven't got enough."

"Too bad. I win."

164

She reached across the board for his money. Mike grabbed her hand. "Suppose we make a deal?"

Maggie shot him a playful glare and bit her bottom lip, trying not to smile. "What kind of deal?"

"My body for another chance." He said it so seriously that if Maggie hadn't caught the laughter in his eyes, she might have thought him serious.

"You mean, strip Monopoly? I never heard of it."

"Sure, it's all the rage."

She leaned back and looked him over. He was leaning on his elbow, his long body stretched out, his feet close to the fire. "I don't know if you're worth it."

"I assure you, I am." Maggie thought he just might be right about that.

"Mmm, a man of confidence. Women like that." She smiled. "All right, let's see if you're worth it."

"What?"

"I said . . ."

"I know what you said. What does it mean?"

"It means, if you take your clothes off, I'll see if you deserve another chance."

"You mean, just lie here naked, and let you have a look?"

"That was the offer, wasn't it?"

"Suppose we start with just my shirt in exchange for Boardwalk."

"Forget it. I've seen a man's chest before."

"All right, my shirt and boots."

"I won. Admit it."

Mike breathed a sigh and came to a sitting position. "I knew we should have played cards."

Maggie chuckled as he helped her put the game pieces

165

back in the box. "You're sure you'd have won if we'd played cards?"

"Maggie, I'm a cowboy," he said, as if that fact should have made everything clear. It didn't.

"So?"

"So, cowboys play cards when they're not . . ."

"Playing with cows?" she offered.

"Working." He frowned, which only made her laugh again.

"Is that all cowboys do? Work and play cards?"

"And rescue damsels in distress."

Maggie smiled and shook her head. "Only I'm not a damsel."

"You're as close to one as I've ever seen."

She smiled, thinking it was lovely that he should think so.

"It smells like it's done."

Maggie breathed a sigh and looked toward the ceiling. "You said that five minutes after I put it in."

"How much longer? I'm starving."

Maggie glanced at her watch. "Ten minutes. And it's impossible for you to be starving . . . you ate enough fried chicken for two men."

Mike grinned. "I'm a growing boy, and that coffee cake smells delicious.

"If you don't watch out, you'll start to grow sideways." Maggie came up from the floor. "I'll make some coffee."

Mike sat on the couch, his feet propped up on the coffee table as he reached for the TV remote and started flicking through the channels. "What do you want to watch?" he called into the kitchen.

Maggie, finished with the coffee, came back into the living room and sat on the opposite end of the couch, her gaze on the TV. The channels were going by at the speed of light. Maggie frowned. She couldn't imagine what he was looking for. And how he could tell whether he'd found it or not. Three times she'd been about to say "Leave this," or "This looks good," but the station was changed before she got a chance to open her mouth.

"Do you know what you're looking for?"

"Something good."

"And you expect to find it by flicking through the channels?"

"Sure."

"Meaning you always do this?"

"How else can you tell what's on?"

"Well, you could read it in the paper or in *TV Guide*," she offered hopefully.

He shook his head. "Don't have either."

The channels suddenly stopped flicking by at the sight of a woman's back. A woman's naked back, as it turned out. A man was kissing her. The camera moved down the length of her, and Maggie discovered it wasn't only her back that was naked; it was her entire body. The angle moved up again and to the side a bit, and her naked breasts came into view. The man's hand came to cup a breast, displaying it for the camera as he brought his mouth to the tip and began to tease it with a flicking tongue. Mike remarked, "This looks interesting."

Maggie knew this movie couldn't be on regular television. "You have cable?"

"A dish."

She watched a moment longer before saying, "She's bound to get a kink in her back, twisted like that."

Mike glanced at Maggie, obviously puzzled. "Think so?"

The couple were standing in a tub. Water was running over the man's shoulder, splashing the woman and allowing the man to run his hand over her slippery body as she leaned back, sort of sideways and definitely off balance.

The camera followed his hand down, while her nude body effectively shielded the lower half of his from view.

Maggie snorted a sound of disgust.

"What?"

"They never show the man, only the woman."

Mike frowned. "You're not one of those woman's lib people, are you?"

Maggie shot him a look of disbelief. "Of course I am. Isn't everybody?"

Mike wondered what he was supposed to say to that. As far as he knew, there wasn't a woman's libber in the state of Wyoming—if you didn't count politicians, that is—not even a liberal, if the truth be told. The men around here were mostly cowboys and ranchers, sort of an old-fashioned breed. They knew the world was changing around them, but they were satisfied to see things stay pretty much the same. Obviously Maggie was unaware of that fact. Mike figured it best to say nothing on the subject. And saying nothing proved to be exactly right.

"Do you think it's fair that a woman should be on display, and not the man with her?"

Mike shrugged. The truth was, he hadn't ever thought about it before. "Maybe men are more shy."

Maggie laughed at that. "Men? Shy? I doubt it."

"Known a lot of men, have you?"

Maggie ignored the question. "I can tell you for a fact, this movie is no good."

Mike frowned. He hadn't missed the fact that she hadn't answered his question. He was sorry now that he hadn't thought before asking it. Her private life wasn't any of his business. Even if they should develop a relationship, and he thought or at least hoped they might, the men she'd known in the past wouldn't be any of his business. "Have you seen it before?"

"No, but when they have to show this much skin, there's usually no story."

"Should I change the channel?"

Maggie shrugged. "It's your television." She looked at her watch again. "The cake should be done."

Mike changed the channel and called out, "You like football?"

Maggie could hear the grunts and groans of players as he watched reruns of a past game.

"Baseball," she called from the kitchen.

"Baseball?" he returned, with some obvious disgust.

"Yeah, and don't you dare say anything about it."

"How are we supposed to get along if you like baseball? This is football country."

"I thought we *were* getting along."

"I mean later, during the season."

"I'll be gone by then."

"Right. It's a good thing."

"And if I'm not, I'll get my own television."

Mike laughed. He liked having her here. Liked having someone to talk to, to tease. Liked her coffee. Liked the way she laughed and answered him back, and the way she smelled, the way she made his house smell, like a woman, all soft and powdery clean. He'd be sorry when it was time for her to go.

Maggie brought in a tray of coffee, cups, and the cake. They sat side by side as they ate. "This is delicious. How did you make the crumbs?"

169

"Crumbs are only butter, sugar, and a little flour."

Maggie laughed as she watched him devour the cake amid a chorus of exaggerated *ohs* and *ahs*. "Stop eating so fast."

"I can't help it. It's delicious."

Mike was in the midst of swallowing a huge mouthful when the phone rang. "Should I get it?"

He nodded and Maggie picked up the phone.

"Hello."

"Hello, bitch."

Maggie froze. She hadn't heard his voice in just over a week. She knew he had this number, but she'd somehow talked herself out of the fear of him ever calling here. She instantly realized her mistake.

She said nothing as he began, "Did you think I wouldn't find you? You won't get away that easy, Maggie. I love you. I'll never give you up."

Maggie opened her mouth to protest, but no words came.

"I took care of the bastard, and I'll take care of the one you're with now."

She glanced at Mike, only she couldn't say anything, and he was busy swallowing another mouthful of cake. "I'm going to fuck him up good, Maggie. Just like I did the other one."

As Maggie listened to his threats and imagined Mike's face crushed as Chris's had been, her eyes widened with terror. It was then, because she'd been silent for so long, that Mike turned her way. He frowned. "What's the matter?"

". . . only I'm going to do an extra special job on him. He'll wish he was dead before I'm finished. You'll wish it, too, bitch."

Mike tore the phone from her stiff hand and heard only the last word before barking, "Collins? Is that you? Come on over, man. Show me what you've got. Let's see how brave you are when facing a man."

The silence that followed was so long that Mike thought Collins had hung up. He almost hung up himself, and then he heard, "I was brave enough to show the last one who fucked her. You're next."

"Why don't you try it?"

"You're fucking her, aren't you?"

Mike purposely refused to answer, knowing Collins would believe what he wanted in any case.

"I'll kill you. I'll kill all of you."

Mike laughed, taunting him to madness, knowing instinctively that Collins was bound to make a mistake if he lost his cool. And he'd never heard a man less cool in his life. "You got no balls, Collins. Let's see you do something about it," he said, just before he deliberately broke the connection.

Chapter Eleven

With an, "Oh, my God," Maggie got up suddenly from the couch and started for the front door. "I've got to get out of here. I've got to get out of here," she repeated, as she struggled with the coat. What was the matter with the thing? Why couldn't she get her arms into it?

Mike was instantly beside her. "What are you doing?"

"I've got to go. I can't . . ."

Mike pulled the coat away. "Calm down. You're playing right into his hands! He wanted to shake you up."

"Yeah? Well he did a good job of it."

Mike figured she was right on that score. He'd never seen anyone shake like this before. "Listen to me," he said, as he threw the coat on the floor and took her against him. His arms held her tightly along the length of his body as his hands soothed her back in a comforting gesture. "It's all a part of the game of terror. He's hoping to scare you into making a mistake."

"I can't live like this anymore. I can't stand it."

"I know it's hard on you, Maggie, but it won't be much longer. He's as mad as hell."

She shuddered and slowly shook her head. "Mike, you don't understand."

"Yes, I do. He's going to make a mistake soon. Because he's furious, he won't be able to think clearly. And then it will all be over."

"*What'll* all be over? He said he'd kill you like he killed Chris. He thinks we're sleeping together."

"He's not going to kill me. And he's not going to kill you." He pressed her face to his chest. His mouth was against the top of her head. "I promise you'll see your grandchildren, Maggie."

Tears choked her as she bit her lips together, holding back threatening sobs. She thought those words were just about the nicest she'd ever heard. It was exactly what she needed. But it wasn't enough to stop her tears.

"Don't cry, darlin'," he said, hearing her sniffles and feeling her shudders against him, as he continued to soothe her fears with gentle strokes over her back.

But suddenly that wasn't enough. She needed more than a gentle touch, she needed to know his warmth, the security of his possession, of losing her fears in his arms, even if it was only for a little while.

She didn't think of her actions as her arms reached around his neck, holding him tightly to her as her lips mindlessly brushed against his throat, his jaw, blindly seeking his mouth.

Mike had realized her terror, but he hadn't imagined that her fears could cause her to turn to him in almost desperate need. He felt her lips on his throat, but pushed aside the very real fact that she was kissing him. She didn't mean it. She didn't know *what* she was doing.

Her lips didn't stop at his throat. She kissed his jaw, his

173

cheek, and Mike felt a low groan begin somewhere in his chest and rise to his throat.

He closed his eyes as he tried to summon the strength, but there was no strength against this. He'd been without a woman too long, and to refuse this woman, this beautiful, enticing woman, was more than he could manage.

Her lips brushed over his, and the pounding of his heart almost choked him at the pure, sweet invitation to bliss. There was no way he could resist.

His hands reached for her head, his long brown fingers sliding into her thick, clean hair as he held her still for the awesome exploration of her mouth.

Maggie felt her knees weaken as the taste and scent of him filled her being, as his tongue ravaged and claimed with devastating sureness the softness of her.

Maggie, had she the ability to think at all, might have thought that she'd never been kissed quite so thoroughly before. This wasn't just a kiss, this was foreplay, a prelude to lovemaking, and Maggie loved every second of it, every movement of his tongue, every sweet breath he took and returned.

She was lost. His wanting had overpowered her own, and she knew only sweet bliss.

He turned her so her back was against the wall. Pressing his hips to hers, he brought her higher, so their mouths might more easily meet, and he kissed her again and again.

Maggie thought nothing could ever be this good. Nothing.

His hands were at her waist, her hips, running over the smoothness found there, cupping her, pulling her more tightly to him. And then she was suddenly alone. Alone, and trembling with a need that had been out of control, a need they'd both known.

Mike leaned against the wall for support, his arms positioned on each side of her, his head hanging weakly from his shoulders as he gasped for every breath. It took a second, but he finally managed, "Not because of Collins, Maggie."

Mike looked into her eyes. Knowing that she was soft and needy, and yet refusing to touch her, was the hardest thing he'd ever done, but he knew he had to do it, or never know the truth. "You have to want this because of me. You have to want *me.*"

Maggie realized his meaning. It was only then that she realized her actions. She did want him, but she knew her emotions wouldn't have been so out of control had it not been for the phone call and her resulting fear. She wouldn't have ended up in his arms had it not been for the fear.

She hadn't been fair, and she knew it. She couldn't make this kind of decision in the throes of terror. It wouldn't be fair to him or to her. Maggie knew a light, casual relationship that included sex wasn't possible between them. It could never be possible. This man, steady and strong, was for keeps. And if she made love to him, it would mean forever.

She'd have to give up something, if it came to that. Maggie wasn't sure she was ready to make that kind of decision, that kind of commitment. At least, not yet.

"I'm sorry," she said, her voice weak as she tried to garner the needed strength just to stand. She'd never known passion could be like this, so overpowering, so overwhelming.

"Don't be," he returned. "Only the next time, if there

is a next time," his voice lowered with emotion, "I won't stop."

Maggie read the promise in his eyes, saw the fire, and knew the meaning behind his words. He wanted her to come to him with a clear mind, in full possession of her senses, knowing exactly her wants. The next time would mean commitment. The next time would be for keeps.

Maggie bit her bottom lip, nodded, and lowered her eyes from his fiery gaze.

"Are you all right now?"

"Yes."

With his hand at her waist, he guided her back to the couch, only she didn't sit. "I'm tired. I think I'll go to bed."

Mike turned her to face him. "Remember what I said. Nothing is going to happen to you."

Maggie nodded and then smiled. "I'll remember."

She left him standing in his living room, knowing there was no way she could forget, no way either of them could ever forget.

It wasn't light yet, but Maggie had awakened early, having tossed and turned most of the night, unable to take her mind from what had happened after that awful phone call.

Maggie stood in the kitchen with a cup of coffee in one hand and the thumb of the other hooked into the waistband of her jeans. She grinned at Abner, watching him roll a cigarette. She hadn't imagined people still did that sort of thing. "You shouldn't smoke, Abner. Cigarettes will kill you."

"Aw, honey, it'll take more than a little ole cigarette to do this old man in."

"You're not old, and that's exactly what they'll do," she warned.

"I'm seventy-two," he said proudly.

Maggie thought because of the devastating effects of the sun he looked more like eighty-two, but he didn't act it. The man was lively and as full of energy and humor as anyone she'd ever met.

Maggie looked into her cup and grinned. "I wouldn't think of getting involved with anyone who smoked."

Abner laughed out loud. "You mean, there's a chance for me?"

"There's always a chance, Abner," Maggie teased. "You're a very handsome man."

"Whoopee!" he almost yelled, as he grabbed his hat from his gray head and snapped it against his thigh. "Just wait till I tell the boy."

"Tell me what?" Mike asked, as he stepped into the kitchen. His hair was wet, and he was buttoning up his shirt, having obviously just come from the shower.

"You lost out, boy. I told you not to dilly-dally, and now it's too late."

"Too late for what?"

"This lady here just spoke her intentions. And I accept."

Mike's puzzled gaze moved from Abner to Maggie. "You did?"

Maggie shrugged. Laughter danced in her eyes. "Only if he quits smoking."

"That's a big sacrifice to make, but probably worth it, if he'll stop stinking up my house."

"What do you know, boy?" Abner frowned and then

looked at his cigarette. "This isn't a stink. It's a smell. The way a *man's* supposed to smell."

"Not if he wants me," Maggie said to the room at large. "I don't kiss ashtrays."

Abner held the cigarette almost at eye level, studying it for a long moment, before he asked Mike, "Is she worth giving this up?"

Mike grinned at the question. "Why ask me?"

Abner's gaze moved to Maggie. Maggie, a redhead with creamy skin, felt her cheeks grow crimson at the question. The color of her face was all Abner needed by way of an answer. He laughed, and Maggie grew redder.

"Looks like she's already spoken for."

Mike didn't respond. All he could do was hope the old man was right.

"And I think I made a mistake inviting you for dinner."

"Now, don't go getting yourself in an uproar, little lady. I was only seein' how the land lays."

"What?"

Mike interpreted. "He was trying, in his sneaky way, to find out if we're involved."

"Oh."

"Tell him it's none of his business."

"I couldn't be that rude."

"If you don't tell him, you'll never hear the end of it," Mike warned.

"And if you don't give me the right answer, I won't believe you anyway." Abner's blue eyes twinkled wickedly.

Mike breathed a heavy sigh. "There's only one thing to do, Maggie."

"Is there? What?" This conversation was getting a bit out of control, and she wasn't sure about the look in

178

Mike's eyes, either. She was even more unsure as he started toward her.

"You want to convince him we're not involved?"

Abner was all eyes.

Maggie thought it possible to convince him they were, but how could they convince him they were not? "How?"

"Kiss me."

"Forget it."

Mike grinned at Abner's crestfallen expression. "See?"

Abner shrugged. "That don't mean nothin'. Some ladies are shy."

"I'm not shy."

Abner breathed a sigh, put his coffee cup in the sink, and said to Mike, "You're a fool if you let this one get away."

Mike knew he was no fool, but did not comment on Abner's last statement. His gaze followed the old man outside before he grinned at Maggie. "I hope that shuts him up for a while."

"I have a feeling it won't."

And it didn't.

Apparently Maggie's staying with Mike was cause for speculation in more than one mind. As it turned out, Abner wasn't the only one who hoped things were growing serious between Maggie and Mike. Miriam hinted at the subject more than once during the late-morning visit.

"Don't you think a man needs a wife?"

"Some men," Maggie said, noncommittally.

"Mike's a good sort," Miriam said, as she adjusted the weight of the baby at her breast and downed half her coffee. "God, this makes me so thirsty."

"He's very nice."

"But you're not interested?"

179

"I don't know him that well."

"Honey, it don't take much to know a man. It takes years of study to figure them out, but only a few hours to know them."

Maggie grinned. "You might be right."

" 'Course I'm right." A moment of silence went by, and then, "He's good lookin', don't you think?"

Maggie nodded as she picked up Miriam's two-year-old who gave up trying for his mother's attention and toddled toward her with a ratty blanket in one hand and a thumb in his mouth. Maggie settled the child on her lap. "This one is adorable," she said, trying to change the subject. "Is this blanket yours?"

The little boy looked at her with huge, slightly suspicious brown eyes, and nodded.

"It's beautiful, isn't it?"

And as if he thought perhaps the pretty lady's interest in his blanket was a bit too avid, the child pulled it tighter against him.

Miriam grinned. "Watch out, that blanket means more to Johnny than I do. One day he got away from me and I found him standing under the clothesline, holding on to his wet blanket while sucking his thumb."

"That was very smart, wasn't it?" Maggie said to the boy.

"Maybe, but it damn near gave me a heart attack.

"Jake, did you find your shoes?" Miriam called into the next room, her voice carrying over the blasting TV. Maggie noticed the baby in her arms did not stir. Apparently he was used to his mother's less-than-soft tones.

"I found one," came a voice from an unseen child.

"Look for the other one." Miriam sighed. "Last week, Johnny put one of Jake's shoes into the broiler. At least,

I think Johnny did it. You can't get anyone to admit to anything around here." She took a deep breath. "I didn't know it was there until I turned the oven on."

Maggie laughed.

"Don't laugh. Kids' shoes cost more than mine." She changed the subject. "You want something special for dinner?"

"No. I ah, well, I thought I'd cook tonight, if it's all right with you."

"Sure it's all right with me. I could use a break. You want to do it every night?"

Maggie shrugged. "Maybe. I feel like I'm not earning my keep. I just sit all day and watch television or read."

"You could come riding with us someday." Miriam got up to refill her cup. She leaned against the counter for a moment as she spoke. "The kids and I go a few times a week. It helps to keep me in shape." Miriam ran her free hand over a plump hip as she said the last of it and then smiled. "Imagine what I'd look like if I didn't ride."

"You look great. After four kids, nobody should look that good."

Miriam looked at her for a moment before saying, "You're going to be my friend for life."

Maggie laughed.

"I don't know how to ride."

"I'll teach you."

Maggie smiled. "Is everyone this friendly out here?"

"Some could be a lot friendlier, if you let them."

Maggie realized Miriam was back to the subject of Mike again. She thought she'd never seen people more intent on matchmaking, and figured they needed something to occupy their time.

"I'd better go. A sauce takes a while to cook."

"Italian?"

Maggie nodded. "Uh-huh."

"Mike loves Italian food."

"Good, because that's just about all I know how to cook."

"With a last name like Smith?"

"My mother was Italian."

Miriam laughed, thinking this woman was just about perfect for her friend. Mike wasn't going to be able to resist her.

Miriam never knew how close her thoughts were to the truth.

Henry Collins drove the fifty miles to Rock Springs. On the outskirts of the city he found a shabby motel. Outside the office door was a newspaper rack. After paying for his room, Henry took a paper and headed for number eight. Inside the room he quickly scanned the paper. He knew his picture would be inside somewhere, and he wasn't disappointed. He was right there on page three. Only the picture didn't look anything like how he looked now. In the picture he had no beard. Henry touched his face, fingering the two weeks' growth. His beard was full. Tonight, or maybe tomorrow, he'd shape it.

And he'd lost weight. Henry figured at least ten pounds, maybe more. Living on his wits and little else had caused him to thin out some. Good.

It wouldn't be all that easy to recognize him now. Especially since he'd bought new clothes and had himself a new car.

Henry had figured that Maggie could identify the car, so he'd found himself another. It was easy enough. All he had to do was stop in one of those rest areas and wait for a woman alone. The next thing he knew, he'd traded the white car for a blue one. By the time they found her body in the Chevy trunk, Henry would be long gone, and no trace of him would ever be found.

Henry lay back on the bed, remembering how easy it had been to kill her. Didn't women know how easy it was to die? He wondered why so many people traveled alone and then shrugged away the thought. It was a good thing they did, or he might have been sitting in jail at this moment, rather than half asleep on a nice, soft bed.

Henry awoke late that night. He was starving. Too late he realized that he should have stopped someplace before taking this room. Henry sighed as he rolled to a sitting position and then got to his feet. He'd have to find a fast-food place or he'd never get back to sleep. And he needed sleep almost as much as he needed food.

He pulled the car away from the window and turned into a parking space. Almost before he stopped he was rummaging through the bag for the hamburgers. He ate three before he started to slow down, before he took a long sip of his drink or touched his french fries.

Now that the worst of his hunger was appeased, Henry began to look around the small parking lot. He watched a woman leave the fast-food restaurant and walk to her car. At the door she fumbled with her keys a bit, but finally, with oversized pocketbook and bag, she got inside. She put a few french fries in her mouth just as she started the car and pulled out of the lot into light traffic.

Henry watched her taillights for a long time, knowing she'd never know how close she'd just come to dying. It was then that Henry realized that he liked killing, especially killing women. He wondered why he hadn't done it sooner. It felt so damn good to be able to control whether they lived or not. It made him feel stronger than God.

People were told all their lives that only God had control over life or death. That was bullshit. Henry had the control, not God. Henry chuckled softly and almost choked on his drink. If there was a God, how come he didn't draw on his mighty sword or whatever crap he had at his command and snuff him out? How come he didn't stop him from killing even one woman? How come he let Henry Collins be born in the first place, especially to that sick, perverted bitch? God. Henry laughed.

Henry thought maybe he should find himself a woman, but almost immediately he changed his mind. He couldn't get it up with decent women, if there were any decent ones out there, and he couldn't stop beating the other kind. If he found a prostitute and started beating on her or killed her, it would be sure to bring attention where he wanted no attention. Henry needed time to rest, to think, to plan on how he was going to get her.

It wouldn't be easy. Not while she was living with the bastard. But he was going to get her. He was going to get both of them. He could hardly wait to watch them die. As far as he could see, there was only one problem, and that was which one he would kill first.

No, he wouldn't look for a woman. He'd do what he always did: he'd watch the news. Maybe he could find himself another love. Maybe she'd smile for him and he'd show her what he had waiting for her.

Henry came from the bathroom, wet from his shower, as a woman took her seat as anchor. He'd been listening to CNN, the words unheard, for his mind took in only sound, only her voice. Soft, sweet, and silky, it had called him from the bathroom. Naked he walked to the bed and sat, waiting as a news clip took over the screen. Perhaps twenty seconds went by and then a short blackout, and there she was again. She smiled into the camera and Henry gasped. He knew what that smile meant. He knew she was interested.

It reminded him of Maggie, the way she smiled. Only she wasn't anything like Maggie. She was dark, and her eyes were blue. Beautiful.

Henry thought he could easily love this one. He'd have to go to Atlanta after his business here was finished, but he didn't mind that. He liked the South. The people there were friendlier, the days and nights comfortable even in the midst of winter.

Henry grinned. No, he wasn't going to mind moving south. He'd finish the bitch off first, and then he'd be on his way to his new love.

Her eyes moved over him and Henry remembered he sat there nude. He didn't want to shock her. It was too early in their relationship. He pulled the bedspread over his lap, lest she see too much too soon.

He had to get to know her first. He had to know her before he could show her a cock so big.

Maggie rested her chin in her hand, her eyes wide with amazement as she watched Mike down his third plate of spaghetti. She never would have believed that anybody could eat that much.

Mike pushed the plate away and groaned as his hand went to an apparently aching stomach. "Now you've done it."

"What?"

"My stomach is killing me."

"And that's my fault?"

"If you didn't cook so good, I wouldn't have eaten too much."

Abner chuckled.

Maggie snorted in disbelief. "You ate three bowls of spaghetti, and what, six meatballs?"

"Eight."

Maggie nodded. "Eight. And because you ate like a pig, I'm to blame?" Again she nodded to his pained expression. "That's logical."

Mike grinned. "You're not very sympathetic, are you?"

"Not when you eat tonight's dinner and tomorrow's lunch all in one sitting."

Abner laughed as he leaned back in his chair and rolled another cigarette. "Before you make any definite plans, maybe you should think things over a bit, boy. It takes a real man to know how to handle a feisty woman."

"And maybe you'd better butt out of my business."

"Leave him alone," Maggie said, coming to Abner's defense. "He didn't do anything."

"He will." The words had a certain hopeless ring to them, as if there was nothing anyone could do to stop what was to come.

Abner chuckled wickedly, the silky, almost suggestive sound oddly strange coming from a man in his seventies. "Now, I've had myself some experience with feisty women. They just happen to be my favorite kind." Abner chuckled again at Maggie's tender grin.

Maggie thought this old man was so cute.

"You two want to be alone?"

186

Both Maggie and Abner ignored the less-than-gracious words.

"If you know what's good for you, boy, you'll snap her up. Once I quit smoking, it's gonna be too late."

Mike shot Maggie a knowing look. "See?"

Maggie laughed and then coughed as she waved away a cloud of smoke. "If smoking doesn't quit you first, you mean."

Mike leaned back and eyed another meatball, but wisely decided he'd wait until later. "Where'd you learn to cook like that?"

"From my mother."

"You should own a restaurant, not work on television."

"You work on television?" Abner asked.

"Local. I anchor the news in Ellington."

"Wow!" Abner's eyes looked like they were ready to pop from their sockets. "Do you know Connie Chong?"

Maggie laughed and shook her head. "She works in New York."

Mike felt somehow obligated to inform her of something that was obviously none of her business. "Connie Chong is Abner's secret love."

"Watch your mouth, boy."

"Too bad she got married. Abner was really hoping . . ."

"I ain't stayin' here to get insulted by some no-account whippersnapper like you."

Maggie thought that expression had probably gone out with Gene Autry and his singing cowboys. She didn't know people actually still talked like this. Dilly-dally, no-account whippersnapper. Amazing.

"I don't see that you're tied to the seat, old man."

"Why, I have half a mind to . . ."

"You're right about that, you've only got about half a mind left."

"You got a smart mouth, boy."

"Smart enough to put you in your place, old man."

"Mrs. Hennesey has been lookin' for a new foreman. I think I'll mosey on over . . ."

"She wouldn't want an old busybody like you. She wants somebody who can work, not talk a good show."

Maggie's head had been snapping back and forth as she'd listened to the trading insults. "Wait a minute."

"What?" both men said at once.

"What are you fighting about?"

"Who's fighting?" Abner asked, even as Mike shot her a puzzled look.

"You mean, you're not fighting?"

"Nope."

"It sure sounded like fighting to me."

Abner snorted, and then said, "Maybe she's not all she's cracked up to be, boy. For one thing, she needs a hearing aid."

Maggie shot the two grinning men long looks of steel. And then, to their delight, she said softly, "At least I don't need a psychiatrist."

Chapter Twelve

"Are you going to get a new dress, or do you have something with you?"

"A new dress? For what?" Maggie asked, as she poured herself a cup of coffee in Miriam's kitchen.

"For the wedding."

"Who's getting married?" For just a second Maggie was almost afraid to hear the answer, lest she recognize one of the names as her own.

"Tommy Harris. He works here. At least, he used to. I guess he'll be working the Hardgrove place from now on."

Maggie never realized her sigh of relief. Sometimes she didn't know what to expect from the all-too-eager romantics around this place. "I don't know if I'm going."

"Oh, you have to go."

"How come?"

" 'Cause everybody is invited. And you couldn't stay here alone."

Both women knew, even if Maggie decided to stay behind, she wouldn't be alone. Maggie never stepped out of the house that two men weren't instantly at her side.

Most always they were state troopers, but once in a while, for reasons unknown to herself, they were the men who worked around the ranch.

"You want to know how it happened?"

"What? The wedding?"

Miriam nodded eagerly. It was obvious the woman was practically bursting to tell it.

"I take it it wasn't planned?"

"I guess you could say that."

"Sure, go ahead."

"Well, it's like this. For the last twenty years, old man Hardgrove played cards at Jesse Stokes' place on Monday nights."

"So?" Maggie asked, knowing something was expected of her at Miriam's dramatic pause.

"So last Monday, Jesse dropped dead."

"Oh, dear. That's terrible."

"Yeah. I guess the boys," Miriam snorted something like a laugh at the inaccurate wording, "they're hardly boys. The fact is, they're a bunch of old men." She took a deep breath and smiled. "It seemed they didn't take Jesse's death as hard as one might have expected."

"Why? What did they do?"

"They moved the game over to the Hardgrove place."

"God, they're all heart, aren't they?"

"That's not the best part."

Maggie smiled a bit sickly. "They didn't take him with them, did they?"

Miriam laughed. "Actually, I'm surprised they didn't just stay at his house and deal around the corpse. No. The best part is what they found when Hardgrove and the rest of the card game got to his house."

"They saw a boy running from the house. Tommy."

190

"Oh, thee of simple faith and pure heart." Miriam shot Maggie a wicked look. "Not even close."

Maggie couldn't hold back her smile, especially since Miriam appeared to be getting such a kick out of the telling. "What?"

"Well, you have to picture this first. Hardgrove's house is set up something like Mike's, with the laundry room out back. Just like Mike's, you have to go through it to get into the house."

Maggie nodded as she pictured the setting.

"Except that there are three steps to the laundry room from the kitchen."

"Okay."

"And Monday is usually the night Ginny does the laundry."

"Yeah?"

"And she wasn't doing it alone."

Maggie shrugged.

"Or with any clothes on."

"You're kidding. What about Tommy?"

"I guess he figured to take advantage of the opportunity and wash his things along with hers."

"You don't mean they were both naked and standing around the laundry room and her father walked in?"

Miriam shrugged. "Well, not exactly. It seems that Tommy got this brilliant idea to carry Ginny to the washing machine, her having no shoes on and all, and him not wanting his sweetheart's feet to get cold."

Maggie forced back the urge to laugh, and her voice was just a bit tight as she offered, "That was very considerate of him. Don't you think?"

"On his shoulders."

It was too much. Maggie couldn't stop the laughter from bubbling forth. "Are you making this up?"

"Swear to God." With her finger Miriam made a cross over her heart.

"That had to be a sight to see."

"So I heard," Miriam agreed. "It seems they were just coming down the steps when Hardgrove walked in, followed by his four cronies. And *voilà*," she made a sweeping gesture with her arm, as if she'd just performed some extraordinary magic trick, "the makings of a wedding."

Maggie tried, but she couldn't stop laughing as she imagined the scenario. "How embarrassing!"

"Especially since there wasn't a towel or scrap of clothing that wasn't in either the washer or dryer, and those dirty old men got themselves an eyeful."

"What happened?"

"You mean after the leering, or after the shouting?"

Maggie laughed again and shook her head.

"Towels were found in the dryer and wrapped around the two youngsters, while Hardgrove threatened to shoot any man caught looking at his daughter."

"And?"

"And the card game lasted until midnight, just like it always did."

"Now I know you're making this up."

Miriam shook her head. "Nope. After the game was over, plans were made for the wedding."

"I assume the wedding is not on a Monday night."

"Saturday."

The fact of the matter was, once you did anything, whether it was riding a bike, frying chicken, or killing a

192

human being, it got easier each time you did it. Easier and better.

Henry stayed at the motel for four days, sleeping and eating. During his waking hours, he watched her, leaving the television only when her broadcast was over, ready and awake again when it was her turn at the desk.

He knew he loved her, loved her more than he'd ever loved Maggie. Only this time, he wasn't going to save himself for her. He'd done that for Maggie and she hadn't appreciated it. Women didn't appreciate anything a man did for them.

No, he'd have his good times as he waited for the opportunity to finish off the bitch and then he'd head south to his new love.

Henry stood before the television and grinned as she smiled. She could see him opening his pants. Slowly, he thought maybe he'd tease her a little, drag out the moment, increase the sexual tension. He drew the zipper down and released himself for her pleasure.

She laughed at something someone said, but that was only because she didn't want the rest of the world to know what was going on between them. She looked at him and Henry's cock felt the full blast of that sweet, secret smile.

He closed his eyes with the ecstasy of the moment. He knew it would be like this. He knew she'd love it, want it, do anything for it. He was happy, now that he'd waited. It was much better that he'd waited these four days.

Yes, he'd wanted her to see it right away, and he knew she'd have been happy if he'd shown it sooner, but this was better. Much better.

Henry pushed his clothes to his knees and sat on the edge of the bed, facing her. Watching her mouth move, he imagined how it would feel on him, sucking him, loving him. She couldn't do that yet, but she would. Henry knew she would. And he lived for the day.

With his legs parted, he exposed himself completely to her, raising his hips slightly to make sure she had an excellent view.

Her eyes widened with surprise, with happiness. She hadn't expected a cock could be this big, he knew.

And then he began to stroke it with loving caresses, showing her how a man liked it best.

"You put your tongue here, sweetheart," he said to the woman in the television set. "And then you start to lick it upward, like this."

A pulse hammered in his throat. His breathing grew harsh, labored. Henry knew he wouldn't be able to hold back much longer. Not when she looked at him like this. Not when she wanted him so badly.

Henry leaned back, supporting himself on his elbow as he raised his hips higher to her view. It was so exciting. It was the most exciting thing he'd ever known. He hardly had to touch himself. Just knowing that she was watching caused the first squirt of juice to fly from his body. Henry groaned at the feeling, the pure bliss of this moment as his cock pulsed and shot forth another stream of sacred liquid. And then came another and then more, until Henry lay there shaking from the trauma, from the unbearable pleasure of her.

Henry shot the woman in his car a quick glance as she fixed her lipstick and dotted a powder puff over her nose and cheek. He wondered if she was going to scream. He liked it best when they screamed. Their fear made him

194

strong. He didn't know how, but it did. And Henry loved feeling strong. It was the best feeling in the world.

He'd driven around the city and its outskirts a few times, becoming acquainted with the area, looking for the best places. The places where there was the most privacy. He was taking her to one of them right now.

"I really appreciate this, mister. I was already late when my car started giving me trouble. It's my kid's birthday."

"No problem," Henry said. "I was going that way."

"Do you live in Warrington?"

"A little north of it."

"Oh." Cindy Bowes frowned. What was north of Warrington? Nothing but a ranch. The Thompson place, she thought.

"You work for the Thompsons?"

"Yeah, just started."

Cindy thought that was odd. The ranches around here didn't usually hire on until spring, which was a couple of months away. She shrugged. Maybe someone had quit and left an opening.

"Do you mind if I smoke?"

Henry shrugged. "Make yourself comfortable."

Cindy lit a cigarette. It wasn't until he reached for his ashtray, pulling it from the dashboard for her use, that she noticed his hands. They were white, soft, and clean, definitely not the hands of a cowboy.

Cindy figured she just might be in trouble. As she replaced her cigarettes and lighter in her bag, she pulled out a small gun and slid it into her coat pocket. If the son-of-a-bitch thought he was going to get some, he could think again. There were plenty of available women in the city, if a man wanted that.

Greg had given her this gun for her birthday, years ago.

So far, she'd never had the need to use it, except for practicing at the firing range. She hoped she wouldn't have to use it today, but she wasn't going to hesitate even for a second if it came down to where she had to use it or be hurt.

"Take the next exit," she said, and then gave a mental groan as he ignored the direction. This was it, then. It would be the first time she shot or maybe even killed a man, but Cindy figured there had to be a first time for everything. "You missed the turn-off."

"I know a shortcut," he said, without a hint of emotion. "Don't worry."

The bastard was cool, she thought, too cool, too confident, only he shouldn't have been. Cindy knew there were no shortcuts. She'd lived in this area all her life, and there was only one road to Warrington.

"Stop the car," she said.

Henry only turned to her and frowned. "I told you . . ."

"I know what you told me. Only there ain't no short-cuts to Warrington. Stop the car."

Henry laughed. "I guess you found me out."

"I guess I did," she returned, and then a second later, moaned at the unexpected blow to her face. Cindy hadn't seen it coming, and it stunned her into silence. That was a mistake; she should have been on guard. She should have been expecting something.

He hit her again, and even as the car went calmly down the highway, he twisted her arm behind her back as he cursed into her face. "If you know what's good for you, you won't fight me. I won't hurt you if you don't fight me."

I won't hurt you? What did he think he was doing now? Cindy figured had she been anybody else, she'd have been as good as dead. But Cindy was no weak, simpering miss. She'd been knocked around for most of her life, until she'd met Greg. Greg had shown her that a woman wasn't supposed to just stand there and take the abuse some men dished out. A woman always had two choices, to leave, or to fight back. Cindy couldn't leave at the moment, so she thought this was the time to fight back.

She reached into her pocket and pulled out the gun. Her teeth gritted together as she shoved it against his belly. "Let go."

Henry laughed in ridicule. Did she think him a fool? Was he supposed to think she had a gun and stop the car? He didn't think so.

He pulled her arm tighter, higher, ignoring not only her command, but her moan of pain.

Cindy mustered enough strength and courage to grit out, "Stop the car."

Henry laughed as he let go of her arm and reached for the painful fist pressing into his belly. They wrestled for a second and then Henry's eyes suddenly opened wide with surprise. She hadn't been lying; she *did* have a gun in her hand. A tiny gun, but a gun nonetheless. The tussle lasted only a moment as he tried to pull it from her. He shouldn't have done that. At least, not in this particular position, because the gun went off and Henry screamed as his hand came away with one less finger.

The car rolled to a stop as Henry grabbed his damaged and already throbbing hand and held it tightly to his chest. He was bleeding all over his coat, but he took no notice. All he could think was that his middle finger was missing and it was all her fault. He was going to kill her for this. With a wild growl he lunged for her, but she was already half out the door.

With his free hand he got hold of her arm and started to pull her back. "You bitch, you fuckin' bitch," he said, trying his best to hold on. But Cindy effectively put to an end any thoughts of revenge as she pulled the trigger one more time.

It was too much. Henry couldn't hold on, not while he was hurting like this, not while his head was pumping blood all over his face and neck. The second shot had grazed the top of his head, almost knocking him senseless. He blacked out, but only for a second, only for as long as it took for her to get free.

She rolled from the car, trembling, almost falling in her terror, perhaps, but holding the gun on him all the while.

"I'll kill you for this," Henry said, as he fought to stay awake.

"Not today, mister," Cindy said, just before she started to run down the highway.

Henry saw her wave down a car. Before the vehicle had a chance to slow down, Henry was doing sixty. He had to get out of here; he had to get back to the motel. He'd park the car around the back, just in case she thought to get his tag number. It would be safe there. He'd be safe there.

It would take him a little longer, now that he'd gotten hurt. He'd have to heal up again before he could finish up here, but he'd do it. Henry had every confidence that he'd finish all business before heading south.

"What the hell is going on? There hasn't been anything in more than a week," Mike barked into the phone. "He can't have just disappeared."

198

Jim Forster sighed from the other end of the line. "He's probably gone."

"Probably? Meaning, you don't know for sure?"

"Right."

Mike took a deep breath, straining for control of his temper. "Tell me."

"We found the car about thirty miles from here. It looks like he was making tracks."

"He wouldn't have just abandoned the car, would he? Out in the middle of nowhere?"

"He didn't. We found a woman's body in the trunk."

"Jesus."

"He probably has her car, only we don't know who she was or what kind of car she was driving."

"Son-of-a-bitch! That's just great, isn't it?"

"Mike, I understand you're worried for her, but I'm doing the best I can. The bastard stripped her. She had nothing, not even a laundry mark for identification. We sent her prints to Washington, but unless she was in the service or worked for some government agency, or had a record, we'll probably never know *who* she was."

"What about television? If you show her picture . . ."

"Yeah, we thought of that, but word came down from the big guys—the mayor doesn't want to scare anybody. Says the tourist trade will fall off if we let it out that there might be a serial killer in the area."

"Stupid goddamn bastard."

"Yeah, but he's the boss. What can I do?"

Mike would have loved to tell him exactly what he could do. Instead he said, "I need a favor."

"What kind?"

"Just a picture."

"Damn it, Mike, if anyone found out, I'd be out of a job."

"No one's going to find out. Just give it to me, all right?"

Jim breathed a weary sigh at the other end of the line. "All right. You going to Tommy's wedding?"

"Yeah."

"Don't come into the office. I'll get a copy to you then."

Later that night, Mike sat in his easy chair while Maggie lay on the couch. Brandy had positioned himself at her side, and with one hand she stroked his thick coat, her attention on the television. She laughed at something, but Mike hadn't been watching the movie. He was thinking. Thinking of how easy it had been to begin to love this woman. How content he felt, how wonderful it was having her here. They were growing closer every day. He wondered if she realized that fact.

He thought maybe she did. He hadn't missed her gentle smiles, nor the few times he'd caught her looking at him with a longing that had taught him the meaning of control. Mike wondered how he'd managed to keep his hands to himself during those moments.

How would she feel when it was time to leave? How would he? Mike shook his head. He didn't want to think about her leaving. Maybe, if things worked out the way he hoped, he'd never have to think about it.

He hadn't mentioned his phone call to Jim yet. He'd have to tell her, he knew, but he kept putting off the inevitable. He didn't want to see her afraid again. He didn't want to watch as she jumped at every innocent sound.

She'd been happy here, he thought. Happy and safe, especially during these last two weeks of silence, and now he was going to have to ruin it all.

Maggie sat up and grinned. "It's so ridiculous," she chuckled softly. "Safe sex, and they're both rolling over the bed wearing full-length condoms. Who thinks of this stuff?"

"Want some coffee?"

"Sure."

Maggie shoved her feet into her sneakers and then frowned as she realized his silence, realized she'd never seen him looking more serious. "What's the matter?"

"We have to talk."

"About what?"

"You and your being here."

"Oh." Maggie looked at him for a long moment before she thought she'd figured out the problem. She swallowed the sudden lump in her throat. She'd known, of course, that she couldn't stay here forever. It shouldn't have come as such a shock that he wanted her to leave. Just because she felt . . . Maggie wasn't sure exactly *what* it was she felt. And it no longer mattered. The man had a life to live, after all, and she was obviously cramping his style. She forced a smile as she tied her laces. "Look, I told you from the first that my leaving is no problem. My car works fine, and I can go tomorrow. All right?"

"No, it's not all right," he barked in return. "What the hell are you talking about?"

Maggie frowned. "What are *you* talking about? I thought you wanted me to leave."

Mike frowned as well. "Maggie, you know better than that."

"So what's the problem?"

Mike took a deep breath and released it slowly.

Maggie's smile was weak at best. "Should I wait for the coffee before we start this?" '

"A drink would be better, maybe."

Her eyes were suddenly dark with fear, her lips pinched into a tight line. "He's been calling again, hasn't he? And you didn't tell me?"

"No. No one has heard from him in weeks."

She breathed a sigh of relief. "Well, that's something, at least. Maybe he took off."

"The police think he might have."

"That's good."

"Only they're not sure."

She frowned. "And you don't think so?"

Mike didn't answer her question. "They found Chris's car."

"Where?"

"About thirty miles from here, in a rest area."

Mike cut off her next question with, "There was a woman's body in the trunk."

"Oh, my God."

"Yeah."

"Why wasn't it in the papers?"

"Because the idiot we call mayor doesn't want to scare away tourists next year."

"What?" she asked, as if the explanation had been so ludicrous she couldn't possibly have heard right.

"That's exactly what I said."

Maggie smiled, knowing he wouldn't have said anything half so mild. "I can't believe this. The mayor is suppressing news? Doesn't he care about the welfare of his people?"

"Apparently he cares more for the welfare of his pocket. He owns a dude ranch about twenty minutes north of my place. If people find out that there's a lunatic on the prowl, his business will fall off."

"I'd like to see him fall off. A mountain, maybe." Maggie sighed. The whole thing was impossible. There was a murderer out there somewhere and all the mayor was worried about was next year's business.

Mike smiled at the comment, knowing by the way she said it that she didn't mean a word of it. Too bad he couldn't say the same for himself. At the moment, he'd like nothing better than to get his hands on the jerk.

"What are you going to do?"

"Well, what I was thinking was, maybe you could do something."

"What?"

"Jim is going to give me her picture." Mike frowned. "I'm not allowed to say how I got it." He shrugged. "Anyway, I was thinking maybe we could drive down to Ellington and you could go on TV and ask if anyone knows her. There was no identification on her. The cops don't have a clue as to who she is."

Maggie gasped. "Oh, my God! What's the matter with me? I haven't been thinking at all." It took only a second for Maggie to understand how her instincts as a reported had been temporarily inhibited. She'd been traumatized, terrified, and it had taken a little time for her to take her life back into her own hands.

She laughed out loud. "I'm not only going to put her picture on television, Mike, I'm going to tell everyone who will listen exactly what happened to her, me, and the Jacksons, and Mrs. Murphy as well."

She grinned and said very softly, "The power of the press is scary, sometimes. The cops won't like it much. They'll be a public outcry, but we're going to get this bastard, and your mayor might find himself out of politics come the next election."

Mike laughed.

"We'll leave Sunday morning."

"We? You mean you're coming with me?"

"Of course. Did you think I'd let you travel alone with that maniac out there?"

A few minutes later Maggie was in the kitchen making coffee when Mike came up behind her. She jumped a little as his arm slid around her waist. "You're not afraid anymore, are you?"

"No. Not here, not with you."

Mike hadn't been sure about touching her. He'd been wanting to touch her for a long time, but wasn't absolutely positive that his advances would be accepted. He smiled as she leaned back against him a bit. The softness of her voice gave him courage to tighten his hold. She was measuring the coffee into the pot. "You made me lose count."

"Do you remember what happened the last time I held you in my arms?"

Maggie's chuckle was low, delicious. "I'm not likely to forget it anytime soon."

"No?"

"Well, not within the next hundred years or so."

"I've been sort of thinking the same thing."

Maggie nodded, her hair rubbing against his chin. When the coffeepot was plugged in, she twisted gently out

204

of his arms, but didn't move so far away that he couldn't have touched her again. He made the attempt, but she said, "We've got things to discuss first."

"What kinds of things?"

"Well, it's an important step, don't you think?"

"Maybe the most important thing that will ever happen to either of us. Falling in love usually is."

Maggie bit her bottom lip. "Do you love me already?"

"I think so."

"And you wouldn't be interested in a short, sort of light affair?"

Mike's dark eyes darkened even more. Maggie wondered how he did that. "Just checking." She bit her lip again and Mike could only wish he was the one doing the biting. "Are you interested in an affair of any kind?"

"No."

"So where does that leave us?"

"Married."

"Fine, but what about me?"

"What about you? If I'm married, you'll be married too."

"Married to a kitchen?" She shook her head. "It's not enough."

Her mouth dropped open a little, as if his words had just sunk in. "Did you just ask me to marry you?"

"It appears I did."

"Did you mean it?"

Mike grinned. "Maggie, I rarely say anything I don't mean."

"Are you always this romantic?"

"You're the one who won't let me touch you."

"Oh."

Mike laughed.

205

"What was I talking about?"

"About us getting married."

"Oh, yeah. You were marrying me, and I was marrying a kitchen . . . I remember."

"Are you telling me no? That you won't give up your career?"

"Will you sell the ranch and move to Colorado?"

"To start all over again? Maggie, do you realize how hard I've worked?"

"No harder than I have. You can't become an anchor on the evening news by applying for the job. It takes years of working and waiting."

"And you want it?"

Maggie shrugged. "I want something."

"Maybe you could work around here."

"As a reporter? Sure, I could report that Mr. Connor's cows were seen in the northern pasture of the Stanford ranch. I could say a few feet of fence fell down and . . ."

"We could work something out, Maggie, if we tried."

"God, I hope so. I won't be happy if I have to leave here, and I won't be happy if I stay."

"You don't like it here?"

"I love it here, only I'm not a rancher. This could be my home; it couldn't be my life."

"Let's take things one step at a time, all right?"

Maggie nodded.

"First, we go back to Ellington and take care of business."

"And then?"

"And then, I don't know for sure, but it will work out. I'll do anything I have to do make sure it does."

"Ellington is only a hard day's drive from here. I could

make it in about twelve hours, I think. That means it would take only a few hours by plane, and I could come home every weekend."

"And what about during the week?"

"During the week?" Her eyes twinkled with mischief. "During the week, we could have phone sex."

Mike laughed. "Just what I always wanted, a long-distance wife."

"You said you'd do anything to make sure it works."

"And I will. Let's try to think of something else."

There was a long moment of silence before he asked, "What are you doing?"

"I'm thinking."

"You could think in my arms, couldn't you?"

"Not about my career."

Mike's eyes widened with interest. "No? What would you be thinking about?"

"I'd be thinking about the things I wanted to do to you."

"What kind of things?"

"I probably shouldn't tell you."

"Why?"

"Because if I told you, you'd want me to do it."

"No, I wouldn't.

"Yes, you would."

"Go ahead and try it. You'll see."

"All right. If you held me in your arms . . ."

"Like this?"

Maggie shot him a hard look as she suddenly found herself pressed against him, his arms around her waist. "Yeah, like this."

"Go on."

"As I was saying, if you held me in your arms, I'd want to touch you."

"Where?"

"Your lips, for instance. I'd like to touch your lips very much."

Mike swallowed. "What else?"

"Your jaw and neck. Your chest and belly."

Maggie felt him shudder against her. "God, don't stop there."

"I'd want to touch you everywhere. I've wanted to touch you for a long time."

"I know, I caught you looking."

Maggie smiled and allowed her body to soften against his. "Did you? You didn't say anything."

"I know. I was waiting for you to be ready. Umm, is there a special place where you want to touch me the most?"

"Yes."

Mike swallowed. His heart was pounding, his voice hardly above a whisper, when he asked, "Where?"

"In the kitchen."

Mike laughed and then pressed his forehead against hers. "This is the sexiest conversation I've ever had in my life. Forget phone sex. I'd never live through it."

Maggie laughed.

"You know you're driving me crazy, don't you?"

"You don't look crazy."

"I am inside."

"Should we call the doctor?"

"He can't give me what I need."

"Can I?"

"Yup."

"Maybe you could show me exactly what it is you need."

" 'Cause you might need it, too?"

"Because I definitely need it, too."

Mike brought her into his arms, holding her high against his chest. "Just one thing."

"What?" she asked, as he headed for his bedroom.

"Don't tell Abner." Mike sighed his disgust at the thought. "He's going to say, 'I told you, boy.' "

Maggie laughed. "I won't, but something tells me he just might notice on his own."

Chapter Thirteen

Maggie stepped out of the spare room where she still kept her clothes, wearing a light green silk jumpsuit. The loose top was gathered at the waist with a silver belt, her hair flowed softly around her shoulders, and watching her standing there in three-inch silver heels, Mike thought he'd never seen anything better in his life.

He'd known, of course, that she was full in the right places, slender in the rest, but she hadn't felt the need to let everyone know exactly how full or slender. And that green outfit hid nothing.

Maggie smiled at his slightly stunned expression. With her hands on her hips, her painted nails sort of tapping on a flat belly, she asked impatiently, "Well, how do I look?"

Mike swallowed. "Ah, maybe we shouldn't go."

Maggie's smile turned into a frown. "You don't like it?"

"I like it too much, and so will everyone else."

Maggie laughed. "You're not going to be one of those possessive, jealous husbands, are you?"

"You mean you're going to marry me?"

"Of course. What kind of question is that?"

"Well, you never really answered me."

"That's because you never really asked me."

"But you're going to marry me anyway?"

Maggie sauntered up to where he stood and with a wicked look in her eyes said, "Try and stop me."

Mike chuckled a low, silky sound as he wrapped her into his arms. He hadn't imagined that he'd be lucky enough to love again. He hadn't imagined that the second time would be better than the first. He was nuzzling his lips to the side of her neck, enjoying the feel of her, when he frowned and said, "Ah, honey?"

"What?"

"The back of this thing is missing some material."

Maggie laughed and spun out of his arms, turning this way and that for his inspection. She shot him a glance and grinned. If she thought he looked stunned before, it was nothing compared to how he looked now. He just stood there, frozen. "I'd ask you if you like it, but your eyes look sort of glazed, and I don't think you can really see it."

"I can see it, all right. And my eyes look like that 'cause your back is naked. And it looks like you're not wearing a bra."

"I am, and it's supposed to be."

"To your waist?"

Maggie laughed.

"You're not dancing with anyone but me," he announced.

She laughed again. "Why?"

" 'Cause there's only one place a man can put his hands without touching skin, and I'll kill the first son-of-a-bitch who touches your ass."

"Mike," she said in warning.

He bit his bottom lip, knowing the answer to his question before he asked. "I couldn't convince you to change into something else, could I?"

"Like what?"

"Like jeans and a shirt?"

Her gaze told of the absurdity of his request. "Wear jeans and a shirt, to a wedding?"

"All right, what about just a shirt?"

"Just a shirt? I think that would show more than . . ."

He cut off her teasing with, "What about wearing a shirt under that?"

"You're adorable, and I love you."

"All right, you can wear it."

"Thanks," she said dryly, as she shot him a look that told him she had every intention of doing just that, no matter what his opinion.

"I just hope you still think I'm adorable with a black eye."

Maggie, with his help, shrugged into her cleaned coat. The fur lining felt luxurious against her bare back. "Why? Do you expect to get one soon?"

Mike nodded as he guided her out the door. "Yup."

"Are you going to tell me why?"

"Maggie, cowboys don't get together much."

"So?"

"So, when they do, they're apt to get a little wild."

"And?"

"And there's bound to be plenty of drinking."

"Mike," she said, losing a bit of patience as she waited for him to get to the point.

"Someone's going to get drunk. And drunk usually means stupid."

"Stupid how?"

"Like hitting on you."

Maggie laughed. "Don't worry. I can take care of myself."

"I hope you can take care of me while you're at it, 'cause I expect I'll suffer a bit for protecting my own."

"You're so cute."

Mike breathed a sigh. "Yeah, I'm cute all right."

The VFW hall was bursting at the seams. There was hardly a place to stand, never mind an empty table. Apparently this was a first-come, first-sit type of affair.

Maggie was surprised at the number of people. Wyoming was huge, but it had always appeared so uninhabited. She could only wonder where all these people had come from.

To her relief, she found two seats saved for her and Mike at Abner's table. Miriam and Jake sat there as well as two other couples she'd never met. Maggie thought she would enjoy herself tonight, especially since she liked to dance and the music, although mostly western and coming from a jukebox, was loud and clear.

The atmosphere was festive, the bride lovely, the groom, although they had just arrived, already eager to be alone with his new wife. Maggie figured Ginny's father clung to some old-fashioned moral codes. The girl looked hardly old enough to be out of school, yet he had forced a marriage simply because he'd found her in a compromising position.

The girl had lost her chance to further her education, to become something other than a wife and mother. Maggie figured being a housewife was fine for some. Miriam, for instance seemed to thrive, loving her life-style, her husband, and her family, but changing diapers, cooking, and cleaning would never be enough for Maggie.

She wanted and needed a home, a man, one particular

man, in fact, and maybe children in the not-too-distant future, but she needed more as well.

Maggie knew had Ginny been her daughter, she'd have allowed the girl more options.

It didn't take more than a few minutes for Maggie to notice the woman at the bar. She was attractive, her hair long and mussed into a sexy style, her gaze coming often to their table, lingering, in Maggie's opinion, just a moment too long on Mike.

From her peripheral vision, Maggie realized Mike had noticed the attention. He nodded and Maggie knew this woman had once been special to him. Oddly enough, especially for Maggie, she felt a flicker of jealousy. She'd never been jealous before, and the emotion caught her by surprise.

A few minutes later, Mike asked her to dance. On the crowded dance floor, she allowed his possessive embrace, delighting in the feel of him against her.

"Who is she?"

Mike did not pretend ignorance. "I used to see her."

"I like that," Maggie said, growing soft in his arms.

"What?"

"That you *used* to see her."

Mike chuckled as he nuzzled his lips to her temple. "Jealous?"

"I never thought I was the type."

"You mean you've never been jealous before?"

Maggie shook her head.

"There's no need to be. I won't be seeing her again."

"Sure?"

"Positive."

Mike did not further the subject, but held her a bit

more tightly to his chest. "Are you sure you're wearing a bra?"

"Yes. Why?"

" 'Cause you feel so soft, so good. I can't wait to get this thing off you."

It wasn't until the end of the evening that Mike's earlier prediction proved true. During the party that followed the wedding, many men gave Maggie hungry looks, but she paid them little attention. She knew she looked good, and a good-looking woman usually caught a man's eye. The fact of the matter was, Maggie wasn't interested in any man but the one she was with. She was having a good time, talking and laughing with Miriam and Jake, as well as Abner, with Mike at her side.

And Mike was even beginning to relax. As it turned out, he'd relaxed a bit too soon.

Even though he had made his intentions clear from the first with evil glares toward any man who showed the slightest interest in his woman, one of the hands from the Dobson ranch came over to ask Maggie for the last dance. The man was obviously drunk, for he couldn't stand still, but weaved forward and back at an alarming degree while awaiting her response. Maggie thought there was a good chance he'd fall over with the slightest touch.

Maggie did not dance with drunks under any circumstances, and she had no intention of following him out to the dance floor. She shook her head and smiled. "Sorry. I'm saving the last one for Mike."

"Take a walk, Charlie," Mike felt bound to interject. Maggie thought his tone as well as his words totally unnecessary and glared at the unasked-for interference.

"No need to act like that, Mike. I only asked her for a dance, not to walk out back for a little fuckin'."

There was a unified gasp as everyone at the table tensed at the easily spoken obscenity. Tensed, because men in this part of the country did not talk like that when a lady was present; because Charlie had, everyone realized the insult. Tensed, because they knew what was in store, especially since Mike and Maggie had stepped out back for a few minutes of privacy and maybe a kiss or two during the evening. The man was clearly implying he wouldn't be unhappy if he had his turn at her. It was a dangerous implication and had he been sober, he might have thought twice about his lack of sense.

A pulse hammered in Mike's brain as he took immediate offense. He was trying to be on his best behavior. He didn't want Maggie to think he was some kind of barbarian. It was for that reason alone that he forced himself to ignore the taunt and smiled. "Goodnight, folks," he said to those at the table, and shoved Charlie aside and backward, into the lap of some unsuspecting matron. The woman yelped her surprise and her husband, Maggie assumed it was her husband, instantly put the drunk from her lap with a mighty and well-placed blow to Charlie's jaw, just before Mike whisked her from the VFW hall.

Maggie sat in his Jeep, laughing, as Mike started the engine.

"What's so funny?"

"You. You wanted to hit him. Why didn't you?"

He looked at her with something like shock. "Did you want me to?"

Maggie shrugged. "He deserved it, I think."

"Then why did you look at me like that?"

"Because I hadn't asked for your help at that point."

216

"Damn." Mike spun the Jeep's wheels as he headed out of the parking lot for home. He figured he owed Charlie one, but he knew it would have to wait. "I wish I'd known."

Maggie unhooked her seatbelt and slid closer to his side, buckling herself again in the middle belt. "What? That I can enjoy a good fight, as long as no one gets hurt?"

Mike looked straight ahead. "I'm going to love you for a long time, Maggie."

"I hope that means forever," she whispered, as she kissed him just below his ear.

"It means for longer than forever."

"Let's park," she said, as she placed her hand on his thigh and began to slowly slide it toward one particular interesting objective.

Mike figured part of the reason why he was so tempted was that you never wanted to do it so bad until you *couldn't* do it. Only that wasn't completely true. He would have wanted to do it in any case. "The guys behind us will wonder what the hell we're doing."

Maggie had forgotten about the state troopers who had followed them to the wedding and were now behind them on their way home. She laughed. "I think they'll know what we're doing. Maybe we'd better get home first."

"Don't take your hand away."

"No?" she teased. "Think you can drive if I keep it there?"

"Honey, I could climb a mountain if you kept it there."

Mike walked on shaking legs as he followed Maggie into the house. Brandy greeted them with a bark and a happy wag of his tail before returning to the fire and dropping down beside it.

"I don't know how I made it home. Everything is a blur. And I'll have to throw these pants out."

"Why?"

" 'Cause Otis, at the dry cleaner's, will know what the stains mean."

Maggie chuckled at his words as she hung up her coat and watched him do the same.

"You told me to touch you."

Mike grinned. "I know. And thank you."

"You're welcome." Maggie laughed.

"What are you laughing at?"

"We sound so polite."

"You mean we don't sound like we've just had sex while I was driving home?"

"We didn't, exactly."

"That's because I couldn't reach you through your pants."

"When are you going to marry me?"

"How's as soon as we get a license sound?"

"That sounds good."

They hadn't moved out of the hallway. He just stood there staring at her as if he couldn't believe that this woman was his. Maggie grinned. "You think we should sit down?"

"What I think is, I'd like you to pull that thing to your waist. And then I'm going to do to you what you did to me in the car."

Maggie slowly did as he'd asked and listened to his gasp of surprise. "You said you were wearing a bra."

"I lied."

Mike breathed out on a sigh. "It's a good thing I didn't know."

"Why?"

" 'Cause I probably couldn't have stopped myself from doing this." He reached for her then, cupping her softness in his hands.

They were stretched out on the floor before the fire, relaxed and a little sleepy, now that their bodies were temporarily satisfied.

"Are you warm?"

"Mmm," Maggie murmured, as he played with her breast.

"How long do you think we'll stay in Ellington?"

"How long can you stay?"

"A week, maybe."

Maggie had been on the phone with her station manager for half the morning. They were set to run a series on her story. Crews were already on their way to Gray Bluff, ready to interview the police and the mayor, to shoot footage of the area, to film Chris's car and anything else that might add to her story. "A week should do it."

"Suppose they don't catch him anytime soon?"

"Then I'll go back and run the series again. Hopefully, I won't have any more murders to report."

"You know, I was thinking."

"About?"

"About the fact that you work in Ellington and I live here."

"And you've come up with a brilliant solution," Maggie teased.

"Maybe."

"What?"

"Suppose you give up your job as anchor."

She shot him a scowling look. "Yeah, that's brilliant, all right."

"I'm not finished. Say you gave up your job as anchor and took another that didn't involve being there every night. You could do, what do they call them, spots, or something. You know, series like the one you're about to do.

"They wouldn't all have to be about murder, of course. You could do them on different topics, say the homeless, or child molesters, or sexual harrassment." Mike shrugged. "Things like that."

Maggie lay there for a long, silent moment, wondering why she hadn't thought of it herself. The truth was, her job wasn't the most important thing in her life. All she wanted was to work in the field of reporting. It didn't have to be every night. And it didn't have to be as anchor.

She didn't have to think long before she knew it was a wonderful idea. She had a gut feeling that her station manager would agree, and if he didn't, maybe she could work in Rock Springs. The city was closer than Ellington, and managing the distance between the city and home would be easier.

Of course, she'd have to travel some, but that wouldn't be all the time. Mostly she could work at home, with a fax machine and a modem for her computer, and travel to Ellington only when the series aired. Maybe, on occasion, they could even tape her at home.

She was excited at the thought, but kept the emotion to herself as she asked, "What made you think of that?"

"The fact that I want to keep you as close to me as possible. What do you think?"

"I think you're wonderful."

"I know, but what do you think about my idea?"

Maggie laughed as she rolled him to his back. She sat, straddling his hips, grinning at his look of surprise. "I think it's almost as wonderful as you."

He was sick, sicker than he'd ever been in his life. And it was all her fault. He was going to get her. As soon as he was better, he'd make her suffer for this. God, he couldn't wait.

The drugstore had delivered bandages, salve, and asprin, but he couldn't go to the doctor, not with these kinds of wounds. A doctor always reported gunshot wounds, didn't they?

His hand was killing him. He thought maybe it was infected. It was red and swollen around his missing finger.

Maybe he'd die from the infection. Henry shrugged aside the thought. He didn't care much if he died or not. All he really cared about was seeing that she paid for what she'd done.

Maggie sighed at the picture of the dead woman. Douglas, KFLI's new station manager, was going to give her a hard time about this. The woman had been badly abused, and Douglas wouldn't like the idea of putting so gruesome a picture on the air.

Only Maggie knew they had no choice. There was no other way to identify her.

Once they managed to do that, they would know what kind of car she was driving. Once the newspapers picked up the story, the cops would have no choice but to follow up every lead and do their job without interference from some greedy, and worse yet, stupid, politician.

They were just ready to leave when Jim showed up.

"Anything happen?" Mike asked, before Jim got a chance to say hello.

"No, not yet."

"Then why . . ."

"I'm here because I got an idea."

"Yeah? What kind of idea?"

"Maggie's going to do the series, right?"

Mike had told Jim about Maggie's intentions last night at the wedding. "So?"

"So, I was thinking . . . it might make Collins mad."

"That would be tough, wouldn't it?"

"I mean, mad enough to come after her."

"He'll never get near her," Mike said, and all three knew he meant it, if he had to put his life on the line.

"I was thinking maybe we could set a trap. Let him think she'd be easy to get to."

"You mean, use her for bait." Mike shook his head. "Not a chance."

"Mike," Maggie said, unhappy at the fact that he was making this decision for her.

"What? Are you saying you want to do it?"

"No, but we didn't hear what Jim has in mind."

Jim shrugged. "I didn't have any real plan. It was just an idea."

"Maybe an idea worth considering."

"Maggie, damn it!" Mike suddenly roared.

Maggie ignored his building anger. "You said it yourself, Mike. Suppose the cops don't catch him? Then what? Will I have to live the rest of my life in fear, with body-guards following me everywhere I go?"

Mike knew there was no sense in arguing with her, at least, not at the moment. They didn't have the time,

222

anyway, not if he wanted to make it to Ellington anytime soon. "Get in the car, Maggie. We're late."

Maggie shot him an angry look and then said to Jim, "We'll talk about it when I get back."

Maggie noticed that the state troopers following them pulled over to the side of the road as they approached the state line. She felt suddenly apprehensive at the thought of traveling the rest of the way alone and then ridiculed her feelings. Henry was nowhere around. He couldn't know they were heading back to Ellington.

Besides, she was with Mike. Nothing was going to happen . . . nothing at all.

They got to Ellington and her apartment in just under ten hours. Maggie was exhausted, not from the long, hard ride so much as from the silence she'd been forced to endure. Mike was angry—furious was probably closer to the truth—and she hadn't gotten him to say more than ten words during the entire trip.

They entered her apartment and she called the station even before taking off her coat. "Yeah," she said to someone, "I have it. Are they there?"

"Good. I'll see you first thing in the morning."

Mike placed their bags against a wall in the living room. "Is who where?" he asked.

"So, you haven't forgotten how to talk, after all. I was beginning to wonder."

Mike allowed her a scowling look and she grunted, "You know, I was thinking, strong, silent types leave a lot to be desired."

Mike gritted his teeth as he said, "The reason I haven't been talking is because you would have gotten even more angry if you'd heard what I had to say. And I'm waiting until we get married for that." And before she got a chance to respond, he repeated, "Is who where?"

"For what? To curse at me? I've heard you curse before. The crew, are they in Gray Bluff?"

"No, I'm not going to curse at you."

"Then what?"

"Nothing."

"Order me? Is that it? Do you think you can order me to listen to you because I'm your wife? You might as well get this straight: a wife is a man's partner, not his possession."

"Somebody's got to make you listen. You're nuts."

"Yeah, maybe. I was going to marry you, wasn't I?"

His eyes narrowed and he said very calmly, "You're still going to marry me."

"I don't think so."

Mike ran his fingers through his hair and sort of collapsed on her couch. He leaned forward and buried his face in his hands. "Maggie, don't do this to me, please."

"Don't do what to you?"

"Put yourself in danger. I couldn't stand it if I lost you."

For the first time, Maggie realized the depth of fear that had been behind his anger. Her voice softened. "You're not losing me."

"You can't guarrantee that, especially if you listen to Jim's stupid plans."

"You don't know that they're stupid."

"Anything that involves putting you in danger is stupid."

"All right."

He raised his gaze to hers. "All right, what?"

Maggie shrugged out of her coat and went to him. She

224

sat on him, straddling his legs as she faced him with a grin. "I'll marry you."

"That's not what I want to hear right now. Besides, I already knew that."

"And I won't go along with anything Jim might come up with."

"Swear?"

"I swear."

His arms moved around her, pulling her tightly against him with a touch of desperation, Maggie thought. "When did you decide that?"

"I never said I would. I said I'd talk about it."

"Then what were we fighting about?"

"You, trying to order me around."

"Oh, God," he said, almost crushing her against him. "I swear, I'll never do it again. Just promise me you'll stay with me forever."

"You mean, I'm supposed to ignore the tendency you have of insisting on your own way?"

He rubbed his face against her breasts. "Well, maybe you could kind of overlook that."

"And your temper? Should I overlook that as well?"

"I'd appreciate it greatly, ma'am."

"Mmm, I thought you might. There's only one thing."

"What?"

"The silent treatment. One more of those and I'm out the door. You want to fight, then fight. I can take anything you dish out. Anything but silence."

"I'm sorry, Maggie. I swear to God, I'll never do it again. I'll never stop talking. I'll talk until you're sick of hearing me. I'll yell, scream, if I have to. When we fight, you'll never . . ."

"Shut up."

Mike allowed her a slow, lazy grin. "Do you usually change your mind that fast?"

"Kiss me."

"Yes, ma'am."

Henry moaned in his fever. He was so sick. So very sick, but his mother was there. She'd help him, he knew. She'd help him . . . only . . .

she was licking his cock and laughing. "My little boy's cock, his puny little cock." God, but he hated her. Hated the nights when there was no one to share her bed and she came to him.

But he hated her the most on nights like these. Nights when one of her friends stood there drunk, watching the things she did to him. Laughing at the things she said. Henry looked at the man's dick. God, he was so big. Would his ever get that big?

He swore he'd kill her someday. He'd kill her for holding onto the man's dick, for kissing it and turning to laugh, comparing it to his. He'd kill her and kill her.

How could he hate her more? He couldn't, except for the times she sucked him deep into her mouth. He didn't want to like it, not with his own mother; but he did. He couldn't help but like it.

He'd hate her afterward, though. He'd hate her more than ever after she was done with him.

But he'd fixed her. In the end, he'd fixed them both. They were drunk again, lying in his bed, sleeping, tired after what they had done. The man had raped him, and while he was caught up against the giant, unable to fight the superior strength, his mother had made him come again. She'd laughed at his cries of pain, enjoying his humiliation. Sprawled on his bed, her hair a mess, her makeup smeared, she'd said, "Henry, we were only having some fun. Have fun, Henry."

He'd waited for them to sleep, and then he'd gotten the gas tank from the garage.

They never felt the liquid splash over them. They never knew they were about to die. He'd remember the screams. Sometimes, alone in the night, he heard them still. And then the fire was on him, his mother kneeling again before him, his dick in her mouth, and the fire from her caught. His body was burning. Burning mostly on his cock. No, God, no. It couldn't burn that. She'd said it was small, but now it would be gone. Now he wouldn't have one at all.

Henry screamed and opened his eyes at the sound of his cry. He looked down at his cock and sighed his relief. It was there. They hadn't burned it off.

He didn't want to sleep again, but he had to. He hadn't dreamt about her in a long time, hadn't even thought about her in years, but since he'd started the killing, her face had been there, laughing at him, delighting in his pain.

And now, because he was sick, he dreamt about her every time he closed his eyes. In one fashion or another, sleep brought the dreams. He didn't want to suffer through them again. But his body was feverish and he needed sleep. Needed it more than he needed to hide from the horror of the dreams.

Chapter Fourteen

Mike watched from a darkened corner of the studio as Maggie finish up her segment, the second night of her series. "Remember, this began as stalking, but a sample of the semen found on the Jackson's bedroom floor matches the semen that had been spread over the dead woman. There's one murderer here, and he fits the pattern of a serial killer. According to his own words and his victim's, he enjoys watching the terror, listening to the screams. If you watched last night, you heard Doctor Black. The victim's fear gives him a sense of strength and confidence, of sexual excitement that he can't get in any other way. So be very, very careful. This is Maggie Smith reporting for KFLI, Channel 6 News."

The camera lights went out and another camera moved to the anchorwoman who'd taken Maggie's place. It was obvious that the woman was badly shaken. She cleared her throat a number of times before directing the camera to pick up the dead woman's picture. "Remember what Maggie said, please. If you know this woman, or have any information that could help, call your local police."

They went to commercial and Maggie was trapped behind the desk as a dozen old friends came to hug her and offer their sympathy, as well as congratulations on a job well done. "Damn it, Mag," an older woman, Jennifer something, who appeared to be in charge of production, said, and gave her a shake and then a tight hug. "Why didn't you say something?"

"You couldn't have done anything, Jen."

"I could have been there for you."

"Thanks."

"You taking care of her?" the woman asked Mike as he stepped closer to the two, his arm sliding around Maggie's waist.

"I aim to."

Jennifer smiled as she looked Mike over. "He looks like he can handle himself."

"He can." Maggie winked before she finished with, "Only he thinks he can handle me, too."

"Can you?"

"I'm learning how."

"Good."

The woman kissed Maggie and then yelled to the set and crew, "Ready people. Five, four, three . . ."

Maggie, with Mike's arm around her waist, walked out of the studio.

"You mind telling me why I'm paying these kinds of prices for something you can cook a hundred times better?"

They were sitting in a quiet restaurant, one perhaps too luxurious for Mike's taste. The atmosphere was all right, he thought, but the food was barely mediocre.

Maggie smiled at his question. "Because you love me and wanted to see me relax over a nice meal. A meal I didn't have to cook."

"Is that why?"

Maggie nodded.

"It's a good thing you told me. I was wondering."

"The next time, you can tell me how to do it and I'll cook."

"Is it that bad?"

"No, I just can't see paying out good money for this stuff. And I wouldn't have to pay if you or I cooked."

"Oh, you'd have to pay, one way or another."

Mike grinned, for her tone had turned decidedly provocative. He ran his fingers over the cool, wet wineglass. Maggie's gaze moved to the glass and didn't miss the way he slipped one finger over the edge, into the wine, and then brought the finger to his mouth. "That sounds interesting. What kind of payment are you looking for?"

Maggie cleared her throat. "Well, I'm wearing a skirt tonight. Why don't we leave the payment to your imagination?"

Mike chuckled at the suggestive remark. "You're blushing."

"No, I'm not. What I'm doing is imagining a payback."

"You know, I was thinking," he teased. "Maybe we should wait on this sort of thing until we're married."

Maggie smiled at his comment. "Odd that you didn't think about waiting the other night in your car."

"Yeah, well I might have had a lapse in common sense that night."

"It's a good thing you thought about it now, though. Of course, that would mean everything would have to wait."

Mike eyed her suspiciously. "What do you mean, everything?"

"Just what I said. No sex of any kind."

"I didn't mean it."

She laughed, a rich, deep, and sexy sound. "I know you didn't."

"Let's get out of here."

"I should have worn boots. That way, no one would have known I wasn't wearing pantyhose."

They were sitting in her living room with the television on, but neither was paying much attention to the movie. They were sipping at glasses of wine while Mike investigated a naked leg with some real enthusiasm.

"No one saw a thing."

"Oh yeah? Then why were those two men looking at me like that?"

" 'Cause you're gorgeous and men will always look at you."

His hand moved under her skirt and he said, as if he'd just discovered the fact, "Maggie, you're not wearing anything under here."

"That's because a man I know tore them off and put them in my coat pocket."

"That was very smart of him, don't you think?"

"I think they cost too much to tear off."

"I'll pay for them."

"You've got that right," she said, as his mouth dropped to her leg and followed the direction of his hands.

* * *

"And you shot him?"

They were still on the couch. The movie that had been on was over, and another was beginning.

"I shot at him. I hit the ceiling and the wall. I don't know who was more scared. He dived under the bed, and I didn't stop shaking for hours." Maggie chuckled. "Even in my terror, I could hear him praying, swearing he'd never drink again."

"Does he still live here?"

"I don't know. I left for home a few days later."

Mike grinned as he played with her breasts. "I'll bet he's not drinking anymore."

Maggie leaned closer and ran her hand from his chest down his body. "And I'll bet you could do it again."

Mike laughed. "Are you sure? We did it three times already."

"So it wouldn't matter if we did it once more."

"God, I'm going to love being married to you."

"I talked to Douglas about your idea."

"What did he say?"

"That it had possibilities."

"I thought so."

"He's going to talk it over with the brass. Mrs. Harris owns the station. The final decision is hers."

"What's tomorrow's piece about?"

"Mrs. Murphy."

"Don't you need her permission?"

"We already have it. The camera crew is out there right now. I'll see what they have tomorrow and work with it."

"What am I supposed to do while you're working?"

232

"Cook dinner?" she suggested.

"We'll have to have steak, then. It's the only thing I can cook."

"Steak is fine." She gave a lusty yawn, and then, "I'm tired."

"I see. Now that you've used me, you want to sleep."

Maggie laughed as he cuddled her close to his side. "I could be talked into using you again."

"Lady, you'll be a young widow, if you keep this up."

After three nightly newscasts in Ellington, the series was picked up by most of the stations in the area and repeated. Only, having slept through the last five days, Henry Collins had no knowledge of it.

He still had a fever, but because of the asprins, felt better. His hand throbbed, but a few more asprins would take care of the worst of it.

He couldn't stay here any longer. He had to get some food, but most of all, he had to find himself a woman.

The dreams might have disgusted him, but they excited him as well, and after days of suffering through them, he had to find someone.

Henry left the motel room. His intent was first to find something to eat, only he saw her hitchiking and knew she'd be the next one. He pulled the car to the side of the road and rolled down the window. "Where are you headed?"

The girl was young. He didn't usually like young girls. It was women that he preferred. Women knew how to please a man. A woman would make him feel good again.

Henry shrugged. It didn't matter. She was available, and that was all that counted.

233

The girl got into his car and threw her bag in the back seat. She huddled before the heater, shivering as gusts of warm air flowed over her. "Thanks, mister," she said, and then, "I'm going to California, but I'll be satisfied if you get me anywhere out of this cold."

"California's a long way off."

"I know, but I want to be a model, and I'll never make it while living on my dad's farm."

"I guess you have to be where the action is."

The girl nodded. "My name is Mary, but I'm going to change it to 'Desiree.'" She smiled. "Don't you think Desiree is better than plain old Mary?"

"I like it."

"What happened to your hand?" she asked, noticing the bloodied bandage.

Henry was wearing his woolen hat again, so he knew she couldn't see the wound to the top of his head. "Got my finger caught while working on the engine."

"Gee, that's awful."

"Yeah, but it's only one finger, and I have nine more."

Mary laughed. "What's your name?"

"John," he said, and then wondered why he lied. She wasn't going to be in any shape to tell anyone what happened. Not after he finished with her. So it didn't make sense to lie about his name.

Henry shrugged, knowing it didn't matter. "You hungry?"

"Yeah," Mary said, as he pulled his car into the fast-food driveway. He was in the midst of ordering when Mary said, "Hey, look. There's Tony, my boyfriend." An instant later, she turned to Henry and grinned. "I've got to go. Thanks for the ride." And before he could stop her,

234

before he dared to stop her, she was out of the car and running toward a ratty old pickup parked in the lot.

Henry cursed as he watched her go and then shrugged, knowing he'd find another. Soon enough he'd have a woman just where he wanted her, just where all women belonged.

It took him longer than he'd expected, a lot longer. It was well into the night before he finally found a woman. She was standing outside a bar in the middle of the city. She leaned down to talk into his window as he pulled the car to a stop. "You need a ride?" he asked.

The woman grinned. She had ugly teeth, crooked and stained. "For fifty bucks, I'll ride just about anything you got."

Henry frowned at the sight of those teeth. He didn't know why, but they disgusted him. He almost pulled away, but thought better of the impulse as he remembered how long it had taken to find her. He didn't care what her teeth looked like. He just wouldn't look at her mouth.

Henry nodded and she got in the car. She was a dirty old whore, Henry thought. She smelled of body odor and sex. Henry wondered how a man could have touched her in that way. She was disgusting.

"You got a place?"

"I don't bring men to my place, honey. Let's go to your room."

Henry shrugged. What the hell did it matter? He was going to kill her, wasn't he? So what if she stank? Still, he might be able to enjoy himself a little first, if she used his shower.

Henry waited for the woman to finish her bath. She

called from the room's open door. "Want to join me, mister?"

"My name is Henry," he said, as he sat on the bed watching television and his love. He flicked the TV off. He didn't want her to see the whore he had in his room. He might not be faithful, but he didn't have to shove his unfaithfulness in her face, did he?

Henry stood at the bathroom doorway. Naked, he leaned against the door jamb and watched the whore soap herself. "You got nice tits," he said.

The whore laughed. "Why don't you come over here and play? I like doing it in a tub."

Henry didn't respond, except to say, "Hurry up." Then he turned and walked back into the bedroom.

The woman shrugged and came out of the tub. It didn't matter to her none the way a man wanted it. All she cared about was the fifty dollars in her purse. Damn, but this was fine. Much better than doing it in someone's car, or standing in the alley behind the bank, giving twenty-dollar blow jobs.

For a change, she'd be in bed. And lying on clean sheets would be a novelty.

The woman grinned as she stepped naked from the bathroom. As a fist contacted with her jaw, she staggered back and muttered, "Sweet Jesus," just before she fell to the floor and hit her head on the tiled floor. Perhaps it was a good thing she'd muttered God's name, for it was the last thing she ever said.

Henry cursed at the sight of the blood. The dirty bitch was bleeding all over his floor. A maid came in almost every day. He couldn't stay here now. He'd have to leave because of the stupid bitch.

Only not yet. He needed sex more than he'd ever

236

needed it in his life. And standing over her wasn't good enough. He forced himself to touch her. He didn't like to touch dead bodies much. The thought of having sex with a dead body caused him to gag. The body would immediately begin to decay, and that decay would get all over his dick. Henry shuddered at the thought. No, he didn't like touching dead bodies, but this one was warm. He could pretend she wasn't dead as long as she stayed warm.

How long did he have? How long did a body stay warm? He'd do it just this once. The fact was, he needed a woman bad, and standing over her, emptying his body into her mouth and eyes, wasn't enough. Not this time. This time he needed to be inside.

Henry studied the dead whore as he pulled his clothes on. It hadn't been bad at all. Maybe he'd been mistaken about using dead bodies. It was the dreams that had gotten him confused, he thought. The dreams when his mother had come to him, engulfed in flames. The sight of her jumping from the bed, screaming. Henry shuddered at the memory. He had screamed for her to die. He didn't want her to touch him, to make him catch on fire, too. Only she hadn't. She'd come for him, reaching out, screaming her agony as she'd tried to bring him with her to death.

The memory disgusted him. She had disgusted him, and he had allowed his fears to rob him of some real pleasure.

Henry thought of all the women he'd killed. Of all the times when he could have enjoyed himself and hadn't because of the fear. Things would change, now that he had discovered the truth of it. He'd enjoy them now, really enjoy them.

The television was on and his love was talking to him, soothing him, telling him not to be afraid, that she was waiting for him to come to her. He was tempted. He wanted to go right away, but he had to take care of Maggie first. The bitch had to die before he could begin a new life with his love.

And then he heard her voice.

Henry swung his gaze to the television, his mouth dropping open in shock as he saw her. He couldn't understand. How could she be on television? She was at the bastard's place, wasn't she? She was. Then how?

Henry sank to the edge of the bed and watched. She was talking about him, telling the world that his love for her was sick. How could she? How could she say those things? How could she do this to him?

His mind roared his hate and pain, and he curled into a ball like a wounded, whimpering animal. It took him a long time before he could think again. Before he knew that she was dirt, that she was lower than dirt. She was worse than his mother and deserved to die more than any other woman. She'd betrayed him, told the world about him, ridiculed him and his love.

Henry's eyes narrowed and his mouth tightened as he imagined killing her, imagined how she was going to beg for mercy. He'd get her for this; he'd get her if it was the last thing he ever did.

He wrapped his hand again and searched the room for his things, stepping over the woman's body a few times as he cleaned out the bathroom and threw his stuff into his bag.

He left her body where it was. It didn't matter anyway.

The maid would have found it first thing, even if he'd bothered to shove her into the tub. There was no sense in that.

Henry smiled as he pulled the car onto the highway, heading east and then south for Ellington, for her. It would be over soon, he thought. And once it was, he could get on with his life again. He could find his new love.

"If you want it that much, sweetheart, I swear, I'll work with you." He took a gasping breath and continued, "We'll go to California together."

At her smile, he said, "We'll get married. I'll work while you get your career started." He grinned down at her expression of delight. "And when you make it, I'll retire."

Mary Gladden breathed a sigh of happiness. Soon she'd have it all, and she wouldn't have to give up this man to get it.

Tony, her boyfriend and lover for the last year, rested full-length upon her naked body. They had just made love when Tony had come up with the idea of leaving his father's place and heading west with her. Tony knew there was no way that he could lose this woman.

"You can be my manager."

Tony grinned at the thought. "Yeah, I could."

The television lent the dark room its only light, and Mary glanced without thought toward the screen. A second later she frowned. "Tony, turn up the volume."

"Why?"

"Hurry up."

Tony did as she'd asked, and a woman's voice filled the

239

room as she held up a police artist's drawing. "If you've seen this man, call your local police."

Tony's gaze moved from the television to Mary's face and then back again. "Do you know him?"

"He gave me a ride the other day. Remember when I found you parked at Burger King?"

"Yeah. You sure it was him?"

"I think so. He has a beard now, but the eyes are exactly the same."

"He looks like a nut to me. Why did you get in his car?"

Mary shrugged. "We had that fight, remember? I wasn't thinking clearly."

"You mean you were on your way to California."

"I wouldn't have gone without you. I was just so pissed off." There was a moment of silence. "What do you think I should do?"

Tony shrugged. "If you're sure it's the same guy, you'd better call the police."

"But what can I tell them?"

"What kind of car was he driving?"

"A blue Pontiac, I think."

"Tell them that."

Mary reached for the phone.

Mike nodded to the guard at the studio door and stepped into a room filled with huge lights, cables, cameras, monitors, a few desks, and lots of milling people. Some worked at computers, others were on phones, still more stood in a friendly circle around Maggie. They were heading back to Gray Bluff, now that she'd completed the series. Mike's Jeep was filled with boxes of clothes and personal items Maggie had wanted to take with her. A moving company would be bringing the larger pieces, in particular, her desk and file cabinets, as well as a dining room table and chairs and a china closet that she'd inherited from her grandmother.

Mike grinned as he watched her talk to her associates and friends. She was moving to Gray Bluff permanently, only to come back on occasion. During those times, Mike would be with her, and for that purpose they would be keeping her apartment. At least, for the time being. They would be leaving the bed, couch, a few lamps, and enough utensils to cook up a quick meal.

Maggie swung her gaze to his as he snaked his arm around her waist, her eyes warm, her happiness obvious at the sight of him. Mike thought he liked the way she looked at him. Liked it just fine, in fact. "How did you know it was me?"

Maggie grinned. "I didn't."

His arm pulled her tighter against him, and she laughed. "Jen told me when you came in, and no one else touches me like you do."

"That's good to know. You ready?"

Maggie nodded and said her goodbyes. Ten minutes later, they were in his car, heading for home.

"I'll have to call Dad as soon as we get back. I never told him about any of this, and I just found out that the stations all the way from Chicago to California picked it up yesterday. He's sure to have seen something."

Mike nodded. "We're getting married Saturday."

"We are?"

"Yeah, I thought I'd make an honest woman out of you," he teased.

"That was very kind of you."

"You don't mind, do you?" Her tone told him she might have minded just a bit.

"It might have been nice to decide together, don't you think?"

"You were busy."

Maggie nodded, knowing she wanted nothing more than to marry this man, and the details of how and when were the least important of all. To Mike's relief, she smiled. "Why Saturday?"

" 'Cause my folks will be back from their vacation on Wednesday. They'd want to be there. And I thought you should meet them first.

"Maybe your father can come."

Maggie laughed, knowing just about nothing would keep him away. "Maybe."

"I got a phone call from Rock Springs, just before we went on the air tonight. The station there picked up my piece."

Mike nodded. "Good."

"They offered me a job."

Mike didn't say anything. He waited for her to go on. And at his silence, Maggie said, "What do you think?"

"What kind of a job?"

"Doing the same things I'd be doing at Ellington. Strong, current pieces.

"You're not saying anything," she said, commenting on his silence.

"I don't want to tell you what to do."

"Just when to get married?" She laughed at his sheepish look. "So what do you think?"

"Sounds good. What do you think?"

"I think the money is better, the driving will take about an hour. I think it's perfect."

"I think you're perfect. I think life is perfect."

"Almost," Maggie said.

"Yeah," he agreed, knowing they were both thinking about Collins and the fact that he was still out there somewhere. "Almost."

They never saw the blue sedan pass them, heading toward Ellington. They never knew the insanity of the driver, the determination that would end only in death. They never imagined what that kind of mad determination could do to their lives.

243

Chapter Fifteen

Maggie glared. There was no way he was going to go shopping with her.

"I'll follow along behind. You'll never know I'm there."

"Forget it."

"I'll close my eyes."

Maggie shot him a scowling look. "Yeah, that would be something. I could just see you walking along the streets of Elster with your eyes closed."

"I mean, I won't look at the dress."

Maggie nodded. "I know, and that's because you won't be there."

Mike continued to nag, to plead, and then, in final desperation, to order her not to go without him, but all to no avail. There was no way she was going to allow him to see the dress before the wedding, and nothing he could say made any difference. He didn't want her to go shopping alone so he managed to convince his sister and Miriam to accompany Maggie.

Maggie reminded him of her bodyguards, but Mike knew he wouldn't rest easy until he saw Susan's car pull into his driveway. He knew as well that there was no way that he could just stay here and wait.

He came to the conclusion that there was little sense in suffering through the afternoon, imagining all sorts of things.

He watched the three women leave, the bodyguard's car close behind them. They were almost out of sight when he slid behind the wheel of his Jeep. He figured Maggie would be a bit upset if she saw him, but he'd chance her anger if he could be sure that she'd be safe. He promised himself that he'd remain a good distance behind the two cars. There was no sense in denying it. He wouldn't be worth anything, staying at home worrying. He had no real choice.

"What's the hurry?"

Maggie smiled at her soon-to-be sister-in-law. "Ask your brother. He's the one who insisted on Saturday."

Miriam chuckled and said only, "Men." Obviously, that word was somehow enough for all three women to understand the need to hurry.

Susan scowled. "It's fine for him to insist on Saturday. All he has to do is talk to the minister, polish his boots, and get his good suit pressed. We've been shopping for hours, and we still haven't . . . Maggie," she said, as her gaze caught the dress displayed in the small boutique window. "Look at that dress."

Maggie followed the direction of Susan's gaze and knew with one glance she'd found what she'd been looking for. The entire dress was made of lace-covered silk. Champagne in color, it boasted long, tight sleeves, a high neckline that ended with a small ruffle almost at her chin, and a handkerchief hemline. Darting points of lace flowed to the mannequin's ankles. Maggie thought she couldn't have found anything more perfect.

As it turned out, the dress, an antique, cost far more than any modern-day wedding gown. Maggie, who was not in the least extravagant, content with her business suits while working and jeans and a shirt while relaxing, rarely bought dress-up clothes. She owned only two evening dresses and the pantsuit she'd worn to Tommy and Ginny's wedding. It was time, she thought, to splurge. This was the dress she'd wear when saying her vows. She didn't care that it cost more than three weeks' salary; it was worth it.

The dress was a little too big in the waist, but Miriam promised she'd take care of the alterations.

Rummaging through the merchandise inside the shop, they found a couple of yards of Irish lace that matched the dress and could be used as a veil. All that was needed now were matching shoes, and they'd look for those, along with Miriam's matron-of-honor dress, after lunch.

They were sitting near a window, enjoying a cocktail before lunch, when Susan almost choked on her drink as her gaze took in the man at the wheel across the street.

"Ignore him," Maggie said, having noticed his presence some time before.

"I thought you said he was staying home."

"You know, they took out the obey part in the wedding vows, probably because of men like Mike."

Susan chuckled. "Yeah. I guess they figured, why bother? He wouldn't listen anyway."

"He's suppose to be at the airport, picking up your mother and father."

Susan laughed. "He asked Pete to do it."

"What's he doing?" Miriam asked, as all three women watched Mike suddenly jump from his Jeep and lunge for a man who happened to be walking, or weaving, at any rate, toward the restaurant in which they were sitting.

Maggie, her eyes wide with surprise, couldn't believe it when she saw Mike shove the man toward his car and force him to lean over the hood of the vehicle as he ran his hands over the stranger's legs and patted down his pockets.

One of the ever-present state troopers who had followed the three women walked over to Mike. The two men spoke for a few minutes before the man offered his identification. The officer shrugged and said something else and Mike scowled as the man was allowed to continue on his away.

The three women grinned at one another. "I guess it wasn't him," Miriam, the most surprised of the three, said.

Maggie laughed as she leaned back in her comfortable chair. "It wasn't. And if your brother had listened to me and stayed home, he wouldn't now be getting an earful from that cop."

"He always was a thick-head." Susan nodded at her own comment. "He deserves it," she said, obviously unconcerned.

The waitress brought their lunch, crisp salads heavily laden with fresh seafood. Everything was delicious. The women soon forgot about Mike Stanford keeping guard, hungry, worried, and just about all-around miserable, as they laughed and talked their way through lunch.

Hours later, Susan dropped off both women, along with armfuls of packages, as she continued on her way home. Maggie brought most of her things to Miriam's.

Tomorrow, the two would get to work fitting the dress. She then headed for the main house.

He'd barely had time to open his door and rush in when Mike turned around and stepped outside. He leaned against one of the posts that supported the porch roof, effecting a nonchalant pose. His arms were folded across his chest as his dark gaze watched her progress. "Have a good time?" he asked.

Maggie smiled as she moved up the three steps to the porch. "Lovely."

"Did you find what you were looking for?"

"Uh-huh."

"Hungry?"

"Tell me you have dinner ready and I'll love you forever." Maggie grinned, knowing, of course, that he couldn't have had dinner ready, since he'd only made it home minutes before she had. But she'd love him forever anyway.

"I could fry up a few steaks."

Maggie allowed him a tender smile. "That would be lovely."

They entered the house, and after the pleasure of a long, hungry kiss, she asked, "Were you busy today?"

Mike shrugged. "Some."

"What did you do?" she asked, as he went about searching the refrigerator for the promised steaks.

"Oh, the usual, I guess."

Maggie pulled off her sneakers and rubbed her feet. She walked barefoot toward the stove. A frying pan was hot and ready by the time Mike gave up his search and took two steaks from the freezer.

Later, sitting at the table, they ate the steaks, which just happened, by luck, Maggie thought, to turn out rare and delicious. A crisp salad was the perfect addition to the meal.

Maggie swallowed a juicy piece of steak, washing it down with a sip of wine, when she said, "You know, something odd happened today."

"Yeah? What?"

"Susan, Miriam, and I were sitting in a restaurant this afternoon when this man jumped out of a Jeep." Maggie shot him a quick look before turning her attention again to her steak. "A Jeep just like yours, in fact." She took a forkful of meat and then said, "This is delicious."

She glanced at Mike's guilty expression. He was obviously wondering just how attentive the three had been and exactly what they had seen.

"You know what happened?" Maggie didn't wait for an answer, but went on with, "He jumped on this man, sort of sudden-like, and pushed him over the hood of his car."

Mike sighed. There was no sense in denying his actions, but he wasn't about to apologize for them, either. "I never said I wouldn't follow you."

"No, you didn't, did you?"

"Are you upset?"

"No." She smiled, and Mike knew she was telling the truth. "What I want to know is, how did you get home first?"

Mike chuckled. "A shortcut."

"Your sister says you're a thick-headed man. I'm afraid I agree."

"And?" he prompted, while wondering if he was going to have to apologize after all.

"I suppose I'll learn to live with it."

* * *

Maggie was a beautiful bride, not a great shock, for a beautiful woman can only be a beautiful bride. The organ began and Mike watched her father walk her down the aisle. He thought she had to be the most beautiful creature in the world, and he knew he was the luckiest.

The vows were spoken in a small church just outside of town. After the bride and groom kissed, Abner, who was Mike's best man, took his turn.

Maggie looked at the older man for a long moment, staring into blue eyes that twinkled with delight and pride, as if he alone had been responsible for the fact that she was now Mrs. Michael Stanford. Maggie laughed and said, "Sorry about this, Abner, but I warned you to give these up." She patted his pocket and the cigarettes that were always there.

Abner shook his head in mock disgust. "And here I was, planing on quitting tomorrow."

Maggie laughed and kissed his scratchy cheek.

"If he don't treat you right, you let me know."

"You'll be the first."

"The first what?" Mike asked, hearing only Maggie's part of the conversation.

"The first to keep you in line, boy. You'd better treat this lady right."

"Yes, sir," Mike said, probably for the first and last time answering him with the respect Abner considered due a man his age. "Mrs. Colton hasn't taken her eyes off you. I wonder what she sees in old men."

"Quality," Abner said, without a second's hesitation and with a definite twinkle in his eyes.

Mike and Maggie both laughed as they led the group of well-wishers out of the church.

It was a warm day, and the wedding guests moved constantly in and out of Mike's house. Maggie's father and his lady friend, Marlee Perkins, had come, as well as her sister, Pat. Her brother-in-law, Andy, couldn't make it on such short notice, but Pat brought her boys. Andrew Jr., was eight, and Paul was five. It was obvious from the first that they loved the ranch. Maggie realized it was a wonderful place to raise children. She and Mike had never discussed a family. That had been a mistake. They had probably hurried into this marriage far too soon. She hoped there wasn't anything else they had neglected to discuss. And she hoped even more that he wanted lots of kids.

Maggie and Mike watched the boys run off for the barn following little Jake's lead. "Which one tells you the dirty jokes?"

"The small one."

Mike nodded. "Yeah, he looks the type."

"What he looks like is a terror."

Mike grinned. "You think we could have one like that soon?"

"Only if we adopt." Mike looked at her for a moment in silence, only then realizing they had never discussed having a family. He thought that omission was pretty dumb on his part. She was a careerwoman. Maybe she wasn't interested in having kids at all. With his arm around her, he moved to a more private corner of the wide front porch. "You don't want to have any children?"

"Sure, but if you want a little boy about five years old, you'll have to wait or adopt one. The thing is, they only come about this big," she said, as she positioned her hands a little more than a foot apart. "So a five-year-old would be hard to come by anytime soon."

Mike smiled at her teasing. "You gave me a scare. We probably should have talked about this before."

"We probably should have talked about a lot of things. Only you were more interested in carrying me off to bed."

"Damn smart of me, don't you think?"

"I think your head is already too big, so I won't give you my opinion."

Mike laughed. "I love you."

Pat was suddenly at their side. "I hate to break up this intimate moment, but you have a phone call," she said to her sister.

Maggie worked her way through the crowd to the bedroom and the privacy she needed. She picked up the receiver, and said, "Hello."

"How could you do that, Maggie? How could you tell them how much I love you? How could you treat me like this? All I ever wanted was to love you."

"Henry?" Maggie didn't know why she said his name as a question. She'd recognized almost immediately the sound of his voice.

"I'll have to kill you for it, you know. I don't want to do it, but now I have to."

Maggie looked around the room with an eerie feeling, as if he might be there, or at the very least, had found the means somehow to see her. She shuddered at the ghastly thought and took several deep breaths. She couldn't panic now, not this time. It might never end if she didn't keep her head, if she didn't talk to him.

Her first impulse had been to scream, but she had somehow found the strength to keep her mind focused on his words, to answer him as if the pounding of her heart wasn't choking her.

"We should talk, Henry."

"About what?"

"About the things I said on television. I didn't mean them."

"Then why did you say them? Why did you tell them I was crazy?"

"I never said you were crazy. I said things, yes, but that was only so you'd call again."

"What?"

Maggie sat on the bed, in control now, her fear of this man fading, for as she spoke, he appeared to grow confused. "I wanted you to call again. I wanted to see you again, only I didn't know where to look."

"Are you telling me the truth?"

"Of course I'm telling you the truth. I want to see you. Where are you?"

"Why are all those people at the Stanford place?" he asked suspiciously.

Maggie felt a chill race down her back. He'd been here, or at least, close enough to see the house. God, how awful. "One of the workers got married. Are you going to tell me where you are?"

"No," he said in a sullen little-boy voice, "I don't trust you."

"You can trust me, Henry, I swear it. I want to see you, please."

"I'll call you back."

"Wait, Henry, don't hang up," she said, as the dial tone buzzed in her ear.

She breathed a deep sigh then jumped at, "You and I have a problem."

Maggie spun around on the bed, nearly falling off in her shock. She'd thought she was alone. How long had he been standing there? How much had he heard? "Oh, hi!" she said, just a bit breathlessly. "I didn't know you were there."

Mike nodded very slowly. "I figured that out for myself."

Maggie knew her smile was weak. She knew he could see through her attempt to make light of the terror every phone call from Henry instilled. It was obvious that he knew what she was about. It was also obvious that he was growing angrier by the minute.

"You wouldn't mind telling me who you were talking to, would you?"

"Ah, actually, I was talking to . . ." Her mind raced as she tried to think.

Mike interrupted with, "Let's make a pact to start this marriage with a promise never to lie to one another."

"Mike," she said, dragging his name into two syllables, in obvious disappointment, as if he'd just gone and ruined everything.

Mike sat on a chair opposite her. "Who was it, Maggie?"

"Do you think we should leave our guests this long?"

"Tell me."

"I don't have to. You already know. Only it's not what you think."

"Isn't it? You mean you're not planing to see him, planing to set a trap for him?"

Maggie shrugged. "Well, the thought might have occurred to me, but . . ."

Maggie never got a chance to finish. Mike was suddenly standing. The chair he'd just been sitting in now lay on its back, forgotten as he began to pace. Pace and curse. As he was mindful of his guests in the next room, though his words were blistering, they were hardly above a whisper.

"I could wring your neck, you know that? *What the hell is the matter with you?* If you think I'm going to let you put yourself in danger, you'd better think again! No wife of mine is going to die before we finish our goddamn honeymoon."

"Mike." She tried to interrupt the torrent of expletives that followed, but he seemed unable to stop.

"Mike, we have guests in the next room."

"They can't hear me."

"We can talk about this later."

"We're going to talk about it now," came a sudden roar.

Maggie gave a great sigh. "I guarantee they heard that."

"Too bad. I promise you this, Maggie: if I have to tie you to the damn bedpost every day, I'll do it. You're not going to get hurt."

"The bed doesn't have any posts."

"Don't be smart."

"That's exactly your problem, I think. You don't want a wife who's smart. You want one who will obey you blindly, be a good little girl, and do what she's told."

"What the hell is the matter with that?"

"Nothing, except in that case, you married the wrong woman."

"I married the one I love."

"Then give me some credit, will you? I'm not going to meet him on some deserted country road."

"You're not going to meet him at all."

"The marriage vows said to have and to hold, not to own."

"I don't want to hold you after you're dead." His voice broke when he said the words, and he looked suddenly beaten, as if already bereaved.

It was then that Maggie understood his anger stemmed from fear, not from the need to control. She moved to him, her arms sliding around his neck. "Sweetheart, don't."

Mike grabbed her so hard that Maggie groaned at the force of his hold. "You can't do this, please. I'd never do this to you. I've never make you so afraid."

"I won't meet him. I swear I won't. The cops can use someone else in my place."

Mike buried his face in her neck. There was no way that he could allow her to come to harm, not if he wanted to live. "What?"

"I'll tell Jim about the phone call. When Henry calls back, Jim can set up something. I won't even be there."

"He's calling back?"

She nodded. "I hope so. I think I surprised him when I told him I wanted to see him. He didn't know what to say."

"And you swear you won't do anything but talk to him?"

"I swear."

He hugged her to him for a long minute before he said, "It's awfully quiet out there. Do you think everybody left?"

"I think they know we were fighting and they probably don't know if they should leave or not."

"What do you think we should do?"

"Well, we could lock the door and hope they'll leave eventually."

"I vote for that one," he said, as his palm ran down her back and cupped her rear.

"Or we could go back out there and make believe no one heard our yelling."

"I still vote for the first one."

Maggie laughed as she reached behind her for a hand that was growing bolder with each passing second. "I thought you might, but I'm hungry and we didn't cut the cake yet."

It was late and starting to rain as the last car drove away from the ranch house. The lights were on there, and in most of the other smaller houses as well. People were getting ready for bed.

Soon it would be safe for him to come closer. Soon it would be safe to look inside and see for himself if she was telling the truth. She'd said she wanted to see him again, she hadn't meant the things she'd said; she'd only wanted to find him. Henry couldn't understand it. Why would she say those things if she wanted him? Why had she called him insane? A serial killer . . .

He wasn't any of the things she said. He'd killed a few people, yes, but they had needed to die. He hadn't wanted to kill them. He hadn't even enjoyed it. Well, maybe he had a little, but not so much at first.

It was her fault. If she had loved him the way she should have, no one would have died.

A dog barked in the distance and a man yelled for him to shut up. Henry smiled at that.

They'd be tired tonight. He'd be able to get close to the

house without any problems because they had partied late into the night. And now that it was raining, no one would think he'd be out here.

The barn door was open. Two cops sat at a small table near the door, drinking coffee and playing cards. They were here to protect her, but they weren't doing much of a job of it. Henry snickered at the thought. If he wanted to, he could kill her tonight and no one would ever know until morning. He thought maybe he should, just to show those cops how stupid they were.

Henry crept closer to the house, to the rainswept window, and glanced inside. He was at the side of the house, looking in the living room.

Maggie smiled, gave a last wave, and leaned against the door in relief as her father, Marlee Perkins, her sister, and her nephews left for the rooms reserved at the motel just off the interstate. She'd see them again tomorrow, before they left for home. And after this mess was over, she and Mike were going to her father's place for a visit, and if the looks she'd intercepted between her father and Marlee meant anything, maybe even another wedding.

"I thought they'd never leave," she said, pushing herself from the closed door, coming toward Mike, who was already in the living room, pulling off his tie and shrugging out of his jacket.

He sat on the couch and kicked off his boots. A second later, he was pulling his white shirt from his pants.

"What are you doing?"

"Taking off my clothes."

"I thought we could have a glass of wine, to celebrate, before we . . ."

"I don't have to be wearing clothes to drink wine, do I?"

Maggie laughed. "You don't have to, I guess."

"That way, I'd be sure not to stain anything, in case it spilled."

Maggie nodded as a tender grin tugged at the corners of her mouth. "I see."

Mike bit his bottom lip and the hunger in his dark eyes belied his words. "I hope you do. It's not that I wanted to get undressed, or anything."

She shook her head. "I never thought you did."

"It's just that I'm trying to save some money."

"On cleaning bills?"

"Of course," he said, as he shrugged out of his underwear and threw them across the room.

Maggie followed the flying fabric and then eyed the spot where they had fallen. She shook her head. "You might as well know right now that I don't pick up underwear."

"I'll get them later."

She touched his throat with her index finger and allowed it to run sort of aimlessly to his chest. "But I do like the way you think."

"And I like the way you touch me." His body's growing reaction to her touch told her he liked it very much indeed. "How come you're still dressed?"

"Well, I thought since you're so good at taking clothes off, maybe you could help me."

"Let me get the wine first."

"Why?"

" 'Cause once I've got you naked, I won't want to leave the room."

"Oh?"

"It's not what you think."

She shook her head. "I wasn't thinking anything."

259

"It's just that I don't want you to get cold, so I'll have to build up the fire. I won't do anything to you, or anything."

"You won't?"

"Well, maybe I could be talked into doing something."

Maggie grinned as she watched him head for the kitchen. "I'll bet it wouldn't take much talking."

"That depends," Mike called from the kitchen. Maggie could hear the clink of glasses as they were held together. He came back with the wine. "If we talk about the space program, I could probably . . ."

She was looking his naked body up and down and very obviously enjoying the view, while Mike sort of rolled his hips as he sauntered toward her, obviously pleased. "You got a thing for astronauts?"

"Not exactly. Just wondered what it would feel like doing it while weightless."

Maggie blinked at that comment, more than a bit surprised, for thinking about making love in outer space was hardly how she began each day. As a matter of fact, she'd never thought about it. Maggie fought back the urge to laugh, enjoying the dry humor here, the teasing and very sexy conversation. "Do you often think about things like that?"

He shrugged. "Now and then."

Maggie shook her head. "Where else do you think about making love?"

"On a horse."

"Really?"

"Get yourself ready for that one, Maggie," he warned, his dark eyes gleaming with promise. "It won't be a dream of mine for much longer."

Maggie felt a thrill race through her at his words and

found it a bit difficult to talk above the trembling in her voice. "Does it take a special kind of mind to do that?"

"What? To think of unusual places to make love?"

Maggie nodded.

"I don't think so. As far as I know, all men think like that."

"I think you're wrong. I think you're very special."

Mike watched her a long moment, his heart filling with joy. "Come over here and say that."

Maggie quickly disposed of the few steps that separated them. Then he said, "But making love in space wouldn't work." At his questioning look, she said, "No leverage."

Mike grinned at her comment as he uncorked the bottle and poured two glasses. He handed her one and they each sipped slowly of the ruby liquid. "But you wouldn't mind trying it, right?"

"You'd have to drug me to get me up there."

"I guess I can get you high enough right here on earth."

Maggie grinned at his confidence, knowing no man had more of a right to boast. "I guess you can."

His dark gaze traveled down the length of her and Maggie felt excitement bubble to life in every nerve ending. "You were a beautiful bride, Maggie."

"All brides are beautiful," she countered.

" 'Cept none of them ever looked like you. But I think that dress has kinda served it's purpose. And being as I'm practically professional at it and all, you want me to help you take that dress off?"

"You mean, you've had so much practice as to be practically professional?"

"Only with my own clothes."

Maggie chuckled. "Good answer."

261

"Now, let's see . . . what would be the best way to start?" he asked, as he studied her dress.

"There's a zipper down the back."

"I'm professional, remember? I noticed that right off." His hands moved around her and lowered the zipper to her hips.

"We could do this in the bedroom."

"Actually, I was thinking about that new dining room table."

Her dress fell to the floor and she stood before him in a white strapless bra, a one-piece lace contraption that ended just above a scrap of lace that laughingly served as panties. Attached to the long bra were garters that held white lace stockings in place. Mike took a deep breath even as he wondered how he managed to breathe at all.

"You like it?"

Mike swallowed. He knew his voice was lower, sort of raw and raspy, but he couldn't do a thing about it. "I'm not sure 'like' is an accurate description."

Maggie smiled. "The woman at the store called it a 'merry widow.' "

Mike nodded. "I understand the widow part. I'm not sure I'm going to live long enough to get this thing off." Mike reached for the garters first and slowly rolled her stocking down her legs. Her hands were on his shoulders for balance as he rolled them from her feet.

Standing again, he felt his hands shaking by the time he reached around her and worked the hooks of her bra free.

"It's a good thing you're a professional at this, or you wouldn't know how to get this off."

"I'd figure out something."

He smiled as the flimsy material followed her dress and

stockings to the floor. He played with her softness for a long moment before she said, "Close the curtains."

Mike's mouth lowered to her breast and he took one long delicious sip of her before he pulled away and said, "Don't move. I always like to finish what I've started."

Just outside the living room, Henry pressed himself to the wall, sobbing his agony as rain mixed with his tears, as his mind howled its pain, as the unseen knife in his chest twisted and turned again and again.

She hadn't meant it; she hadn't meant any of it. She was a whore, just like his mother. Letting a man take off her clothes, letting a man touch her. He hated her. Hated her more than he'd ever hated anyone in his life.

Henry walked back to the car, parked behind the hills. Inside he let the emergency brake go and smiled as the car rolled down the slight incline and away from the ranch. He wouldn't start the car now. In the darkness, in the night, sound carried, and he didn't want them to know he was wise to what she truly was. Dirty pig. Dirty, vile bitch. He was going to get her for this. He didn't care if he had to die doing it. Getting her was more important than living.

Mike leaned over his wife and amid desperate attempts to breathe, groaned his exhaustion against her breasts. "I've been known to have some great ideas, but this one amazed even me."

"Except that the table is harder than it looks."

"Next time, we'll put a quilt over it."

"And I'll slide off."

Mike groaned as he tried to hold himself above her. "God, my legs are about as strong as jelly."

263

"Then how come you're still standing?"

" 'Cause I've got my knees locked. But if I try to walk . . ." He shook his head, and despite his best attempts, leaned heavily on her.

"You were suppose to carry me, and now you can't even walk."

"Was I? I didn't know that."

"Over the threshold?"

"You were already in the house."

"Into the bedroom, then. That's how they do it in the movies."

"Oh, that. Well, just this once, maybe you could carry me."

Maggie chuckled softly. "I took a course once and learned a fireman's hold. I could probably do it."

"And mouth-to-mouth resuscitation?"

"Uh-huh."

"You might have noticed that I'm having a hard time breathing."

"Now that you mention it, I did notice that."

"I wouldn't mind if you gave me some of that mouth-to-mouth about now."

"Now?"

"Right now."

Chapter Sixteen

It was mutually agreed upon that the best thing to do, the safest thing to do, would be to wait until Collins's capture before leaving on a honeymoon. Obviously, the police couldn't follow them out of the state, but Collins could. According to his last conversation with Maggie, he had seen the party. He might not know all, but the fact that he'd been that close was enough to give everyone the shivers and put them on their guard.

Noisy dogs were no longer told to shut up. Now when one barked, women grabbed guns and sat on their children's beds, while men from the bunkhouse to the small houses that dotted Mike's property left with powerful lamps to search every corner of the ranch. They searched until they were sure no one was there who did not belong. They searched until they found the cause of the alert.

Maggie had shivered her horror when they'd found footprints in the ground just outside the living room window. The dirt there was soft and the rain had turned it softer yet. But it hadn't rained hard enough to obliterate the prints. He'd been closer than any of them had suspected or imagined.

Maggie was clearly upset. It had been three days since the wedding, two since finding the footprints, and she had yet to calm down. She jumped at every sound and found herself unable to eat. Her nerves stretched to the limit, and she snapped at Mike over the smallest things.

"Do you have to do that?"

"What?"

"You know what. Make that much noise with those ice cubes."

Mike put the glass of iced tea down and brought his bride into his arms. "Take it easy, Maggie. Nothing is going to happen to you. I swear it."

Maggie shuddered at the thought. She couldn't go through the horror. She'd rather die than know that kind of hopeless fear again.

Mike knew a sense of helplessness. His wife was terrified—on the edge of hysterics, in fact—and he couldn't do a damn thing about it. "You know he's doing this on purpose just to rile you, don't you?"

"I figured as much."

"He's in control again and he knows it."

"I can't stand it, Mike. He was outside the window." Maggie couldn't hold back a shudder of disgust. "Why didn't he try to come in? What stopped him?"

"Us, probably."

"What do you mean?"

"I mean, he probably saw us, after everyone left that night."

Maggie's eyes widened with shock. "You mean . . ."

"I closed the curtains, remember? There wasn't much to see before that."

Maggie did remember, but she couldn't relax. There might not have been much to see, but there had been enough. She had been wearing only a brief pair of undies by the time she'd realized the curtains were still open. And then she remembered something else. "Mike! If he saw us, he won't believe that I want to be with him."

"It doesn't matter."

"That means if he calls at all, it will be to set up a trap to kill me."

"That doesn't matter, either. You won't be anywhere near the meeting place. Jim has already found a policewoman from over in Rock Springs who looks enough like you to fool even me."

Maggie shot him a look of disbelief.

"All right, maybe she wouldn't fool me, but she'll fool Collins. By the time he realizes she isn't you, there'll be a couple dozen cops around him and it'll be too late."

Maggie gasped and then glanced at Mike as the phone rang. She licked her bottom lip as she reached a trembling hand toward the phone. Mike pressed the mute button on the television. Next he pressed the record button on the answering machine and Maggie picked up.

"What took you guys so long to answer?" Susan's voice held a suggestive tone. "I didn't interrupt anything, did I?" By the sound of her, she hoped she had.

"I wouldn't have answered it, if you had."

"Mmm, too bad."

Mike could hear both sides of the conversation, since the record button was still pushed. He smiled and said, "Ask her if she wants anything in particular, or if she's just being her usual annoying self."

"I heard that. Tell that brother of mine . . ."

"He can hear you."

"Fine. I was going to bring over a tray of my lasagna. I made extra. Only now I've changed my mind."

Mike laughed. "Tell her to come over anyway. This waiting is driving me nuts."

Susan was aware that they were expecting another call. Everyone was aware of the fact that Henry Collins was out there waiting and perhaps watching for the right moment. Still, Susan teased, "You mean you can't think of anything to do to occupy your time?"

"It's too early for that." Mike grinned at Maggie's look of surprise. He knew she was thinking it hadn't been too early yesterday when they had eaten dinner in bed, or this morning, or this afternoon.

"It's never too early for that. Maggie, you poor thing."

Maggie laughed.

"It is when nosy sisters call and . . ."

"All right, all right, I'll be there in a half hour."

Maggie was checking a coffee cake in the oven when Pete and Susie walked in. Abner, also invited, soon followed.

Maggie poured Pete another cup of coffee. Pete had been grinning since he'd first entered the house. Maggie was beginning to wonder what was so funny when he asked, "What do you put in this stuff? It's great."

"I got the recipe from Miriam. There's a secret ingredient."

"Vanilla?" Susan offered.

"Right."

"So when can we expect to see a baby on the way?" Abner asked, to Maggie's amazement. People simply didn't ask those kinds of questions. At least, the people she used to know didn't. And especially when the bride and groom had been married only three days.

268

"Abner," Susie said to the suddenly silent room, "Don't you know you're not suppose to ask questions like that?"

"I'm too old to wait. How much longer do these two think I have?"

"I figure you'll be around for the next twenty years," Mike said, his voice holding just a touch of despair. "And you're not supposed to ask stuff like that because it's personal."

"Yeah," Susan agreed. And then went and ruined it all with, "So answer the man."

All five laughed, and Mike said, "After you, little sister."

"Then you'd better hurry up. I'll be on my second before you even start."

"Your second?" Mike looked at his sister for a long moment and then burst out laughing as he stood and pulled her from her chair and into his arms. "You little brat. I was wondering why you and Pete couldn't stop smiling. Have you told Mom and Dad?"

"Just came from there," Pete said proudly. "They sorta took to the idea."

"I thought they might." Mike squeezed his sister again and then shook Pete's hand.

"When?"

"Not for a while, so you two have time to catch up. Almost."

Mike grinned. "If you get out of here, we could get to work on it."

Maggie was just about to offer her congratulations when the phone rang. Conversation came to an instant halt while every eye in the room moved to the shrilling object.

"I wish I could stop my voice from shaking. He's going to know I'm afraid."

"Don't worry about it. If he knows you're afraid, he might get careless. He might make a mistake." Mike took her hand in his and pressed the record button, just before he nodded to his wife and said, "Go ahead."

Maggie picked up the phone. "Hello?"

"Maggie?" came a deep, rough voice, and Maggie closed her eyes and leaned against her husband as she nodded.

Susan reached for Pete's hand as everyone listened to the voice of insanity.

"Yes, Henry. I was waiting for you to call."

"I saw you with him, Maggie. You're a whore. A dirty bitch of a whore."

"Wait, Henry. It's not what you think."

Henry laughed wildly. "Are you telling me I didn't see him take off your clothes?"

Susan made a soft moaning sound and Mike shot her a sharp look.

"Yes, he did. He took off my clothes, but I couldn't help it. I couldn't stop him."

Mike tightened his hold on Maggie's waist and nodded for her to go on. They had thought this out earlier. They had carefully planned for this phone call.

"What do you mean?"

"I didn't want him to do it. I'll explain everything once I'm with you again." Maggie couldn't control her shudder at the thought.

"He forced you?"

"Please, Henry, I can't talk about it. I can't. Let me see you again. Please, just let me see you."

"I'll kill him for touching you. I'll kill him . . ."

270

"Henry, listen to me. He'll be back in a minute. I haven't got the time to tell you now. Where can we meet?"

Everyone in the room held their breath.

"Tomorrow night."

"Where?"

"Out on Maples Road. Halfway between . . ."

Mike shook his head. He knew Jim wouldn't be happy with that kind of meeting. The suggested meeting place was a deserted country road, the land around it flat. There would be no cover, no place from which the police could watch.

Maggie tried to think. Her eyes grew desperate, darted to the left and right as she searched for an answer.

Mike shrugged, shook his head again, and raised both hands silently, telling her what to say next.

"I don't know my way around here. Please," Maggie prayed the desperation she felt was evident in her tone, even as she prayed Henry would never know, until it was too late, the truth behind that desperation.

"I can't come there."

Mike mouthed the word "town."

Maggie seemed to calm a bit then, apparently remembering their plan. "In town, Henry. I could meet you in town."

"Where?"

"I don't know. Anywhere."

There was a moment of silence and then, "All right. Behind Lanie's place. In the parking lot."

"When?"

"Ten o'clock, tomorrow."

The conversation ended with an abrupt click and the ensuing sound of a dial tone. Mike cursed. "The bastard."

His arms were around his wife, holding her shivering body tightly to him. "He knows the place. He knows it's wide open behind the bar, that he could take off in any of three directions at a second's notice."

"Jim will take care of it," Susan offered. "He'll work something out."

The evening ended soon after the phone call. Even the fact that a new baby was due to arrive couldn't disperse the sudden gloom and ever-worsening fear.

They called Jim and told him of the phone call, while he, in turn, reported that a young girl had seen the piece Maggie had done, since it was being telecast all over the area. The girl had been interviewed and had described Henry's car. Every cop in the state was on the lookout for it. Jim thought they might have Henry even before tomorrow night.

Maggie didn't sleep until the sun came up the next morning. She lay in Mike's arms during the night as they spoke of their dreams for a future, of the children they hoped to have, of life's sweetness.

Neither mentioned the coming night and the hopes that it would not end in tragedy. All Mike could do was to hold Maggie closer as he imagined the policewoman and the danger she faced. He could only wonder how the man who loved her could stand it.

"You'll have to add onto this house eventually."

Mike smiled at the thought.

"How many kids do you think we'll have?"

"We both come from families of two. Do you think that's enough?"

"Well, I sort of had my heart set on six."

"Six!"

"But I'd settle for four."

Maggie laughed. "You did that on purpose. So I wouldn't be shocked and would gladly agree to four."

Mike didn't answer her. His low chuckle was answer enough. He breathed a great sigh of satisfaction. "Truth is, I wouldn't mind having six."

"That's because you wouldn't be the one doing the having."

Mike glanced down at her. "You're starting to sound like Abner."

"No, I'm not. I haven't once called you 'boy.'"

"Because you know better."

Maggie ran her hand down his body, gently cupping his sex before she said, "This doesn't feel like a boy."

Mike grinned as he rolled to his side, allowing her easier access. "No? What does it feel like?"

"A stick shift."

Mike laughed in delight. "You mean, like a four-on-the-floor stick shift?"

"Sort of. Only . . ." her fingers did some investigating. "I think in this case, it's two, and they're not on the floor."

Mike laughed. "Now that you mention it, it sort of works like a stick shift."

"You mean, if I move it right, it can drive you?"

"You might say that."

"Mmm, interesting."

"It could be."

"Interesting?"

He nodded.

"I've always wanted to learn about mechanics. Do you mind if I check this out?"

"I wouldn't mind," he said, trying not to sound too eager.

"You're sure, now?" Maggie teased, as she ran her fingers over the length of him, measuring from top to bottom and liking very much what she found.

"I'm very sure."

No one slept the following night. The men who had been on alert now sat in the dark at the window of their living rooms or hidden behind shrubbery, or on their bellies upon roofs and waited for Mike to announce that all was finally safe.

The ranch was quiet and the tension almost unbearable as the hands on the clock finally approached ten.

Ten miles away. In the center of a one-street town, eight cars sat in Lanie's parking lot. Four of them belonged to the patrons inside. Four of them belonged to the police department, at least for the night.

Gray Bluff was a small town and had no unmarked police cars, so the cars belonged to the policemen themselves.

Inside each car a man crouched in the front, another in the back. To say they were uncomfortable was putting it mildly. They were dressed in heavy clothes, with added socks and thick gloves, but nothing could protect them from the cold night air that seeped into each car.

Of course, heaters could not be used. The cars had to appear as if they were empty. Henry would have to believe that they belonged to the people inside the bar.

Hidden in the shadows of the bar's roof, two men lay flat. Sharpshooters, they watched through a night lens the comings and goings in the parking lot.

A blue car drove in and stopped. The two men on the roof tensed as they directed their high-powered weapons to the car's windows. Through the nightscope they could see a young man and a girl fall instantly into one another's arms. One of the men whispered, "Lovers," into a button-type microphone fastened to his collar, and a dozen men cursed.

Within minutes the windows were steamed and every man who watched knew there wasn't a thing they could do to hurry them on their way. If they dared to approach the car, the whole operation could fail, and if they didn't, these two young people just might be caught in the midst of flying bullets.

As it turned out, there was no need to do anything. Within minutes, five to be exact, every man there breathed a sigh of relief as the youngsters apparently finished with their business in record time. Without ever knowing the danger they had inadvertently flirted with, they suddenly put the car into gear and were driving out of the lot.

A collective sigh could almost be heard from behind the garbage pails to the roof of the building.

At ten o'clock, Maggie's car was driven into the parking lot. It rolled to a stop, once the driver came deep into the shadows of the building.

"Anything?" Jim whispered into his collar.

His question was answered by a woman's voice. "Nothing. No sign of a blue car anywhere. If he's going to show, he's probably already waiting in an alley someplace."

Jim could only thank the Almighty for the cloud cover tonight. Had the moon not been more than half covered, there wouldn't have been a chance of hiding anywhere but within the cars. And inside the car, lying on the floor, a cop couldn't see a damn thing.

At 10:05, a man whispered into his collar, "A blue car."

Everyone within hearing tensed, every cop's finger reached for his gun's trigger, until they heard: "Forget it. He drove by."

A white van with shaded windows entered the lot. It drove toward Maggie's car and Jim realized almost too late that Collins, just as he had the first and second times, might have changed cars.

"Watch it," Jim said, knowing the van had moved too close to the back of Maggie's car. There were a dozen or more parking spaces, yet the van had headed directly for her car. There had to be a reason why. "This could be him."

A nightscope proved useless. It couldn't penetrate the darkly tinted windows—at least, not enough for them to be sure.

The man inside made no move. From what the sharp-shooters could see, he merely sat there. There was no way they could shoot. The guy could be doing anything, from jerking off to waiting for his kid to return from a church outing.

All anyone could do was sit and wait.

A horn honked.

Jim whispered, "Danny, was that you?"

"No, the guy behind me. I think it's him."

"Don't move."

The horn honked again.

"What the hell am I supposed to do?"

"Just sit there," came Jim's response.

"He'll leave."

"We'll stop him down the road. Don't get out of that car."

The men watching held their breath, waiting for something, anything, to happen. And then they heard, "All right, it's got to be him. Go for it."

A dozen armed men ran forward. They jumped from cars, ran from behind the garbage pails, from within the shadows of the building.

The van's car was wrenched open to a man's high-pitched scream.

Maggie and Mike sat in the living room, waiting for the phone to ring. Every five minutes felt like an hour, every hour like a century.

Jake lay upon the roof of his house. He blew on his hands, trying to bring them some warmth. Damn, tonight it was colder than his first wife's lying heart. He wished to hell it was over. He wished to hell he'd never see that kind of fear in Miriam's eyes again.

He'd go inside in a minute and warm up a bit. Miriam would have coffee waiting for him. He could see as much, at least, almost as much, from his living room window. Inside, he'd be warm.

Jake frowned as his glance moved to the cop crouched in the bushes at the corner of Mike's house. Steve was probably freezing his ass off, Jake thought, and like him, trying to find another position to relieve his stiffness.

And then suddenly, silently, Steve's feet came from the bushes as if he'd just rolled forward, as if he'd fallen asleep, as if the ground wasn't hard and cold, but as soft as a feather mattress.

Jake's heartbeat picked up as adrenaline rushed

277

through his body. He didn't feel the cold now. All he felt was nervous energy. Steve might look like he'd fallen asleep, but Jake knew better. The son-of-a-bitch was here. God damn it! He wished he had the means to let the others know.

Jake inched his way to the edge of the roof and rolled over the side. With his gun in his hand, he jumped and then cursed as pain sliced up his legs. His feet were so damn cold that the jump caused what felt like thousands of pieces of broken glass to come shooting from his soles to his knees.

He limped as he ran forward. Bent almost in half, he headed for Mike's house. Jake passed a shed on the way and from out of the darkness came a gasp and a man's shaken voice. "What the fuck are you doing? Jesus, I almost shot you."

"He's here. I just saw Steve go down. He's behind the house."

"Christ! What are we going to do?"

"Go to the right and pick up Harry on the way. Jimmy had to have seen me come off the roof. He's probably right behind me. The four of us should be able to take care of this bastard."

Joe glanced over and nodded. Just before he began to move, he grinned at Jake's words, "And for Christ sake, don't shoot the wrong guy. Especially not me."

Joe nodded again and almost instantly disappeared into the night.

On silent feet, Jake ran to the edge of Mike's house. He leaned his back, against the building. His heart was pounding so hard, he couldn't breathe, which was probably a good thing, because the bastard would have heard that.

Jake peeked around the corner. Nothing. God, no! Could he have been mistaken?

And then he saw him, in the shadow of the fireplace chimney, trying to see into the house.

Jake saw the gun. The bastard was aiming it through a slit in the curtains. "Stop," Jake called out, only to see the man swing around in shock and face him.

"Put the gun down."

Inside the house a woman screamed, for Jake's call could easily be heard in the silent night. Mike cursed as he lunged to his feet. He shoved Maggie into the bathroom, slamming the door behind her, and ran outside, but he hadn't gained the doorway when a shot went off and a man in obvious pain cried out a stream of vile curses.

All Mike could do was mutter, half in prayer, half in frustration, "Christ," as he ran toward the sound of the gunfire, praying it was Collins out there and not one of his own men.

"I swear to God, I don't know what you're talking about." The man was spreadeagled over the hood of a car as eight hands patted down his sides, his back, his legs, tearing off his shoes and socks.

"Then what are you doing here?" Jim asked.

"I thought she was someone else," the man said, as he nodded toward the policewoman and then grunted as a heavy hand shoved him harder against the car. "What's this all about?"

"You didn't answer my question. What are you doing here?"

"Oh, please, don't tell my wife. She'll leave me if she

finds out," he pleaded, and two cops cursed in disgust as they relaxed their arms and allowed the weapons in their hands to fall to their sides. Two more took a few steps back. Another grabbed the man's arm and pulled him from the hood of the car, just as another cop who had given the van a quick search cursed with shock and came running.

"A woman and a kid are in the back, dead."

When they had dragged him from the car, the cops had been so anxious to gain control, to spread him over the hood, that each had thought the other had check his front. As it turned out, none of them had.

Danny Edwards, the woman posing as Maggie, was wearing a bulletproof vest. When Collins was spun from the car, he reached into his belt and pulled out the gun. She didn't for a split second know fear.

The fact of the matter was, if he'd been allowed to shoot, she'd have taken a blow that would have probably knocked her down, but would have caused little more than a bruise. It didn't turn out like that.

One of the officers surrounding him saw the gun at the exact moment she did. He lunged for Collins's hand, trying to wrestle the gun from his grip. It went off and the shot that might have hit her in the chest hit her in the neck instead.

Danny cursed as she staggered back and watched ten men fall upon the bastard who'd just shot her. But none of them knew yet that he had just shot her.

Another, slightly muffled shot came amid curses and grunts of pain. "Christ, watch out, will ya? That's my hand," one of the men said, as his hand was almost cuffed, and Danny started to smile.

"Jim," she whispered to the officer in command, as she

reached for her throat and held her hand over a gaping wound. The wound was serious, she knew, but it hadn't hit her spinal column. She was still standing, still able to use her hands.

"Yeah," he said automatically, never taking his eyes off the struggling officers, praying none would get shot.

"I got a problem."

"What?" Jim asked, as he glanced in her direction only to find her hand at her throat and blood pumping like mad from between her fingers. "Jesus, I've got an officer down. Get the fuckin' bastard. I don't care if you have to kill him, just do it."

There were an ambulance and an emergency team waiting just outside the cordoned-off area. "John, get that ambulance in here. Now!" Jim screamed into the button at his collar.

Danny watched the goings-on as if from a distance, as if the happenings had not affected her in any great degree. She was hurt. Maybe badly hurt, for the blood pumped out of her throat at an alarming pace. She needed immediate care, and yet she felt somehow strangely detached from the entire happening.

And then the shock of what had just occurred seemed to penetrate her mind and she felt her legs weakening. It was from the injury, of course. She couldn't be expected to withstand this kind of trauma without her knees growing a little weak.

She felt Jim reach for her, but she couldn't help him. She couldn't let go of her neck.

Jim struggled with an awkward hold to keep his officer from falling on her face. He held her against him and screamed again for the ambulance. He never realized the

281

curses, never stopped cursing until the emergency unit had her in the ambulance, heading for the hospital.

Jake spun around in shock at the sound of a gun going off inches from his ear. He hadn't heard Jimmy come up behind him. All he knew was that Steve had been standing at the window one minute and was rolling on the ground the next. Jake shook his head, feeling like he'd somehow gotten lost in some sort of Keystone Kops movie. What the hell were they doing out here? What the hell were they doing with guns? He could count on two fingers the men who were adept at using firearms, and here they were, lying in wait for a killer, just like Top Cops or something.

"Did you get him?" Mike yelled, as he came around the corner of the house.

"Yeah," Steve said with some real disgust, "he got me, all right. Damn near shattered my arm."

Jake grinned. "It's a lucky thing Jimmy shot you and not me. I was aiming for your heart. What the hell were you doing, skulking around out here?"

Steve breathed a sound of disgust. "I thought I heard something."

It took only a second for Mike to realize one of the officers guarding his place had been accidentally shot. It took only one more for him to realize that he'd left Maggie alone with the doors open.

He was gone around the side of the house as fast as he'd come.

He entered his house with a roar. *"Maggie!"*

He was at the bathroom door. God, why had he left

her? "Maggie," he said again, terrified to open the door, afraid of what he might find.

"Mike?" came a soft response.

"It's all right." Mike knew a relief so great, he couldn't have stood on his own if his life had depended on it. He leaned heavily against the wall and watched Maggie slowly opened the door. "You can come out now."

"Did you get him?" She was in his arms, talking into his neck.

"No. Steve got shot."

"Oh, my God!"

"He'll be all right. One of the men will take him to the hospital." He made a soft moaning sound, and then, "I've got to sit down."

Maggie smiled and then said, "I'll help you."

"Thanks," he said, as he made it to the couch at last.

"You want a drink, or something?"

Mike shook his head. "No, just you."

Maggie sat at his side just as the phone began to ring.

"We got him," Jim said, and Mike thought it was something close to a miracle that he was able to hold back his tears of relief.

"Thank God," he whispered, and then nodded to Maggie's questioning gaze. "They got him."

Chapter Seventeen

"Don't let him know you're afraid."

Maggie glanced at her friend and grinned. "You mean, if I tell him I'm not, he'll believe me?"

Miriam laughed. "No, but if you tell yourself you're not, you'll believe it."

Maggie, with one foot in the stirrup, allowed Jake to help her up. It took another minute for her to find the other stirrup and get her foot securely into it. "I'd have to be pretty stupid to believe that. My God, it's so high up here. How come he didn't look this tall when I was on the ground? What is he, six feet?"

"It's not feet, it's hands."

"Hands what?"

"A horse is measured in hands."

The horse stirred beneath her, and Maggie tensed. With a plastered smile and a slightly shrill voice, she said, "How nice."

"Sugar is as calm as a baby. I promise, you don't have a thing to worry about."

"Then why can't he know I'm afraid?"

" 'Cause horses are a little like men." Her gaze caught

her husband's tender smile as she spoke. "No matter how gentle they are, they just might take advantage if you allow them the upper hand."

Maggie followed Miriam's instructions and the two horses walked around the paddock for close to a half hour.

"Getting used to him yet?"

"I guess," Maggie said uneasily.

"All right, then we'll ride up to the northern pasture and back." Miriam saw the doubt in Maggie's eyes. "It's a short trip."

"And I had to go and marry a rancher. Gee, that was brilliant of me."

"After a few times, you'll be begging me to go riding with you."

Almost two hours later, back at the stable again, Maggie slid off the horse and groaned. "I think you can forget the begging stuff. I can't see when I'll ever like this."

"Take a bath. You'll be hurting by tonight."

"By tonight?" Maggie touched her painful bottom and tried to will away the rawness and throbbing ache in her thighs. "You mean it's going to get worse?"

Miriam laughed. "Until it gets better."

By the time Mike came back from town with a truckload of wire, Maggie was in her bathrobe, limping into the kitchen. Her thighs were on fire.

"What's the matter? Are you sick?"

"No," she said unhappily.

"Hurt?"

"I went riding today."

Mike smiled and Maggie thought he looked ridiculously proud. What difference did it make if she could ride or not? What difference could it possible make? And why was she bothering to try?

285

"I love you."

"Why? Because I'm learning to ride?"

"Because you're working at being a rancher's wife."

"I won't ever be the 'good little woman,' if that's what you mean."

"It's not what I meant and you know it." A gleam entered his eyes and Maggie figured she knew what he was going to say even before she heard the words. "I could massage it for you."

"Mike, don't fool around. I'm really suffering here."

Mike lifted her into his arms and carried her to their room. She lay on the bed as he went to the bathroom and rummaged in the medicine cabinet. He came back with two bottles and a towel.

"I guarantee this stuff will work. Roll over."

Maggie did so with a groan, only to find a few minutes later that Mike had been right. Whatever was in that bottle worked. Her rear and legs felt measurably better. The aching soreness was almost completely gone.

"Ah, that feels good. What is this stuff, liquid opium?"

Mike laughed. "I don't know. I just know it works."

"Did you see Jim while you were in town?"

"Yup."

"What did he say?"

"He said Collins was going to make it."

Maggie digested this information in silence. Then, "How's Danny?"

"Jim can't say enough about her. If I wasn't positive that Joan of Arc was dead, I'd think maybe . . ."

Maggie smiled at the thought of a possible romance between the two. "Do you think . . . ah, God, that feels good."

Mike moved closer, his knees between her thighs.

286

"Yeah, I think maybe they have something going there."

"That's nice."

"Is it? Why?"

"Because everyone should know how good it can be, when you find the right man."

"Or woman."

"Or woman," she agreed.

"I saw Steve, too. He's wearing a sling, but he's back at work. Behind a desk, for a while, at least."

Mike stopped for a second, wiping his hands free of the ointment. He started again, his hands more slippery than ever. Maggie smiled and then groaned as he massaged a particularly sensitive spot.

"How does this feel?"

"It feels wonderful, but that's not where it was hurting." She sighed. "How long does this stuff last?"

"A few hours. Why?"

"Because now I'll be numb, and things were just about to get interesting."

"I haven't been using the ointment there."

Maggie glanced behind her and saw the bottle of oil. She laughed. "We didn't have dinner yet."

"We'll eat later."

And they did. Much later.

Henry came slowly into the light, into the pain. He blinked his eyes open to find himself completely enclosed in white. The ceiling, the walls, the bed—everything was white, including the woman who was standing at the side of his bed, writing something onto a chart.

She glanced in his direction and nodded. "Good, you're awake."

"No, I'm still sleeping, you stupid . . ." Henry never finished the thought as he drifted back to sleep again.

It wasn't until the next morning that he awakened again. He could breathe, but just barely. It felt like something heavy lay upon his chest. No, not something heavy; something painful. A tube had been pushed up his nose and down his throat. His throat was sore because of it.

His wrists were handcuffed to the sides of a criblike bed. Both arms were connected to tubes that dripped liquid into his veins. Henry might have laughed. Might have, had he the strength. They had handcuffed him. Were they all as stupid as they looked? Did they think he had the strength to get up and run?

A man leaned over him, a man in a white coat. Henry figured he was a doctor, but he couldn't get his eyes to focus enough to read the black lettering on the gold pin attached to his coat. "How do you feel?"

"Like shit."

The man nodded. "Cough."

"Go to hell."

"You came closer than I'd ever like to come to dying, pal. You want pneumonia to set in and kick off, after all we did to save you?" the man shrugged. "I guess that's your choice."

The doctor filled a syringe with something, a painkiller, probably, and injected it into the tube that was already dropping something into his arm. He then flipped the chart shut and left the room. It was only then that Henry coughed.

Henry hadn't remembered at first. He didn't know why he was here, didn't know what had happened to put him here, but as he waited for the needle to take effect, flashes of memory began to return.

288

They had jumped him. Something like six or eight cops had jumped him, digging their knees into his back, twisting his arms so tightly behind him, he thought they might pop from their sockets.

Henry grinned. He'd almost had them for a minute there. It was the wife bit that had nearly convinced them that he was on the up-and-up, that he was just an innocent—well, maybe not so innocent, but a bystander who'd gotten caught up in the middle of something he knew nothing about. That had been good thinking on his part.

It had been a mistake to shove the bodies into the back of the van. The woman hadn't stayed warm, anyway. Henry shivered his disgust as he remembered trying to do it to her. The bitch had almost spread her death over his dick.

He should have dumped them on the side of the road. Fact was, if they hadn't found the bodies, he might have walked away from the trap, instead of shooting himself in the chest.

It had taken something like a full minute, what with the screaming curses, punches, and kicks he was taking to his head and back, before he'd realized that the gun had gone off.

It was only then, when he'd found himself gasping to breathe, that he'd realized the bullet had smashed into his chest.

He'd given up then. He'd allowed them the control they wanted, knowing when this was all over, he'd be the one in control again. He'd be the one to win.

He was going to show them. He was going to live. He had things to do. There was no way he was going to die, at least, not yet.

289

Three student nurses peeked into the room. No, they weren't nurses, they were Candy Stripers. Henry figured not one of them was over eighteen. He felt like a freak at a sideshow when their eyes rounded in surprise. "He looks so normal," one of them said from the doorway. Another shook her head, "No, he doesn't . . . look at his eyes."

Henry said. "Bring your pussy over here, girlie, and I'll show you . . ."

With a shriek they ran from the room.

Henry lay there, staring at the ceiling, grinning. At least they wouldn't bother him again. He was sure of that.

Suddenly a cop was standing beside the bed. "You want that mouth of yours taped shut? Just keep it up."

Henry would have liked to tell him where he could put his tape, but decided feigning sleep would better serve his cause. Besides, it would frustrate the bastard, and Henry, whenever possible, enjoyed annoying those in authority. He closed his eyes, saying nothing.

"Dirtbag" was whispered just before the cop's footsteps moved to the hall.

Henry lay there for a long time before he slept again. During that time he allowed his thoughts to wander. Carefully he controlled the hate. It had all been a plan to get him, of course. He should have known better than to trust her for a second. He never should have called back. What he should have done was to kill them both the night he'd crept to the window.

Henry smiled as he put aside his rage. He'd have to think a bit and rest a lot, because he wasn't finished with her yet. His turn was coming. And this time, he wouldn't be fooled into believing. This time, he knew her for what she truly was. This time he'd be patient and wait.

During the next few weeks, those thoughts would

become a definite plan. And when one has a plan, nearly anything is possible.

"The next time, I'll follow you in my car."

Mike shot her a look of surprise. "Why?"

"Because that way I won't die of thirst before we get to Dad's."

"Meaning?"

"Meaning, I'll give you ten dollars if you stop at the next truck stop."

"I stopped about . . ."

She glanced at her watch. "Three hours ago," she finished for him. "Are we in a hurry or something?"

They passed a hitchhiker, who flicked them an obscene gesture at being passed up, and Maggie grumbled, "You're better off, buddy, believe me.

"How about twenty?"

Mike grinned. "No wonder it takes you days to drive a couple of hundred miles. What do you do, stop every ten minutes?"

"If I feel like it. At the moment, I'd like a cup of coffee and maybe lunch, not counting the fact that this seat is going to be wet if I don't find a bathroom soon."

"We'll stop, honey. I just want to . . ."

Maggie reached across the small space that separated them and pressed a knuckle into his side. "If you don't want this gun to go off, mister, take the next exit."

Mike grinned. "Yes, ma'am."

A half hour later, after a trip to the bathroom and a relaxing lunch in the truck stop café, Maggie leaned back against the ripped vinyl seat and sighed.

"Better?" he asked her.

"Much."

She smiled as she watched him look longingly through the window to the highway and the trucks and cars that were speeding on by. "Are they overdosing on testosterone?"

Mike frowned. "What? Who?"

Maggie shrugged as her gaze followed a speeding truck. "There's got to be some reason why men feel it necessary to make good time. Ten dollars says that's the first thing my father asks you when we get there."

"We won't be getting there for a while."

Maggie laughed in disbelief.

"I thought maybe we could stop somewhere, for a little while."

"Stop? You? You mean . . ." Her voice took on a whispering quality. "Stop the car?"

Mike chuckled at her dramatics. "Like, say, in Reno. We could get a room with a tub big enough for two. Take in a couple of shows, and maybe just relax and have a little fun."

Maggie smiled at the delightful thought. "Only Dad's expecting us tonight."

"Well, the fact is, honey, I called him before we left and told him we'd be there in a few days."

Maggie grinned at the hungry look in his eyes. "So all this hurrying was to get us to Reno?"

"Do you mind?"

Maggie's expression grew decidedly wicked. "I imagine I could bear up under the strain."

The room wasn't anything like Maggie had ever seen before, and she had done quite a bit of traveling in her work. But while traveling, usually on a restricted expense account, she had stayed at motor lodges or motels, never in a luxurious hotel.

The bed had mirrors over it, but she'd sort of expected that. What she hadn't expected was the private terrace facing one of the most beautiful sunsets she'd ever seen. She hadn't expected a bar in their room, nor a small pool and fireplace in a glassed-off area. She hadn't expected a bathroom bigger than any she'd ever seen before, containing a Jacuzzi and separate shower. She hadn't expected the little things like three choices of bubble bath, heated towels, and silk robes spread upon the bed, to lounge around in.

"This is really something," she said, her eyes widening as she took in the luxurious amenities, the satin-covered pillows, the thick white carpet. "The honeymoon suite?"

Mike nodded, watching carefully for her every expression.

"It's good thing we didn't meet ten years ago and marry then."

"Why?"

"Because I wouldn't have appreciated this as much then."

"Maybe, but we could have come back for a second honeymoon."

Maggie laughed. "I love you."

"I can count on one hand the times you've said that."

"Meaning you'd like to hear it all the time?"

He nodded. "I expect it wouldn't hurt none."

"And you won't grow bored hearing it?"

Mike gave her a long, lazy grin as he started to undress. "Are we having a glass of wine?"

"I was thinkin' on it, among other things. Why?"

"Because you're taking your clothes off again."

"Am I? I didn't notice."

"You'd notice if I took mine off, though?"

"I doubt it."

Maggie laughed. "Really?"

Mike shrugged his arms into the larger of the two silk robes spread out upon the bed. "Really," he returned "go on and try it, you'll see that I won't notice a thing.' He left the robe untied as he moved to the bar. Looking over the display, he asked, "What'll you have?"

"You wouldn't be trying to tempt me, would you?"

His gaze moved to hers at the question and his voice lowered a notch. "The thought never crossed my mind,' he said, his eyes darker, hungrier than ever before.

"White wine," she said, as she closed the drapes.

"What are you doing? No one can see us up here."

"What about low-flying planes?"

Mike laughed and took his time preparing their drinks. He took his time because he mostly watched her as she took off her clothes and slid into the remaining robe. Lik him, she didn't tie the belt, but let the material flow behind her as she moved toward him.

She sat on one of the two bar stools. Facing him, sh sipped at the crisp, dry wine.

Mike ran the tip of one finger over the edge of the rob that barely covered her breast. "You wouldn't be tryin to tempt me, would you?"

Maggie chuckled. "You said you wouldn't notice."

"Notice what?" he teased.

"You mean, it's not working?"

Mike chuckled a low, almost painful sound. "It's work ing, all right. If I stepped around this bar, you'd see ju how much."

Maggie smiled. "So, are you going to stand there all night?"

Mike smiled, and without a word, came toward her.

Maggie allowed herself the pleasure of a long, leisurely look before saying, "I see what you mean."

"I've been like this for most of the drive up here."

"So it wasn't seeing me like this?"

"It was imagining you like this. But now that I've seen you, I'm having a hard time making him behave. He sometimes has a mind of his own, you know."

Maggie brought her gaze to the object in question. "It's he?"

"I'd be mighty surprised if it wasn't."

"What is he thinking about right now?"

"I want this evening to last a bit, so let's not ask him, all right?"

Maggie laughed.

"What do you want to do first?"

"I thought maybe a swim."

Mike nodded and moved off to light the fireplace. He turned out every light and watched as she came to join him by the pool.

"And you weren't the least bit interested?"

"Sweetheart, a hundred bouncing boobs are surprising at first, and maybe a little interesting at that, but once you've seen them, you know," he shrugged, "you've sorta seen them."

"Meaning, they become less than mysterious?"

Mike grinned, figuring she got the idea, as he let them into their room. "Now, if it was you dancing up there, you wouldn't have gotten me to look anywhere else."

"You'd have liked that?"

"No, but I'd like it if you did it now."

"Forget it. I'd end up throwing out my back. There'
no way I could slither around the room like that withou
doing myself some harm."

Maggie dropped her bag on the bed and Mike reache
for her, wrapping his arms around her waist, slowly drag
ging a finger over her midriff as he rested his chin on he
head. "Are you happy?"

Maggie nodded. "More than you could ever know."

"You know, I was thinking . . . if you hadn't bee
running from Henry, we might never have met."

"Are you saying we owe him?"

Mike scowled at the thought. "We owe him, all righ
and I hope he gets everything . . ."

"You don't believe in fate?"

"You think we would have met anyway?"

"We'll never know now."

"It doesn't matter. It only matters that we did, n
matter the circumstances."

Two weeks of lying in bed was about all he could take
Two weeks of snotty nurses, of doctors who didn't give
damn if he lived or died, was more than any man coul
take. Still, he managed to get through each day with a
little trouble as possible, except for that dragon wh
worked the graveyard shift. Henry would have liked noth
ing more than to see that one in a grave.

She'd just held the bottle before him so he could pe
and was covering him again when he asked, "Can't yo
let one arm free? I ain't going anywhere."

"Sorry."

296

"Lady, I need my hand."

"For what? I do everything for you."

"I need it to jerk off, all right?"

The dragon shot him a hard look. "You're wasting your time and mine if you're trying to shock me. I've heard it all before."

"Maybe, but by the looks of you, you ain't done it before."

Henry sighed as he watched her walk out of the room. The fact was, he hadn't been trying to shock her; he'd been telling her the truth. He'd never gone more than a week before, never mind three, and he had a hard-on that just wouldn't quit.

Not counting the fact that because he couldn't use his hands, he had more itches than he'd ever had in his life. Damn, it was like being tortured.

Henry rubbed his nose against his pillow, trying to ease at least one of the many itches that tormented him, wondering if, after he escaped—and he knew without a doubt that he would escape—it wouldn't be possible for him to come back here and do the bitch in. He could almost taste the pleasure of doing that one.

Chapter Eighteen

"You're happy," Frank Smith said to his daughter.

Maggie smiled as she sipped her coffee, her gaze moving to the window and her husband, who was showing both Pat's boys the correct way to hold a bat. She realized his words were less a question than a statement of fact, and said, "There's no way I can hide it."

"You shouldn't have to."

"You don't look like you're ready to cry, either."

Frank smiled at her. "I guess we've both got a lot to be thankful for."

"So, when are you going to marry her?"

"I take it you don't mind."

Maggie covered her father's hand with her own. "I'm happy for you, Dad, I really am. She looks like a wonderful woman."

"She is." He smiled again. "We were thinking maybe the end of June."

"So far away? Why wait?"

"Because Marlee wants all of her children there. Two of them live in New York and can't get away from their jobs before then."

Maggie nodded.

She and her father went on to discuss the coming nuptials, as well as Marlee and her three children and two grandchildren. Maggie thought life couldn't be sweeter; as soon as she was sure she was pregnant, it would be sweeter by far.

Later that night, while she and Mike were in bed, snuggled together, they spoke about stopping off in Rock Springs on their way back home for an interview Maggie had set up with the station manager there.

"I'm nervous."

"Are you? You shouldn't be. Cliff Walters has to know you're the best, or he wouldn't have offered you the job."

Maggie smiled. "I wish I had your confidence."

"You'll be wonderful, Maggie. Don't worry."

"I told him I want to do a piece on the homeless."

A few seconds ticked by before he asked, "What does that mean?"

"It means that I can't possibly know what they feel like unless I go undercover."

"Meaning?"

"Meaning, on the streets."

"And?"

"And live either with them, or like them."

"How long is that going to take?"

"Two weeks, maybe a little longer."

Mike sighed. "I'll have to hire someone to help Abner."

Maggie snuggled closer to his side. She thought Mike would give her a hard time about it, but it sounded as if he was going with her without a single complaint. "You don't mind coming with me?"

"There's no way you could keep me away."

"I love you."

"I know. What I don't know is when you're going to tell me."

"Tell you what?"

"About the baby."

Maggie made a soft gasping sound and pulled back a bit, trying to see his grin in the dark. "How did you . . ."

"Simple. We've been together for more than a month. And you haven't had your period yet."

Maggie chuckled. "I was waiting to be sure."

"And the home pregnancy test didn't make you sure?"

"How did you know I used . . ."

"You left the package in the bathroom wastebasket."

"Did you ever think of becoming a detective?"

"I wasn't searching for clues. It was only covered by a tissue, and that sort of blew off when I waved my hand over the basket."

Maggie laughed. "I wanted to surprise you."

"Well, I guess you could say I was surprised, only not much."

"Because I didn't have my period?"

"That, and 'cause I want a baby. 'Cause I can't wait to see you all round and maybe a little plump, but gorgeous here." His hand came to lie against her still-flat stomach.

"You'll be all right, won't you?"

"You mean, living on the street while I'm pregnant?" She could feel Mike's nod.

"It will only be for a few weeks, and I'll be fine, as long as you're with me."

"Then you'll always be fine." His arms tightened around her. " 'Cause I ain't ever going to be without you."

300

Today was moving day. It didn't matter to the bastards that he complained of pain, that he was obviously weak; they were moving him to the county jail to await trial.

A male nurse shook him awake and Henry saw the orange one-piece coveralls hanging over the bars of his hospital bed. They were moving him, despite the pain in his chest, despite the fact that he'd probably die.

"Come on, wake up," the nurse said, and Henry had no choice but to open his eyes. The sheet was flung back and a pair of briefs were shoved up his legs and fitted around his waist.

"I'm too weak," Henry said, knowing it wouldn't matter to them if he was at death's door. He was going to jail, and nothing he could say would stop them.

"You're not that weak," said one of the two cops standing opposite the nurse.

The truth was, Henry felt stronger every day, but continued on with his constant complaints in hopes of delaying the inevitable. He didn't want to leave the hospital. He didn't want to sit in a cell, waiting for his trial, waiting for the obvious conclusion of the trial, waiting for the end. His only hope had been to stay here, to somehow find the means of escaping from this bed.

But after three weeks of planning, he'd come up with nothing. As long as they kept him handcuffed to the bed, there was no way. "I can't sit up."

"You'll be in an ambulance," said the other cop. And then it came to him. Henry knew without a doubt that all hope was not lost. He'd escape. Somehow, he'd find the means to escape, but first he had to make them think he was in real bad shape.

Apparently they believed he was. Henry clung to that hope, for there was no other way.

His hands were handcuffed, not to the bed, but together. Henry reached for his crotch. God, but it felt good to be able to touch himself again. He didn't care that three men stood at his side. He didn't look at them, he didn't think about them. All he knew was that he was able to touch himself and it felt better than good.

Apparently all three thought he was just scratching himself, for Henry heard no disgust in the man's voice when one of them said, "Come on, let's get him onto the gurney." Henry was lifted on the count of three and placed upon a hard bed and transported quickly from the room to an elevator.

From the elevator he was pushed down a long hallway and then into the back of a waiting ambulance.

The door was shut after both cops entered the vehicle. Beside the cop sat an attendant. In the front was a driver. Henry couldn't see whether the driver was a cop or not, and he didn't want to appear too inquisitive by twisting in order to do so. It didn't matter, at any rate. If he got the chance to escape he'd take it, only . . .

Four men. How the hell was he supposed to overcome four men? All right, so maybe he wasn't as weak as he let on, but four? Even if he had all his strength, he didn't think he could overcome all four of them.

The ambulance started down the hospital drive, stopped for a light, and then took a left. Henry knew the road to the county jail would be barren and mostly empty. He figured he wouldn't get a better chance. Once he got to the county jail, he might never find a way out.

The two cops talked. Soon the attendant and then even the driver joined in their conversation.

"A man's got to be careful, 'cause a piece of ass will do him in every time," the driver remarked.

"Especially the piece I had last night," another returned. "Damn, I'd give up everything for that one."

"What? Ten years of marriage and two kids for pussy?" The man's partner couldn't have been more amazed.

The cop's eyes went a little glassy with the memory. "Man, I never had it like that before."

"Bullshit. Stand them all on their heads and you can't tell them apart. There ain't no way I'm giving up what I got. There's no way that I'm sharing my pension, either. Guys like you have nothing in the end."

"Maybe, but at least I can say I've had the best." The cop grinned. "He'd probably be out there with me if Erma hadn't scared him shitless."

The cop nodded to the chuckles of the three men. "That's right. She'd kick my ass if she ever caught me with a woman."

"Bob ain't bullshittin' ya'," his partner felt the need to add. "You've never seen his wife."

"Don't start," Bob said.

Henry groaned, the sound calling an instant halt to the men's conversation. "What's the matter?" the attendant asked, as he leaned over Henry's prone form.

"My chest." Henry panted. "I can't breathe."

The attendant instantly placed an oxygen mask over Henry's nose and mouth.

But the mask didn't seem to help. Henry moaned, gasping for air, apparently in severe pain.

"What's the matter with him?" the cop closest to Henry asked, as he leaned forward.

"I don't know," the attendant said, and then, "Move back. You're in my way."

Bob moved back, but not soon enough. Henry took the opportunity offered and with shackled hands managed to unsnap the button that held his gun in place. In an instant the gun was in his hands. The men didn't have a chance to offer an objection. Bob didn't have a chance, because of the seatbelt, to reach for his own gun as Henry simply, deliberately, and quickly shot each man.

The driver yelled something, but Henry never heard what it was. The ambulance wobbled, as if top-heavy, out of control as the man driving figured a bullet would hit him in the back of his head at any second. But before Henry got a chance to unstrap himself from the stretcher and kill the man, the car hit an embankment and rolled over.

Henry was lucky because he was tied in. The driver wasn't nearly so fortunate.

With the ambulance on its side, Henry quickly undid the straps that kept him on the stretcher. The moment he did, he fell upon the two cops.

Henry hadn't planned on this. He'd known that he would take the first opportunity offered, but he hadn't expected it could be this easy. He worked quickly. First, and most important, he found the key to his cuffs. Next, he stripped off his overalls, and then, figuring the cop closest to him was nearly his size, he stripped him of his uniform.

The back door was locked or jammed, he didn't know which. All he knew for sure was that he couldn't get out that way.

Henry crawled forward, through the small opening and into the cab. The driver wasn't anywhere around, at least, not that he could see. From the cab, he slid out a window.

The driver hadn't gone far. The upper part of his body

as pinned beneath the vehicle. Henry nodded and then hid his grin as a passerby stopped to offer help.

Minutes later he laughed as he drove the pickup truck away from the overturned ambulance. Henry glanced into his rearview mirror and saw another car stop and then another. He chuckled at his luck and then reconsidered. No, it wasn't luck; it was intelligence that had gotten him out of that. Intelligence, and cops who were less than on guard.

He could have told them he'd escape. There was no way he was going to prison. No way.

"Oh, God," Miriam moaned. "I didn't miss him while I was doing the laundry. I thought he was watching television."

"Don't worry, honey," Jake said, as he mounted his horse. "We'll find him."

"I'm not going to live through raising this kid," Miriam said, as she, too, mounted a horse.

Mike was in town. Everyone on the ranch was either preparing to leave, or had already left in search of Little Jake. Maggie, who had been practicing her riding just about every day and had managed at last to sit a horse quite comfortably, joined her friend. Miriam left the rest of her children with Joe's oldest girl. She figured Jake had been gone for close to an hour and a half. She was clearly close to panicking, realizing that by now he could be just about anywhere.

"Take it easy, we'll find him," Maggie echoed Jake's words as they started out for the pastures north of the ranch house.

The southern part of the ranch was mostly mountain-

ous. No one thought Jake would have gone in that direction. The terrain was difficult, almost impossible to rid
through in certain places. No, the boy would have heade
for the pastures north, east, or west of the ranch hous
There he could ride like the wind over more even land
scape.

Everyone knew they'd find him there.

Mike returned from town to a nearly deserted ranch
Marie, Joe's wife, told him of Little Jake's disappearance
and that Maggie had gone with the others to look for him

Mike ran into the house and grabbed his gun from
behind the back door. He almost shut the door before h
remembered his flashlight. It was in the kitchen cabine
A second later, he was running toward the barn and hi
horse. Mike had never saddled a horse so fast. He neve
thought to question the pickup out front.

He left so quickly that Marie never thought to tell hir
about the cop who was waiting inside. She shrugged. H
must have seen him. Mike had gone inside for a minute

Mike had been visiting Jim when the call had come in
Neither man had to say it. Both knew Henry would b
heading for Mike's place. Both knew the man's obsessio
with Maggie.

Again officers were assigned to the ranch, but Mike pu
the gas peddle to the floor and beat them home.

Marie thought that, just in case Mike had run in an
out too fast to notice the cop inside, she'd tell him tha
Mike had been there but had been called away, an
probably wouldn't be back for a while. She was on he
way to the house to do just that when her daughter calle
from across the yard. She stood at the door of Miriam'
and Jake's place, obviously in need of her help. "Mom
come here a minute, will you?"

306

Marie hurried toward her daughter and the three little ones in her charge. By the time they had gotten the baby cleaned up and to bed, and the other two bathed and sitting before the television, Marie had forgotten all about the cop waiting in Mike's house.

It was dark when she left for her own place. Marie glanced at Mike's house. No lights shone from inside. The cop had probably already left. She went home to start dinner.

Mike was relieved to find Jake holding his son. The boy had fallen from his horse, and according to him, had been stepped on by accident. His leg was broken.

Mike and Jake both knew the ride back was going to be difficult. There was no way the child wouldn't be bounced around, and his leg was going to give him a lot of pain before they could get him to a car and then finally to the hospital.

Shots were fired, signaling the others that the boy had been found. Jake and Mike started back.

The men had gone off in small groups to search for the boy. Mike had come across Jake alone, but he knew the others wouldn't separate. At least, he prayed they wouldn't.

It was getting dark. She couldn't be out here alone. *Please God, let her have stayed with a group.*

Mike wouldn't know until he got back if his prayers were answered or not. And even then, he couldn't know for sure, because Maggie and Miriam had yet to return. "Maybe they didn't hear the signal?"

Joe shrugged. "Maybe. They might have been on the west range. If they were searching in the gully over there, the sound might not have carried."

"I'm going to find them," Mike said, as he mounted h[is]
horse again.

"You got a light?" Joe asked.

Mike reached for his belt and touched the flashlight h[e]
had taken with him. "Yeah. If they get back before I d[o,]
tell Maggie not to go anywhere."

Mike was fearful, but not terrified. By last count, ther[e]
were still five men plus Miriam unaccounted for. N[o]
doubt they were all together. Mike wouldn't, couldn'[t]
think beyond that hope.

Mike finally got to the west range, and just as he'[d]
hoped, he saw figures atop their horses. He shot his gu[n]
into the air and the three came riding forward.

Soon another two followed, and Mike smiled as h[e]
spotted Maggie riding beside Miriam.

"They found him?" Miriam asked, as she pulled th[e]
horse to an abrupt stop.

Mike nodded. "Jake brought him to the hospital." H[e]
could see Miriam suddenly stiffen and said simply, so a[s]
not to cause her even more worry, "Broken leg. Othe[r-]
wise, he's fine."

"Thank God," Miriam breathed, as Mike turned wit[h]
the others heading back to the ranch house.

He held back a little, riding alongside his wife, allowin[g]
the others to gain a bit on them, but only a bit. Mike kne[w]
it wasn't safe out here alone, but he had to tell he[r.]
"Collins escaped." Maggie gasped, and for just a secon[d]
lost her hold on the reins. She grabbed them again, thi[s]
time a bit too sharply, and the horse came to a sudden an[d]
dangerous stop.

Mike reached instantly for the reins, his low voice calm[-]
ing the animal. Maggie only wished he could calm her a[s]
easily. "What happened?"

308

"He shot two cops and an ambulance attendant."

"Dead?"

"No, but one of them is in bad shape."

"And they don't know . . ."

"Only that he's wearing cop's clothes."

"God," Maggie groaned. "I can't go through this again."

"Easy, honey. Everything will be all right. The cops are probably already at our place."

Maggie nodded. She might have said that she couldn't go through this again, but what choice had she? None. At least, none until they found him again. Maggie knew they'd find him; they always did. Only this time, she prayed they'd kill him. She smiled at the thought, while wondering how she had the nerve to pray to God for a man's death.

When they got back to the ranch, Maggie dismounted. Mike took the reins from her. "Go inside. I'll take care of this."

Maggie nodded as Mike took her horse with his into the barn.

She saw the two cops standing outside their car as she walked the short distance from the barn doors to the house. She waved. They waved back.

Mike finished with the horses and stopped to have a word with the cops before entering the house. "Everything all right?"

"Quiet. No problem," Steve said, leaning his hip on the hood of the car and crossing his arms over his chest. "They'll probably get him by tonight. He stole a pickup. There's an all-points out for it."

"There was one here before," Mike said, more to himself than to the two officers.

"What?"

"Oh, nothing. It's gone."

Mike never thought to ask if they'd been in the hous[e]
It was an error in judgment on their part that they hadn['t]
and an error on Mike's to assume they had. "I'll brin[g]
some coffee out later," he said, as he moved off toward th[e]
house.

He entered the kitchen and called out, "Maggie?"

She had already been in the bedroom. She was swea[t]
from riding all afternoon, and covered with dust. Besid[e]
the fact that she probably smelled like a horse, she wante[d]
nothing more than to sit for a while in a warm tub [of]
water. She gathered a change of clothes and from th[e]
linen closet took a few fluffy towels with her into th[e]
bathroom.

Maggie reached behind the closed shower curtain fo[r]
the faucets and turned them on. A minute later she wa[s]
naked, and shoving the curtain aside, stepped right int[o]
Henry's arms.

Maggie screamed, but the sound went nowhere. H[is]
hand was instantly over her mouth as he dragged her int[o]
the tub and against the tiled wall.

Maggie never knew a heart could beat so hard or s[o]
fast. She'd been afraid before. The first time he'd foun[d]
her stuck in the snow, she'd been terrified. But this tim[e]
was worse. This time, she knew him for the killer he wa[s]
This time she knew not only her life, but Mike's, too, wa[s]
in jeopardy.

She tried to think, but couldn't. She couldn't manag[e]
even one thought outside of running for her life. And wit[h]
his arms around her, pressing her to the wall, there wa[s]
no way. No way.

The water was loud, but not loud enough to blot out h[is]

310

ted voice. "Hello, Maggie. Have you been waiting long
r me?"

His question was a taunt, one that needed no answer.
e laughed and grabbed her by the hair, slamming her
ad against the wall.

Thud. Thud. He did it twice, and Maggie couldn't
derstand why he stopped. He wanted to kill her, didn't
? Then why stop?

And then she heard Mike calling her. "Maggie?" came
s voice over the running water. "You in the bathroom?"

"Answer him, bitch," Henry said, as he hit her head
ainst the wall again.

"No," she returned.

Mike walked through the kitchen and almost fell.
esus," he said as his feet almost slid out from beneath
m. It was only then that he noticed it. Something dark
s seeping from under the door to the broom closet.
mething red and . . . Mike's heart sank as he opened the
or and found his dog inside. The dog's throat had been
t, and the blood had run under the door to his kitchen
or. Mike didn't know if Brandy was dead or not, and
didn't have the time to find out.

He glanced at his gun, still in the closet, and frowned.
enry was in the house; Mike knew that for a fact. He'd
led his dog, shoved the body into the broom closet, but
t the rifle behind. That had to mean he already had a
n—the cops' gun.

Mike leaned against the cabinet for a second, trying to
se the panic in his mind. He had to think. If he could
ink, they might get out of this alive. But only if he didn't
nic.

Mike called her again. *"Maggie?"*

Water was running in the bathroom. *Please God, don't* *him be in the bathroom.*

With his rifle aimed, Mike searched each room. It w only after he had searched the last closet that he kn Collins was in the bathroom with her.

Mike knocked on the door. "Maggie, you in there?"

"Tell him to come in," Henry whispered near her e

Maggie shook her head in refusal.

Henry smiled. She was terrified. Her eyes were wi She was scared, all right, but she was still protecting t bastard.

Henry snickered. It didn't matter; he was going to I him anyway. He was going to kill them both. But t bastard first.

"Call him," Henry warned, as he hit her head agai the wall again.

"Mike," she said softly.

"Louder, bitch. Louder," Henry said, as he slamm her head again.

"Mike," she said, unable to withstand any further pu ishment. "Mike," she called, as he hit her head one m time before the blackness began.

Maggie could feel her legs weaken. She was passi out, and there wasn't anything she could do to stop i

And then, suddenly, her mind grew clear.

Mike heard her call.

He heard the distress in her voice and knew she w being forced to call out. He heard the thudding sounds something hit the wall. The bastard was hitting her a knocking her head back, Mike thought.

Silently—and, he prayed, without too much of draft—he opened the bathroom door and slid into t room.

The shower curtain was pulled closed, but Mike knew Maggie was in there. The problem was, he didn't know exactly where.

He moved back and to one side. From this position he could see into the mirror over the sink, just a bit behind the curtain. Henry was there, all right. He had his hand over Maggie's mouth, holding her against the wall.

Mike couldn't shoot him. If he did, he chanced hitting Maggie, for the man stood right in front of her.

As far as he could see, Henry's gun was probably in its holster. Mike had only one option.

He tore the shower curtain aside. Collins jumped and spun around. Maggie slipped and fell. Mike's rifle was less than a foot from the man's chest. The sound of a gun echoing in the small, tiled room left all three of them momentarily deaf.

Chapter Nineteen

Henry laughed. Did he think it was so easy? Didn't he know that only Henry had the power over life and death? It wasn't time yet. Not nearly time yet. He had to get the bitch first. He had to see her dead. Then, maybe, when his work here was finished, he could die, but not before. Never before.

Henry reached for support. He'd taken a powerful blow to his chest, but if the bastard thought that was enough to do him in, he'd have to think again.

His mouth curved into a grotesque grin and his hands closed around the shower curtain as if that would keep him upright. It didn't. Henry used all the strength he had, but slumped backward anyway. He pulled the shower curtain with him as he dropped into the tub half full of water, splashing Mike and Maggie as she screamed and hurried from his side.

Henry couldn't understand what was happening. He saw Maggie jump from the tub. He saw Mike's arms come around her naked body. But he couldn't figure out how that had happened.

Mike's arm was around her, and they both watched as Henry went slowly under the water.

Mike shut the faucets and Henry was floating silently on his face as Mike guided a sobbing Maggie from the room.

Mike grabbed the quilt from the couch and wrapped it around her shivering body. He held her tightly against him again and whispered, "Damn, that was close. That was closer than close."

"I thought he was going to kill you."

Mike nodded as he held her closer than ever and breathed in her scent. God, he'd almost lost this. He'd almost lost her forever. Mike wasn't sure he'd ever get over the terror that shook him from head to toe. "He might have, if it hadn't been for you and Brandy." Mike figured he'd tell her later about the dog.

"Let me call Steve," Mike said, as he tore himself from her warmth, her living warmth, and helped her to the couch, hating to leave her even for a minute. "Are you all right?"

Maggie nodded.

Mike turned for the front door, but he had taken only one step when there was a roar of hate such as Maggie had never heard in her life from behind them. Henry's wet, injured, but insanity-filled body flew over the couch and knocked Mike to the floor. Maggie screamed as both went down to roll around in a flurry of curses and flying fists.

She panicked for a second, unable to believe he was still alive. Blood was everywhere, yet he was still alive. And then Maggie realized he was beating Mike's head into the floor and she had to do something.

Maggie ran for the fireplace poker. For the second time

since she'd come here she held it over her head and brought it down with a powerful grunt.

There was only one problem: in the midst of her swing, Mike and Henry had suddenly changed places and she hit the wrong man. But the poker came down on Mike's shoulder, rather than on his head. Maggie could only think that that was something, at least.

Totally shaken, not only by what had happened, but by what she'd done, Maggie dropped the poker and backed up as Henry shoved Mike's groggy form away.

Henry came to his feet, the poker now in his hands. He looked her over and grinned. He couldn't wait to bring the poker down, to hit her again and again.

He took a step and the front door smashed open and two police officers filled the hallway.

Maggie screamed again, but they didn't stop shooting until Henry was down, until he was finally, absolutely dead at last.

Mike rolled into a sitting position and groaned at the pain in his shoulder and arm as Maggie, realizing her nakedness, reached for the quilt that had been around her shoulders. She huddled at his side.

"Are you all right?"

Mike nodded and said, "God, I never saw it coming. I didn't think he could hit me that hard."

Maggie did not correct his erroneous thinking. Instead, she said, "Now that I've given half this town an eyeful, I'd better get dressed."

Mike nodded, but groaned again at the movement.

Maggie bit her lip as she went into the bedroom. It was difficult to dress, what with her hands trembling, but she managed at last.

When she came out of the room, the house was just

about filled with ranch hands. More cops came, and they were ushered outside.

Maggie spotted Mike on the couch, holding his head in his hands. He was talking to Jim.

She couldn't help but glance at Henry's body as she walked by. Mostly she looked, just to be sure he was really dead this time. She joined Mike on the couch.

"I don't know," Mike was saying. "I thought I saw his hands, but he got me from the back, somehow. All I know is the man had a punch that would rival Ali."

"That was me," Maggie said, as she shot Mike an apologetic look. "I'm sorry, but I was trying to hit him and you switched places at the last second. It was like in the movies or something. I couldn't believe it."

Jim smiled. "What did you hit him with?"

"The poker."

"Oh God," Mike moaned. "Not again."

Jim looked confused, and Mike said, "It's a long story."

It took more than an hour before they finished taking Mike's and Maggie's statements. A car arrived to transport the body. Soon after, everyone finally left.

Maggie thought that would be it for the night, that she'd finally get a chance to recuperate from the horror, to rest, safely enclosed in Mike's arms, but Mike insisted that they take a ride to the hospital. He wanted to make sure she was all right, and nothing she could say made a difference. Mike wouldn't be satisfied until he heard it from the doctor himself.

317

Epilogue

"You're sure you're all right?"

"He only hit my head a few times. I'm fine."

"No dizziness?"

"No dizziness."

"Are you sure?"

"Mike, we went to the hospital. The doctor said I was fine. What else do you want?"

"I want to make sure, and I want you to rub it there some more."

Maggie chuckled. "You wouldn't be milking this for all it's worth, would you?"

"I wouldn't think of it."

"I don't understand why it was necessary to get naked just to rub your shoulder."

Mike laughed into his pillow. "Really?"

Maggie grinned. If she didn't understand at first, she understood at that wicked laugh. "All you had to do was open your shirt."

"If I did that, I couldn't feel your breasts rubbing over my back."

"You haven't felt them yet."

"Lean down, and I will."

She did as he'd asked and listened to his low groan of enjoyment. "Does that hurt?"

"More than you know."

"Are you sure you're hurt too bad to do anything?"

"Positive. Didn't I tell you?"

"Yes, but you're not acting very hurt."

"How should I act?"

"Well, for one thing, you keep rubbing your backside against me."

Mike chuckled. Since she was straddling his backside, he figured she knew what he was looking for.

"And I don't think an injured man would try to grab me every chance he gets."

"You haven't been around injured men much, have you?"

"Does it really hurt?"

"It's getting better."

"Oh, Mike, I can't tell you how sorry I am."

"You could show me."

"How?"

Mike rolled to his back and grinned. Maggie couldn't help but notice his excitement.

"Why don't you use your imagination?"

Maggie tried not to laugh. "Are you sure? I have a very good imagination, you know."

"Darlin', I was counting on it."